Ravens Deep

by

Jane Jordan

**Grosvenor House
Publishing Limited**

Jane Jordan is hereby identified as author of this
work in accordance with Section 77 of the Copyright, Designs
and Patents Act 1988

The book cover picture is copyright to Jane Jordan

This book is published by
Grosvenor House Publishing Ltd
28-30 High Street, Guildford, Surrey, GU1 3HY.
www.grosvenorhousepublishing.co.uk

A CIP record for this book
is available from the British Library

ISBN 978-1-906645-06-9

Prologue

There are those amongst us who seek unconditional love, an objective that could either be construed as wise or foolhardy, but regardless of individual perspective many of us search for a like-minded being; someone to return our affection, capture our heart or comfort and encourage when all others may criticize or condemn.

A few relationships are to be considered unusual or diverse, but although cultural difference and personal preference may be argued; our unions typically conform to the rules and moral values that we make.

After all, most strange deviations in love can be explained ...Ordinarily.

CHAPTER ONE

The Invitation

Time had simply vanished, for it was almost midnight when I looked up at the clock and realized that the constant drone of city life had long since diminished. Now, only an occasional car stereo or siren in the distance disturbed this warm summer's night.

I rose from the table and moved across the room. Leaning heavily against the window frame I stared unblinking out into the darkness; it was as though there was an inexplicable need to commit to memory as much detail as possible. The customary sight of the undulating rooftops and historic buildings seemed to convey a sense of reassurance, and that perceived encouragement reminded me that I really did belong to this place.

London was a beautiful city with its hundreds of lights glistening in the darkness, and it was almost hard to believe that in only a few hours from now this darkened multitude of shapes and infrequent figures would again become a seething mass of people rushing through their daily routines of business and pleasure. This vast capital was an urban playground where the attractions were many, from the lure of the West End high life to the charming, traditional markets and culture of the East

End and I could easily summarize that this city had something to entice everyone.

At its very core there is a persistent part of London, whether it is the fundamental structure or the Londoners themselves, which attaches itself and after a while that unfathomable something refuses to relinquish its hold; it becomes a permanent imprint on the hearts of those that it has reached out to. I was one such person and perhaps that was why I was now experiencing a sudden reluctance to leave, to just turn my back and walk away for an unknown period of time.

I was caught up in the nostalgia of the moment and closed my eyes, but that did not ease my feelings of uncertainty. Instead I believed that I could almost feel the pulsating beat in the many exotic night clubs and fashionable bars, or imagine someone playing a piano in a traditional East End pub. This culture was like no other; but more importantly, it was my life.

Tomorrow would come and I would leave this city, with all its noise and commotion, far behind and reluctantly I allowed the memories of earlier to fill my head, which in turn begged the question of why I still felt so unprepared. I remembered the empty suitcase and clothes strewn around the bedroom and I forced myself to glance back to the table and to my research notes spread out in a chaotic mess, but deep down I knew that it was more than the packing and the clutter that continued to trouble me; I still had to resolve the persistent emotional conflict inside.

All evening I had tried to forget my earlier conversation with Charlie, but now alone in the semi darkness and stillness of the night I was again confronted with it.

I thought back to the few simple words that he had spoken; words that had disturbed my insular world.

This afternoon had begun like any other when Charlie had arranged to meet me after work and we had gone out to an early dinner. We had chatted casually about the events of our respective days, but as the evening approached his conversation took on a more serious nature.

In hindsight, I should have known what he had been leading up to, but caught up in my own thoughts I had missed the obvious signs, enabling him to take me completely by surprise when he had shocked me with his question.

"Will you marry me?" he had asked.

I had paused at first and then that hesitation had developed into an awkward silence. I knew that Charlie expected a favourable response, but I had only been able to sit motionless, caught up in the astonishment and the accompanying panic I had felt. When I finally did respond, it was a hasty dismissive reply that told him I wasn't ready and then I had side-tracked and fought to find a better excuse. I told him that it was too soon in our relationship to think about marriage, but we both knew that this explanation was weak and not believable.

However, it was when I witnessed the obvious disappointment and hurt that he could not mask I had realized that I meant more to him than I had ever imagined.

With that knowledge, I found myself abruptly shaken from the comfort level which I had grown accustomed to in our relationship, for I had never assumed he would ask me that question and if the truth be told, the subject had not even crossed my mind. I had thought, like me, he was happy the way things were, after all we had what I would describe as a casual relationship. It had lasted nearly two years, but there was nothing abnormal about that and I was too independent to be tied down. I did not want to commit to a serious involvement because I liked living alone, but more importantly I needed the freedom that came with that solitude.

During the previous two years I had been careful not to let our relationship develop into more than I was ready for and I had carefully constructed my own safety zone, not allowing anyone to get too close, but now it seemed as though Charlie was trying to break down my unseen barrier and I was struggling with the concept of that.

Why did he have to say anything? Today of all days.

It was not as if I was having second thoughts, but if I was honest with myself, I did feel guilty at the way I had reacted; he hadn't deserved my bluntness and lack of sensitivity to his proposal. Charlie was after all a nice person; he was reliable and sincere with a secure future in store. He had worked in his father's publishing company since leaving school and there was no doubt that he would take over the business completely in a few years from now.

However, for me life with Charlie would be too reliable, too predictable. There was no fire in him, no intensity. Surely you needed passion, either about something or someone to make you feel alive and I didn't feel passion when I thought of Charlie. When I was with him I felt safe and I was looking for more than safe. In his world, by his side I would forever be a bystander, suffocating and screaming in silence; my own identity lost in a life that wasn't my own. But despite my innermost feelings I was now being forced to face the question that demanded an answer.

Was it really Charlie that I was reluctant to leave?

Yesterday I had been so certain of my direction. So why did a marriage proposal make me question my own feelings and force me to reconsider the consequences of my answer? I shook my head in despair at my own confusion. I was normally decisive and logical, but I didn't feel that way right now. The voice in my head told me that it was no coincidence that Charlie had picked this day, the eve of my departure, to make his intention known. Then it occurred to me, that this was his way of keeping me in London. If that really was the reason behind his proposal then I knew I had clearly made the right decision.

I had to exist on my own terms and I refused to allow any other influences to change my mind. Besides that, I knew that I would only bring Charlie unhappiness and I wouldn't be witness to somebody else's heartbreak, for I knew all too well what it was like to pay that ultimate price.

I had witnessed first-hand the rise and fall of my own parents' tragic lives. I still had memories of my mother, an accomplished artist, painting away hour after hour in the spare bedroom she had used as her studio, and during those final years she had watched my father's once profitable and successful business decline deeper into debt. Always resourceful she had paid off many of the undesirable sources from whom my father had borrowed money. She had kept the bailiffs from our door with the proceeds from, so I believed at the time, all of her most prized paintings and possessions.

Unfortunately even she could do nothing when the various bankers called in their debts and my father was finally forced into bankruptcy. Our family home was sold at auction, for a fraction of its market value and we found ourselves living in a two bedroomed flat.

It was then that my father's downward spiral accelerated, dragging my mother with him. She by this time was too exhausted to paint, instead she could only watch helplessly as my father turned away from her and to a bottle for comfort.

Two years later, my father died from liver failure brought about by alcohol poisoning and my mother, seemingly unable to cope with the loss, lost interest in everything she had once loved, including life itself; almost a year later she died of unknown causes.

For me, the memories of finding her lifeless body lying peacefully on the bed were still vivid and only I knew that she had died of a broken heart, as I believed such things could happen. I had experienced initial horror and sadness, but that had turned quickly into extreme anger. I had failed to understand how she could have acted so selfishly, and her action only seemed to convey that I was not an important enough reason for her to remain living.

Charlie had been my emotional strength and had given me the much needed comfort. He had reminded me that I was important to him at least, and he helped me deal with the effects of such a tragic loss. It was because of that episode in our relationship that I did feel somewhat indebted to him and after today's events I recognised that I was suffering from a self induced guilt trip.

After my mother's death, I discovered a cache of paintings in the attic of their rented flat. I could never be sure if these paintings had been concealed on purpose for me, as there was no other will or provisions made and it was quite by chance when I finally found the courage to return to that flat that I had even bothered to search the attic.

That had occurred nine months ago, since then I had used the proceeds from the sale of some of the paintings to buy the fashionable London flat in which I now lived.

Several others of my mother's paintings still adorned the walls; they were all I had left to remind me of her. Every time I looked at them, I still could not quite believe how valuable they were, their worth having increased substantially with her death.

Because of these very paintings and the others I had sold, I didn't need to rely on another's good fortune as I now had my own means, which also meant that I wasn't about to settle for anything or anyone other than a perfect match. I knew that my soul mate would be someone to intrigue me and capture my imagination; he would have passion and be someone who would inspire me to attain my dreams, but I had also realized that person was not Charlie.

It was my good fortune that I had inherited some artistic talent, not with a brush, but a pen. My father could write and I had seen beautiful letters from him written to my mother before they were married and now I knew that I also possessed the capability to transport a reader to another time and place.

Charlie was always second to my writing and he had called it a hobby, but to me that was an insult. He simply didn't understand me at all. I wondered again why I had hesitated, when tonight would have been the right time to break off the relationship.

I should have told him.

Resolutely I started packing up the papers laid out on the table, trying to dismiss the continuing thought that reminded me of my lack of courage. I reasoned that he would have been upset, even angry and although I had hurt him deeply, the thought of him hating me completely did not make me feel good about myself. Instead I had chosen the easy option; to postpone that particular disclosure.

When I got back I would tell him, I sighed.

When would that be? ... he will just have to wait.

Right now I had more important things to think about, like the journey on which I was about to embark. This new and uncertain course had occurred coincidently because of my writing. In recent months I had been fortunate enough to have several short stories published. With that small amount of success my confidence level had increased considerably and now I knew that I was capable of a defining piece of work; I just needed the inspiration to create it. That encouragement had come about in the most unusual of circumstances. I thought back, astonished that only five weeks had passed; it really seemed much longer.

I had been working part-time as a hotel receptionist, people were friendly and interesting and I enjoyed my job, but an added bonus of working part-time was the freedom to write.

On one particular afternoon, just as I had been getting ready to leave for the day, one of the hotel staff informed me that collected guest magazines had been delivered to the lounge. Hotel guests invariably left magazines in their rooms, and we often selected the ones in like-new-condition for other guests or staff. This information had prompted me to visit the lounge before I left the hotel that evening, I had often acquired research materials for varied writing projects in this manner, and quickly looking through the pile I saw that they were the usual kind of publications, mainly fashion and various business periodicals, but one, *Ancestry, Your Link To The Past,* did catch my attention.

I had retrieved it from the pile and taken it with me.

That had been it; a simple thing like picking up somebody else's unwanted magazine had put me on the path that I now found myself. That same evening, I sat down to continue my research on an article that I was currently writing and not feeling particularly creative I had eventually laid it to one side; instead I poured myself a glass of wine and picked up the magazine.

As I began to thumb through its pages, the inspiration for a story started to unfold in my mind and I began to absorb as many details as possible on how to research a family tree. My own interest grew considerably as I read more interesting facts, although I was more than a little curious and intrigued by the readers' letters. Many were from people that were trying to find connections to their lineage and I found them to be sad, amusing or even bizarre. It seemed one individual was looking for his royal connection as he was certain he was of blue blood. That particular letter made me smile and I wondered why some people were always desperate to find a connection to royalty.

But it was when I read the letter from a gentleman named Mr. Chambers, that my heart skipped a beat. His letter indicated that he was looking for a connection to the surname *Shaw* in the West Country; Exmoor to be precise.

My father's family had resided in the West Country and our family name was *Shaw*. I re-read the brief letter.

To whom this may concern,

I am searching for any living relatives relating to the name James Shaw. They resided in the West Country near the village of Beaconmayes, Exmoor. I have expansive research that encompasses the Shaw Ancestry Line.

Contact address: 27 Parson Place, London SW3
Sincerely,

Mr. Chambers.

The letter was short and to the point, there was no e-mail address or telephone number, but I found myself drawn to its content. I re-read the letter several times and decided that I would get in touch with this Mr. Chambers.

It was the strangest thing; the whole plot for a story had suddenly hit me like a bolt of lightning and I felt a sudden burning desire to make this connection and to use the research. It would become the foundation for this work of fiction that was now racing through my head. I also felt certain that it would be a great opportunity to make a connection to any existing family, as I needed to find out how to search back through ancestral blood lines in order to complete a family tree for this dark tale that was taking shape, and now I could not think of a better way to educate myself than to delve into my own family history.

I took out a pen and paper and began to write a response to the letter. A deep rooted feeling told me that this had to be a genuine connection for I knew that I had heard the name Beaconmayes somewhere in my past and the facts staring me in the face were obvious. The region of England known as the West Country was where all my father's ancestors had resided and both he and his father had shared the same name; James Shaw.

I felt from that moment, the story I had spinning around my head would be my defining piece of work—my first novel.

I posted my letter that same day and each day after I had checked the mail hoping for a reply from Mr. Chambers; twelve days later it arrived.

That was the beginning of the strange correspondence and relationship between myself and the mysterious Mr. Chambers. I will call it a relationship for although I had never met him he was like no other person I had ever conversed with, even if it were only through paper and ink. In the weeks that followed and led up to this present moment, he had given me a rare insight into his life and in return I responded with revelations of my own past.

To an onlooker it might have been seen as a risky undertaking; giving a complete stranger personal details and information, but the truth of the matter was, Mr Chambers did not ever appear to pose any type of threat; he never asked any leading or uncomfortable questions, instead he had the reverse effect, he made me feel comforted by his words and he seemed genuinely interested in my thoughts and views; he asked for nothing more than that.

Our frequent writings mirrored fascinating glimpses into our individual lives, although mine seemed hardly engrossing; instead it was somewhat dull in comparison with his. Mr. Chamber's letters were beautiful, almost poetic, yet he wrote in the manner of a much older time;

a bygone era which seemed both old fashioned and charming in today's modern world. Although he never divulged his age I estimated that he had to be at least in his eighties.

I deduced this fact because he had knowledge of so many places and experiences, but he recalled that he had not travelled for many years; instead he preferred to shut himself away from the world. I could only guess that this was brought about by his age and his indication that he had some kind of illness. My own good manners and my wish to remain tactful with my mature friend meant that I did not delve into what exactly was wrong with him, for I also sensed in his words that he had no desire to discuss this matter.

However he did reveal that he rarely left his house and he did not receive visitors.

That revelation was fine by me; the mystery and the magic might not have been so vivid had I actually met my mentor in person for I did not want to imagine a sick eighty something recluse, penning these exquisite writings. Instead I preferred to imagine him always as my mysterious Mr. Chambers, for he had indeed become a mentor of sorts. While I struggled to match his perfect english and his fine style of writing, he gently chastised me when my words or phrases were not quite correct, but he would also encourage my efforts.

He described in detail his work as a travel writer, which in turn had led him to research his own ancestry. Of course, the majority of this research had taken place many years ago, but now he felt it was appropriate to complete his work, and I could fully understand that statement knowing that he probably did not have much time left.

He had lived abroad for years and he named many places I had never even heard of, mainly in Eastern Europe; he had spent several months in Italy and lived in Paris for a short while before returning to England.

Although I certainly found this information interesting it was his ability to capture my imagination that I found to be his most irresistible quality; he had a way with words that few can ever master with a pen. We did establish that I was the very last of the Shaw line. My family name would disappear forever should I get married or—a more sobering thought—when I died.

I quickly verified that we were related, but very distantly: I would have to go all the way back up my line to about 1812, and all the way down again to find him. I must admit, I was astonished at the information, to think that I could go that far back in history and find out who my ancestors were. I had never really spoken to my parents about family trees or such, being the only child of parents who were both only children themselves; there had never seemed much point. Now, how I wished I had asked questions when I had the chance, for there was no longer any one left to give me any answers; except perhaps Mr. Chambers.

I tried to do my own research, but the records I found were very incomplete and most only went back to the year 1861. Instead I relied heavily on the information I had been given by Mr. Chambers, who had visited many graveyards, searched out ancient parish records and studied long forgotten archives, and he had done all this research without ever touching a computer.

"Too complicated," he had said.

He preferred to put ink to paper and partake in writing, but despite the indication that he was old and sick he had beautiful handwriting, reminiscent of an old scripture that had been penned in ink by ancient monks; each letter perfectly formed in graceful curving strokes reminding me of some exquisite calligraphy that I had once admired. Even his choice of stationery seemed appropriate for the style of writing as it had an expensive heavy quality, which seemed to give each letter an air of mystery. I delighted in these letters and I kept every one of them safe and secure in a wooden writing box that had been my mother's.

In turn, I composed each of my letters to him as though they were ancient sonnets. He brought out a certain creativity in me, as I tried to match his beautiful words and poetic style with my own imaginative, yet humble offerings.

We continued to keep up the correspondence, long after we had established the last details of the ancestry link and I believe that indicated just how special our relationship had become, in as much as I began to feel that I really knew him, and that he certainly understood me. I had mentioned my hopes for my story that I still had to begin writing, then during the frequent correspondence between us, he had encouraged me relentlessly; always he asked in his letters, "When will you start your book?"

In one of my last letters to him I had finally confessed that I was struggling with inspiration. I wanted my book to be captivating, intriguing, a tale of corruption, mystery and murder that would shake the foundations upon which our country rested. I told him that this book was to be a defining piece of work, a true masterpiece that would elevate me into the realm of a serious author.

I also revealed to him that London was not inspiring me, as I imagined my heroine in a gothic mansion, a sixteenth century manor house or at the very least, a beautiful windswept cottage with roses around the door. I knew that I needed to immerse myself completely and to look at the world from a different perspective, if I was to identify with my main character.

It was therefore, an unexpected surprise when I received his strange invitation.

27 Parson Place
London, SW3

Dear Miss Shaw,

As always your letters capture my imagination, and you continue to hold me spellbound with your words. Your thirst for knowledge is inspiring, as it is, you possess a rare gift that awakens my senses.

Creativity is in your blood, as it was in mine and I can sense the creativity waiting to emerge in you. If you allow yourself to start this book, I am certain it will become your greatest triumph.

Perhaps you would permit someone who once long ago wrote with a passion similar to that which you now possess to help you in finding your inspiration. I still own a house on Exmoor. It is located close to the village of Beaconmayes and although it is very old it is intact and furnished. A magical place where you would find all of the inspiration you will ever need. There is an extensive library in the house and many extremely rare and beautiful books, to fuel both your creativity and knowledge. I am certain, that in this location you will find the peaceful ambiance you so desire, and nothing would give me more pleasure, than to know that you may emerge from this experience with your masterpiece, as you so eloquently use the term.

Although hidden by hedgerows and woodland; on the north side of the property you will find the panoramic view across the moors and down to the sea is unobstructed. The house is named Ravens Deep and has been in my family for generations. Directions on the back of this letter, and the key to the front door will be found hanging on an iron hook inside the porch.

I sense that you alone could breathe life into Ravens Deep, which has stood abandoned for many years. I am also confident in my expectation that you will appreciate the unrivalled beauty of the wild countryside.

Although fate has caused our paths to cross, your destiny is as yet, still to be discovered. Perhaps at Ravens Deep you will find it. You will delight me with your acceptance of this invitation.

Yours Very Sincerely,

Mr. Chambers.

A sudden chill had passed over me, but I had shrugged it off. This invitation sparked excitement and appealed to my sense of adventure. I knew instantly that I would accept.

CHAPTER TWO

Ravens Deep

I had taken an extended holiday from work under the pretext that I was visiting an old friend in the West Country, but had told no one of my real destination. I had chosen to conceal the relationship with Mr. Chambers from everyone, we shared an unusual understanding and I didn't want to answer curious questions.

I knew that Charlie would have been suspicious as to why I would want to write to a complete stranger. Everybody else would have posed their own doubts and opinions on the matter and I did not need, or want to hear them. I saw it differently from how they would; this was my opportunity to escape from the world I had known and to immerse myself completely into another.

The journey through London was tedious and painfully slow; the constant stop, start of the traffic felt as if it was deliberately trying to hinder my progress and I longed to be on the less congested country roads and leave the chaos of the city far behind. I relegated any previous doubts or negative thoughts to the furthest corner of my mind, but every so often those uncertainties came creeping back to make me anxious about what exactly waited for me at the journey's end.

By the time I arrived on Exmoor I had dispelled those imaginings and replaced them with feelings of excited anticipation. I was fatigued from the long drive, but the picturesque landscape all around boosted my stamina and could not fail to impress me; I had never visited anywhere quite as beautiful. I marvelled at the rolling moors and steep valleys and as my car climbed above the tree line, the landscape took on a windswept, desolate appearance. From my vantage point, I could see down to the coastline and along the cliff face to the jagged rocks that protruded out into the sea. It was a wild place and it would be easy to believe, were it not for the occasional farm tractor or car that passed by, I was totally alone in this wilderness.

The road continued to wind dramatically as the varied elevation changes took me down through tree covered valleys and back up again over the gentle slopes of the moors, I passed through villages filled with red sandstone buildings that displayed their distinct round chimneys and miniature turrets, then later the smaller hamlets with their clusters of cob and thatched cottages, which reminded me of the perfect chocolate box images that had inspired poets and artists alike.

Following the directions I had been given, I eventually turned from the main road onto a narrower side road, the instructions indicating that I should drive exactly three hundred yards. I drove slowly, my foot hovering above the brake, not wanting to miss my turn.

I counted slowly in my head as I gauged the exact distance; believing my judgement was accurate, I pressed harder on the brakes to bring the car to a standstill.

The road should be right here.

But there was no road. I stared at the directions again. I had made a mistake and must be on the wrong road. My first impulse was to turn the car around, but intuitively this location felt right and I looked up and peered deeper into the mass of hedges and trees. It was then that I saw a small wooden sign which was so faded with age that I could barely decipher the letters scrawled upon it.

Rush Lane.

I looked beyond the sign and saw that it really did not look like a road at all, it appeared to be more like a narrow gap between tall hedgerows, but I calculated that it was probably wide enough to allow a car to pass and I doubted that anyone else realised this road existed, let alone ever travelled it.

I breathed an immense sigh of relief; I was in the right place.

I turned the car into Rush Lane, although I felt a little nervous at how overgrown and impassable it looked, but I assured myself that roads as narrow as this one, were completely normal in the countryside.

As I passed an old, rusty farm gate pushed back into the hedge, I realised that it had probably not been closed in a long time, as it was probably too difficult to keep opening and closing a heavy gate like that, and I was glad that I didn't have to tackle it.

This location was very remote and the nearest village, Beaconmayes was four miles away. It was a small village that I had just driven through and I had been pleased to see that it did contain a grocery store and a few other amenities that I might need during my stay.

By this time Rush Lane was getting narrower by the second, and I felt my car rumble over a cattle grid that had become very overgrown, making it invisible to the eye. I felt that the hedgerows were closing in on me and I wondered what I would do if I were to meet another vehicle; although that possibility seemed unlikely.

Who in their right mind would drive up here, unless they had a reason to?

After three or four minutes of negotiating my car down the narrow lane, it widened slightly and I saw the remains of an old cobbled driveway which led to the right. A battered wooden sign standing close to the ground informed me that it must be a neighbouring property: Ravens Farm. I tried to locate the farmhouse, but nearly everything beyond the driveway was concealed from sight, all I saw were some sheep in a distant field.

I continued forwards and began to wonder if I should have turned into that driveway at the farm, but I couldn't attempt to turn my car around now; there was no room for manoeuvring. I knew that I had no choice but to proceed and see where this lane took me. I reminded myself that Mr. Chambers would have told me if I were not to have brought a car down this far.

"Just keep going Madeline, it can't be far now," I said in a firm voice to reassure myself. Although my voice sounded more confident than my feelings at this time, for the hedgerows were too high for me to judge how far I had come or how far I still have to travel. My only company was a constant, gentle tapping from the shrubs and nettles that brushed my car as I passed by.

I had pictured the house long before it came into view and from the description I had read and the image in my mind, I knew it would be beautiful and ancient, a rambling relic rising up from the landscape of the moors.

I imagined there would be roses clinging to the stonework and a sprawling garden filled with lavender and hollyhocks, but now I was starting to wonder if the access to the house was just too difficult, and the location too remote.

I had driven a long way down Rush Lane and I was starting to feel slightly doubtful about staying in such a secluded spot especially because I was alone, but just as those doubts began to multiply in my head, the lane opened up and my fears disappeared in an instant; before me stood Ravens Deep.

My expectations were not disappointed, for it was no exaggeration to describe it as breathtakingly beautiful, just as I had imagined it would be.

I had been told that the main part of the house dated back to the fourteenth century; and it certainly looked every bit that old. The soft grey coloured stonework complimented the dark grey slate roof and the gothic leaded windows. There was a long stone wall in front of the building, interrupted by a metal scroll top gate leading into the garden, and a path led up to the front door past a lichen covered stone bench which sat outside the open porch. Wisteria adorned most of the front aspect; unfortunately it wasn't in flower right now and ivy clung to all of the four chimneys covering one complete side of the house. The garden wall disappeared from my view and I supposed it encompassed the back garden as well.

I saw that a pale pink rose had climbed up and over the porch and was now competing for space with the wisteria branches, but adding to this vast array of colour, purple lavender and yellow hypericums hid the base of the stone walls. Long ago, this had been an organized and manicured garden; now it was a jumble of flowers, weeds and nettles.

I parked my car on a patch of gravel to the side of the garden wall, and walked up the three stone steps that led through the gate into the garden. I really had not believed that places like this still existed, so perfect and untouched by modern encumbrances.

"This is beautiful!" My exclamation at once startled a small chaffinch, happily hopping along the stone wall, into taking flight.

I turned and looked back down over hedgerows and across moors filled with heather and gorse to the sea in the distance. Apart from the occasional bleating of a sheep or the insistent humming of bees in the lavender, there was complete peace and tranquillity.

Walking up to the house, I took a seat on the stone bench to enjoy the view and I saw that the house was the end of the lane, as woodlands blocked all further progress other than on foot. The hedgerows which ran opposite the house seemed to divide and an overgrown footpath led between them. I thought then that it may have been a public footpath, but I had seen no sign. The air was intoxicating, with the scent of lavender and roses that drifted lazily around on the warm summer breeze. I sat unmoving for several moments gazing across to the sea which shimmered and sparkled brilliantly in the sunshine, but soon my curiosity to explore further and to see the house drew my focus away from the surrounding landscape.

The key to open the heavy oak door was hanging on an iron hook, just as Mr. Chambers had described in his letter. The key fitted perfectly and the door, despite its age and thickness, opened easily. Inside, the house had a slight musty odour from being shut up for so long and I entered into a small passage which opened into a large sitting room. Across from where I was standing a large stone inglenook dominated the wall. Two large windows adorned with heavy red velvet curtains flanked the fireplace although the curtains were partially closed, so very little sunlight shone through giving the room a dark and dismal aspect.

I moved across the room and pulled open one of the curtains, immediately a cloud of dust showered down upon me; it was obvious that no one had touched them for many years. Shaking the particles from my hair, I surveyed the scene in front of me and noticed that a thick layer of dust covered everything. Now, bathed in the brightness of the sunlight, the room was very inviting and filled with antique furnishings that belonged to another era. Everything had been forgotten and was now succumbing to the ravages of time. The feeling that time had indeed stood still was evident, for the beautifully inlaid French bracket clock had ceased motion long ago and now stood in silence on the mantle.

I lightly struck one of the chairs and as the hazy cloud rose into the air, I could see the details clearer. The fabric of the vintage chair was fashioned out of a dark red brocatelle, the deep relief was an exquisitely woven pattern of horsemen and deer which seemed reminiscent of fabrics found in ancient castles. The fireplace had seen extensive use in the past, as evidenced by a sooty stain on the back wall of the chimney, but hiding part of that chimney wall was an ornate cast-iron wood burning stove.

An opening inside the fireplace seemed obvious that its purpose once served to bake bread, as it looked like a crude stone oven. Two additional recesses in the stonework were visible and still held remnants of wax candles. I wondered how many years ago they had burned out because these days, even in a house this old, thankfully electricity had replaced the need for candles.

Two lovely watercolour landscape scenes were the only wall decoration in this room and they appeared to have some crazing upon their surface, indicating that they were in need of some careful restoration. Dominating the space in front of the fireplace was a large olive-green overstuffed sofa. Vintage carved side chairs covered in deep red brocade flanked the sofa, each having its own matching side table, one of which supported a cranberry coloured glass lamp.

Across the room, a highly carved sideboard decorated with a panache of five ostrich feathers stood against the wall and two large gold candlesticks rested on top, adding drama to the overall appearance.

This room connected to another and I approached this connecting doorway, intrigued by the door casement. Its surface was a raised wood relief, so intricately detailed that it reminded me of a pagan style carving as it depicted a stag's head and hunting horns. On entering this darkened room I was able to see two pieces of furniture; a carved desk and matching chair. I walked across to the window and pulled the heavy curtains back, which at once revealed the room's purpose.

"The library," I observed to myself and I wished at that moment I had someone with me, to share in this wondrous discovery. Bookcases filled to capacity from floor to ceiling ranged along the entire back wall and far side and Mr. Chamber's words rang true; he had said that there was an extensive library.

The books I picked up and examined were beyond antique and very rare and I delighted in reading the names of poets and authors of long ago. Dante, Coleridge, Shakespeare, Thackery, Keats, the names were all here; classics before our time, written by masters whose influence shaped our literary imaginings. This collection had been languishing away here for so many years, and I felt very privileged to be given the opportunity to access a library such as this. Besides the timeworn classics, there appeared to be modern books on every subject imaginable. Strangely enough, neither the books nor the desk seemed to have collected much dust and I noticed that large Turkish rugs slightly threadbare in places covered the flagstones, which did nothing to conceal the unevenness of the floor underneath them.

Reluctantly I left the library behind and moved back across the sitting room to another ornately encased doorway that led through to a carved staircase on the left. I peered briefly into the functional bathroom that lay straight ahead before entering the kitchen.

I found myself in a large rectangular room that contained what I could only describe as a medieval banqueting table which had seen a lot of use, judging from the various cuts, scratches and the occasional gouges on its surface. An old Aga stove was at the far end of the room, positioned next to the back door which still had its original key in the keyhole.

As I walked through the kitchen I brushed away the large cobwebs that hung down from the ceiling; this room was worse than the others in terms of neglect and

I realised that no-one had walked through here in years. I unlocked the door at once to reveal the remainder of the garden, although quite impassable as nettles were waist high, but it appeared to be a very big garden with mature trees. An old wooden hut, reminiscent of a potting shed, was the only exterior structure. I noted that I had been correct in my earlier assumptions, the stone wall did run all the way around the house and completely enclose the garden.

After locking the door again, I saw that there were high cupboards above the Aga and a deep cast iron sink fitted into an old floor cabinet, giving a small amount of work surface. There was also a small refrigerator that had certainly seen better days, which despite its age still appeared too modern and decidedly out of place in this room. I thought it all looked quite basic, but seemed functional.

I just hope everything still works.

The large kitchen window above the sink made this room feel sunny and bright and looking out I saw that it commanded fine views down over the moors to the sea in the distance. The whole aspect of this house was enchanting, but I brought my attention back to the structure of the room that I was standing in.

Throughout the rooms I had seen so far, there was a continuity of exposed beams that ran the length of the ceilings and down the walls at intervals. The walls had some unevenness about them, but the house had definite charm, although it was an odd layout and I would have expected many more rooms in a country house such as this.

As I turned to leave the kitchen, I noticed a door that I had not seen earlier. It was heavy and creaked a little when I opened it. On entering into the room beyond, I found myself in a large walk-in pantry big enough for several people to have stood in there with me. Five deep shelves jutted out from the stonework and the two lower shelves were stacked with exquisite china and several sets of fine crystal which apparently had gone untouched for years; a film of grime and dust covered everything. I picked up an old plate, wondering if I had brought enough cleaning supplies with me.

"This place is filthy." I muttered tersely as I became aware of the enormity of the task that appeared before me. This room had a distinct chill to it, probably the reason it had been used as a pantry, but I was glad to shut the door firmly behind me.

I left the kitchen behind and walked up the staircase, mesmerized as I progressed by the decorative details. A mixture of different wood, panels of maybe oak and elm, formed a continuous rhythmic pattern of curling acanthus leaves that carried my eye upwards and peering out from the leaves were several fox heads, their eyes watching my continued progress upstairs. The details were fascinating and I ran my hand lightly over the carved wood and smooth banister. There was something so appealing and addictive about touching wood, perhaps because it had once been a living thing, or the carpenter who once worked upon it had put so much feeling and commitment into the fine details that it still seemed to have a living form.

I reached the top of the staircase and found myself on a small landing with one door, which was the first of two bedrooms. I entered the darkened room and immediately went to the window to open the curtains and allow the light to shine through. But once I pulled aside the heavy blue and gold damask curtains, I was surprised to find the room still so dark. Then I realised that the ivy had almost covered the window; I knew I would need to trim it back if this room was ever to see the sunlight again.

Despite the gloom, I could see the bedroom suite had covers that matched the blue and gold damask fabric of the curtains and on closer examination, I realized the furniture was all made from some exotic wood, covered with artistic carvings depicting birds of paradise and butterflies in deep relief on the headboard and legs of the bed. A scroll design adorned the wardrobe and it was framed by another bird of paradise in deep relief with its wings fanned, with a matching dressing table completing the scene. As I left the room, I felt sad that everything had been allowed to decay, as if someone long ago had walked away and never returned. These beautiful pieces deserved appreciation, to be used and loved, not just left and forgotten. It was quite a depressing notion and I wondered what had happened. Someone had used them once; someone had carefully selected each piece for each room.

The landing on which I stood had an additional four steps which led up to a corridor roughly twelve feet long, containing two doors. The first led into another bathroom, not quite as basic as the one downstairs; it contained an ornate Victorian bathtub and pedestal basin; its decoration was simple and elegant, as the cream panelling on the walls complimented the white mouldings on the coving.

At the end of the corridor was the door to the main bedroom, but I was totally unprepared for the magnificence that lay before me when I first entered into this room. Leaded gothic windows curved in a semicircle to form a bay window, from which curtains cascaded to the floor in waves of heavy silk. The curtains were well aged and their rose pink colour had faded considerably. I noticed that there were fine details in the ornate alabaster fireplace, which was partly obscured by a pale pink boudoir chair and matching footstool. Silk wallpaper the colour of the palest pink rose, worn and faded in places, hung on the walls and in the corners of the room where the sunlight had never shined, I could still see the rich vivid hues of the pink and green butterflies, with delicate lacy wings that entwined the oriental flowers and adorned the background.

Above the fireplace hung a portrait of a pretty young girl, maybe eighteen or nineteen, her pale flawless skin almost matched the colour of the old fashioned ivory dress that she was wearing. Her eyes seemed to beckon me to come closer, I obliged and stared at the image. I got the distinct feeling that I had seen this portrait before, there was something very familiar about it and I searched for some clue on the canvas, but I could not find the name of the painting or the artist.

After a few minutes I turned away, but I was almost certain that the girl's eyes were firmly fixed upon me as I moved around the room. I tried not to feel intimidated, after all, it was only a picture. Instead I turned my attention to the sumptuous four-poster bed adorned with more of the heavy silk curtains that dominated the main area of this room. Laid across the bed was a bedspread of silk to match. On closer inspection, I realized the fabric contained hundreds of tiny embroidered flowers in tones of pink, green and gold. The bed frame and headboard were made of exotic carved wood, with a relief of vine leaves that complimented a matching wardrobe and dressing table. This room felt as though somebody of great importance should have slept here and I was awed by the fact that this would be my bedroom.

I continued with my inspection of the room and noticed an opening set into the wall, a small arched recess to the side of the dressing table, similar to what you could sometimes find in old churches; a niche to hold a candle, but this was different in that it grew narrower towards its furthest wall and it had a glass inset, like a tiny window. I studied it in detail and as much as I looked, I could see nothing but blackness.

Maybe the ivy has grown up and hidden its true purpose.

Although I wondered what purpose it could have possibly served, perhaps a candle being placed there, maybe to light the way to the house. I liked the idea of that thought; a beacon of illumination rising out of the mists of the moors or a glimmer of light for those travelling home to Ravens Deep so many years ago.

I looked at my watch; it was already mid afternoon and I knew that as beautiful and decadent as this room was, I could not sleep in this ancient bed without changing all the old linens and removing some of the ingrained dirt. Besides, I had no idea when someone last slept here and for all I knew, the bed could be full of bed bugs and other creatures. I was glad I had the foresight to bring clean sheets and linens with me. However, the bed would need some thorough cleaning, to dislodge any unwelcome occupants it may have contained, but I decided that job could wait until tomorrow. I could easily make up a temporary bed on the sofa in the sitting room for tonight and I would worry about my future sleeping arrangements tomorrow. My priority would be to unpack and clean at least some of the kitchen, as I did not relish the thought of eating or drinking out of any of the crockery in its current state. But despite the years of neglect and decay, the house felt welcoming. I could even believe that I felt its embrace as I moved through each room and I knew that I was the right person to breathe new life into Ravens Deep.

CHAPTER THREE

In the Night

I made my way back down the stairs and a feeling of unreality settled over me.

Had I really been in London this morning?

It was hard to believe that now, because city life felt like a million miles away.

A little later I turned my attention to unpacking the car, grateful that I had brought some basic supplies with me, because getting to and from Ravens Deep had proved longer than I had anticipated. I would have to get used to driving the extra distance to get anywhere. Along with my few groceries, I had also thought to pack various items that I assumed I might have needed: candles, matches and a good torch. Although I was relieved to find that I wouldn't be forced to use them, except perhaps in an emergency. Ravens Deep did have functioning electricity and I had quickly tested all of the taps; water did still run through all of the plumbing. I was probably just being over anxious for I was certain that Mr. Chambers would have informed me if there had been no basic facilities.

It was unclear when he had last paid a visit, and I hadn't considered the possibility that the house had been completely abandoned, but it certainly appeared that no-one had maintained or even entered into this building in a very long time. I wondered what would become of this house when Mr. Chambers passed away, or if there were any living relatives? Then it would probably become part of their inheritance, but maybe there was no-one, maybe it would just fall into ruin.

I had only been at Ravens Deep an hour or so, but already this house had given me a most peculiar feeling, as though I belonged here and that was something I had never experienced anywhere before. The very structure itself seemed to wish me to remain within its walls, and I felt slightly disturbed at such a strange perception. I had never considered myself susceptible to energies of the paranormal, but I could not deny that from the moment I had stepped over the threshold I had been enticed by the heart and soul of the house.

I smiled at my own interpretations; did houses have souls? This one felt like it did. I wondered if Mr. Chambers would ever consider selling Ravens Deep.

"Probably not, it will get left to some relative no doubt," I muttered in answer to my own question. Then I questioned the sensibility of living out here permanently; although wonderful in the summer, it would be very isolated and lonely in the winter months.

A little later I threw all the windows wide open to get rid of the old and musty air, and reset the clock on the mantle which instantly filled the peaceful room with a constant reassuring tick. The house was already starting to feel alive once more, and I knew it wouldn't take long to make this a beautiful place to live in as it had been so long ago.

For the remainder of the afternoon and most of the evening, I dedicated myself to washing the china and crystal until they shone like new. The years of neglect had left a tough grime on all the surfaces and floors, but undeterred by that fact, I cleaned and polished until the kitchen and its contents were transformed into something far more appealing.

Too tired after all that to do much else, I made myself a bed on the sofa in the sitting room and sat down to relax for the evening. I turned on my portable television and was pleased to find that I could actually get adequate reception here. I knew before arriving that modern amenities would be limited, so along with the television I had brought my laptop computer and a cell phone in case of emergencies.

I lay back on the sofa feeling tired, vaguely aware of some news program in the background, and lost in my thoughts of the day's events and Ravens Deep, I must have drifted off to sleep from sheer exhaustion.

It seemed that only a few moments had passed, but I woke suddenly.

Instinctively, I checked my watch still feeling slightly dazed. It was just after three in the morning and I absently acknowledged that I must have slept for at least four hours.

My attention was drawn to the television that was still turned on, but now the picture was gone and it had been replaced by a quiet hissing that emanated softy from its depths. I sat up wondering if, in fact, it was the television that had roused me from my peaceful sleep. My eyes slowly adjusted to the light from the table lamp and as my initial confusion subsided, I became acutely aware of my heart racing as I realized something other than the television had disturbed me.

The prickles started on the back of my neck and ran all the way down my spine and I fought to bring under control my growing fright. I sat very still, straining my ears for the slightest sound.

Was there an animal outside, an owl perhaps?

I searched for something that would give a reasonable name to my fear as I tried to remain calm and analyze exactly what I had heard.

Was someone in the house?

I knew that I had locked all the windows and doors.

For goodness sake, it was probably the television!

I found the television remote and pressed the off button. The hissing ceased and the room became peaceful and quiet once more, allowing me to collect and organize my thoughts.

The prickles started to dissipate and I began to relax even though anxious thoughts continued to meander through my head. I sought to make sense of the fact that you could be alone somewhere during the day and not the slightest sound or movement disturbs your peace of mind, but in the middle of the night when dark shadows shift unnaturally and the smallest of disturbances can become construed as a menacing force, then perceived fear could overwhelm rational thought. The voice in my head told me that my imagination was working overtime and the hissing from the TV had allowed strange noises to infiltrate my vulnerable dream state of being. Now, I was sure that's what had happened and I began to feel much calmer. It was only a dream.

Another sound …

The prickles were back and all of my senses were horrifyingly alert.

The creaking continued in clarifying detail and I was certain that it was not the usual expansion and contraction noise that sometimes occurs with temperature changes; this was different, it sounded more like a door being opened very slowly.

I strained my ears listening as the noise continued and all my previous thoughts seemed irrelevant; I was confronted by the frightening reality that this noise was not imagined—it was real.

Something is here!

I shivered inwardly as the spine tingling sensations of fear threatened to take over my entire being.

The source of the noise was coming from the kitchen and I turned towards it in alarm, my eyes fixed on the passageway in an unblinking stare. Slowly I rose from my sitting position. Glancing around the room I noticed the heavy gold candlestick on the sideboard and quickly and silently as possible, I crossed the room and snatched it from its resting position. I gripped it tightly in my shaking hands and pressed it to my body.

What should I do?

I knew that I had to do something.

"Calm down, you have to calm down," I repeated quietly to myself.

With every moment that passed my feeling of dread grew, knowing that I would have to confront whatever, whoever was there. I quickly looked around for my phone and then remembered that it was in the kitchen, along with the key to the front door. The awful realization hit me; I was trapped and somebody else was in this house.

"Bloody hell," I uttered under my breath, realizing the horror of that thought.

My throat seemed to tighten unnaturally and my skin flushed with a sudden intense heat. I moved towards the passage, but my progress was not quick, knowing that each step potentially brought me closer to meeting someone that wished me harm. My eyes were transfixed on the open doorway and I did not dare to even breathe.

Cautiously, I looked through the opening into the kitchen, seeing nothing but the sinister blackness that obscured the majority of its contents. I stared harder, searching through the darkness for a shape that would confirm my suspicions.

Even the air had a chill to it—a consequence of something evil about to happen? I felt my self grow pale as I could hear breathing—something was close to me and the blood seemed to drain from my skin. Terrifying images of murderers and madmen stalking me in the shadows flew through my mind before I summoned the courage to think more rationally and pull myself together. I knew there were knives in the kitchen drawer; if I could reach them, then at least I might be able to defend myself if the candlestick failed. I frantically tried to remember the location of the kitchen light switch—it was just inside the door.

I had to turn that light on, but the fear kept me frozen to the spot.

Another noise!

I recognized that someone was opening the pantry door! All at once, cold logic tookover—whatever it was, *it* was at the pantry door, and that was at least six feet away from the light switch. I knew I had no other choice and moved as fast as I could. Reaching into the kitchen, I quickly found the light switch and flicked it on, simultaneously aiming my candlestick to strike the intruder that was almost certain to appear before me.

The room was empty. Half relieved, half terrified, I took in the whole room with one look. Nothing seemed out of place but the pantry door was slightly ajar.

I know I closed that door!

I hadn't realized that I had been holding my breath, and I started breathing again slowly and quietly, but it sounded loud and laborious to my ears. The deafening sound of my own heartbeat was adding to the din, but one question raced through my mind and demanded an answer: *Why has no-one come out?* I approached the pantry as steadily as my trembling legs would allow, candlestick at the ready.

Whoever was in there could surely hear my heart beating by now and I hoped that my courage would not fail me. I took a deep breath and somehow, I found my voice.

"Come out, I know you're in there," I said loudly. The silence was deafening and no sound or movement came to my ears. I thought then that maybe I should just grab my phone and key and run.

But where would I run to?

I could see my car keys, lying on the surface at the far end of the kitchen. It was a long way to the other end, I had no choice but to confront whoever was in the pantry. At least maybe then I could retain some control over the situation. I edged closer. I knew what I had to do.

Taking a deep breath, I moved very fast and kicked the door as hard as I could. It slammed back against the wall with deafening bang and something shot out of the pantry! I screamed and pressed myself to the wall, wishing I could disappear into it. The candlestick was now gripped tighter in my shaking hands and I forced my eyes to focus on what had come out. There before me was a mouse, huddled in the corner under the cabinet.

It took a moment to register that my imagined axe murderer was nothing more than a field mouse and I cautiously moved forward so I could see entirely into the pantry.

It really was empty. I felt the colour creep back into my skin and I began to breathe properly again. A mixture of shock and relief overcame me, followed by a delayed reaction in which I didn't know whether to laugh or cry, as the adrenaline left my body. My legs felt strangely weak and I sat down at the table to regain my composure. It was obvious to me now that there was bound to be the odd mouse or two in a house this old.

It was only a mouse! You idiot, a murderer would have just killed you while you slept.

I reproached myself severely, annoyed that instead of behaving rationally, I had allowed my imagination to take control and scared myself half to death with all my thoughts of imagined breathing and unnatural noises.

The pantry of all places, why would anyone go in there?

I had been reading too many Victorian novels; in real life there was not an asylum down the road and no escaped murderers waiting to kill beautiful women in the middle of the night. This was just an old house, it was remote, but the odds of anyone waiting around to kill the latest occupant now seemed absurd.

The mouse had recovered from the fright I had given him, and was now scurrying around the floor, in search of food no doubt. On the whole I didn't mind mice, but I knew where there was one, others would follow, and sharing a house with a whole colony made me shudder. I resolved to buy some mousetraps and deal with them in the daylight. As all my apprehension disappeared, I turned on every light and walked around the rest of the house, keeping my candlestick for company.

I laughed at myself for thinking someone was in here with me, for I knew, I had locked every door and window; nothing could be here. I went back downstairs and feeling much calmer, I made myself a cup of tea and sat at the kitchen table to drink it, knowing it would be impossible to sleep now. My thoughts came back to that pantry door. It hardly seemed logical that it would have been so easily opened and I went to examine it. After opening and closing it, I noted it really was a heavy door and not easily pushed open, just as I had suspected.

Surely a mouse couldn't have opened it.

"I probably left it open," I muttered to myself in resignation.

After all, I had been tired; that must be the explanation. I tried hard to convince myself of that fact, but somewhere in the back of my mind I remembered actually closing that pantry door.

CHAPTER FOUR

Darius

I took my tea and opened the front door, it was almost four o'clock. A single bird song resonated shrilly though the silent air and a moment later another joined in; the dawn chorus had begun.

The weather had been very warm for the last few weeks, even at this early hour it felt comfortable to be outside. I walked to the little stone bench and sat sipping my tea, gazing towards the sea which was as yet invisible. The strange swirling mists that hung over the moors obscured my distant vision, instead it gave the landscape a surreal quality.

Suddenly, out of the corner of my eye I saw a movement. I turned my head and stared into the shadows of the trees. In the dim half-light I thought I saw the shape of a person. The sight made me catch my breath and I sat unmoving trying to focus my eyes. The shape moved further into the tree line, away from me, but almost instantly a deer emerged from the same place. She seemed agitated, and rapidly moved towards the gap in the hedgerow—something had spooked her.

A moment later two smaller deer appeared and followed the same path as the first one. I pondered the thought that I must have witnessed a trick of the shadows and light, causing the dark shapes to shift and take on different forms. Or perhaps it was in light of the recent episode that I was allowing normal things to manifest themselves into something sinister.

I pushed all other dubious thoughts away, instead recognizing how delightful this situation was; I never saw deer in the city.

I must have sat for an hour or more, witnessing the magic of the mists rising over the moors, until finally the sun broke through, replacing the shadowy mystery of the landscape with a bright new morning. Slowly the air came to life around me, from the incessant songs of the birds to the first insects as they were energized by the rays of sunlight, motivating them into a frenzy of activity. Life was apparent all around.

Back inside, I began to think about the task at hand; making Ravens Deep a living, breathing house once more. I cleaned and polished the floors and the usable surfaces, I took the cushions and anything else I could carry into the garden to shake and hopefully remove the years of ingrained dust. In the master bedroom, I decided to take the beautiful linens and put them away, rather than try to wash them. The fabric seemed so delicate that it might disintegrate in my hands. I left all the curtains intact, including the ones on the bed, as I could see no way of removing them.

A few hours later I had transformed the interior from the previous day. The surfaces shone like new and now with most of the dust and grime removed, the whole house took on a more dignified quality.

It was early afternoon and I had been working all morning. I was eager to explore the village and decided that I had had quite enough of house cleaning for one day. I locked up the house and drove back along the winding lane to the main road that led to Beaconmayes.

The village had most amenities; a small grocery store, a baker, a hardware store and chemist, even a little park. I spent an enjoyable hour walking the length of the village high street and visiting the various shops, and eventually I bought a sandwich from the bakers and went to sit on the park bench.

Several fat ducks were swimming in a small pond close to where I sat. They were very tame and upon seeing I had some food, waddled out of the water and stood watching me expectantly. Obviously they had become accustomed to being fed by the locals. As I gave the last of my sandwich to one of the more persistent ducks, an older man whom I had noticed earlier in the village walked up and sat at the other end of my bench. He had a bag of breadcrumbs and sat patiently feeding the ducks. We both smiled, as the ducks squabbled amongst themselves for the crumbs. He glanced in my direction and acknowledged me with a nod.

"Good Afternoon," he said cordially.

"Hello, isn't this is a lovely place?" I replied politely. He turned to me, the sunlight catching his silver hair and making it seem almost white.

"Yes it is, one of the few unspoiled villages. Are you visiting?" he inquired.

"Well, not really, I am staying in the area for a while..." I paused, "up at Ravens Deep." The man did not seem to give any indication that he recognized the name, so I continued. "It is about four miles from here."

He gave a nod of acknowledgement and hesitated for a moment. "Is that a holiday place?" he asked in an enquiring tone. I smiled at him.

"No, it's just an old house, belonging to a friend." I felt that this was not much of an explanation, so I continued. "It is quite hidden and remote, off the beaten track a bit, but the views from up there are beautiful."

The ducks, realizing we had nothing more to offer, had gone back to the pond. After a few moments, I turned to him. I sensed that he was a local and he might be a useful person to tell me more about the area.

"How long have you lived here?" I asked. The man seemed to think for a bit.

"About sixty two ... three years," he laughed. "Too long ... I should have left long ago."

I smiled in return, but thought that it was a bit of a strange comment.

After a few minutes my own curiosity got the better of me. "Don't you like living here?" I asked, hoping that I didn't sound as though I was prying. He seemed to think about the question in detail before he answered.

"I have always loved the countryside, but it can get very lonely and sometimes beautiful can get boring," he concluded with a knowing look. I saw a look of sorrow lurking in his eyes as he continued on. "I was going to leave, just never got around to it." He fell silent for several more moments and I thought that perhaps I was being too forward, I should not push him any further.

"Have you been up to Selman Point yet?" he asked pointedly, changing his train of thought and mood completely.

"No I haven't heard of that, what is it?" I replied with interest.

"It is the highest point on this coast; you can look down to the sea and across the moors for miles, there is a signpost on the other side of the village."

"I will certainly drive up there, thank you. I'm Madeline by the way, Madeline Shaw." My companion turned to me and extended his hand.

"Samuel Dunklin," he replied. We shook hands, then sat quietly just enjoying the peaceful afternoon. As reluctant as I was to leave, I knew I should get back, so I stood up.

"It was nice to meet you Samuel."

"Likewise, Madeline, I hope you have a nice stay in ...what did you call it?" Samuel was trying to recall my earlier words.

"Ravens Deep," I offered.

"Ah yes ... I cannot ever remember hearing that name before though."

"It belongs to Mr. Chambers, I believe the family has owned the house for years," I said patiently, in an effort to jog his memory.

"Chambers?" He looked at me sharply. "There was a family, I don't think that was their name though, they owned everything around here." He seemed thoughtful as if he were trying to recall a memory. I was interested to hear that fact and sat down again, shifting my position on the bench to face him.

"Does the family still live close by?" Samuel paused for a moment.

"It's just an old story," he said a little dismissively, but he saw my inquiring look and obvious interest. "It happened a very long time ago, before my time." He hesitated again.

"What happened?" I moved slightly closer to him. Samuel had undoubtly sparked my interest with his few curious words and now I found myself eager to hear this old story.

"I only remember the stories that my grandfather told," he said looking at me cautiously, "and I am not even sure if there is any truth to them," he added, by way of an explanation. I smiled in encouragement as I waited for him to begin.

"The family was wealthy; they owned houses, farms and much of the land for miles, there were many stories that surrounded the family, but one story began to circulate around the village that caused a stir in the whole community. It was said that the family disappeared one night. Some speculated that they had simply moved away to another county, but others believed in a darker reason for their disappearance; they believed they had been murdered. This speculation was fuelled by the fact that several people died mysteriously in the village around this time and then the animals began dying in the fields for no apparent cause," he paused, "the local people believed they had been put under a curse!" he concluded dramatically.

I tried not to, but the tone of his voice and words made me smile. Samuel saw my look.

"You have to remember people believed in dark magic and even today you would be shrewd not to dismiss that thought completely. Most villages have rituals that they uphold to chase away the evil spirits and this one is no different." He considered for a moment. "The times have changed, but many still believe."

I felt an odd sort of shiver from that revelation.

"What is the curse?" I asked softly, catching my breath in anticipation. Samuel looked at me for a long moment and then he took his focus to the duck pond.

"I don't remember," he said a little too quickly, "it all happened too long ago," and in that answer, I knew he wasn't going to tell me.

I stared at him, while I digested this curious information. He didn't appear to be joking, or trying to scare me, he really believed something sinister happened here and the subtle indication was; it was still occurring.

My thoughts on the subject were more rational.

"I have read that this village was once a leper colony, so some of the village people could have died of the squalid living conditions that they had to endure," I reasoned. Samuel pursed his lips, thinking.

"Ah well, some say that was what happened," he replied. "I cannot seem to recall the family's name though. Was it Chambers?" He appeared to have had enough of this line of questioning and had brought the conversation full circle back to the family name.

"I don't think that was the name," he said at last.

I began to feel that perhaps Samuel was slightly senile, as sensible people didn't really believe in such stories. After a few moments more I asked what he thought really happened to the family as the land and houses had to belong to someone today. Samuel's mood visibly lightened. "Ah, no one knows for sure, some must have survived and it is thought they came back to live in these parts. One thing I can tell you, all the land you see around here is in some sort of trust, can never be sold. Still owned by descendants of the family, if any remain."

Samuel had definitely sparked my interest and I wished he could have remembered the name of the family, at least I would be able to research the history myself. I knew that even though the story was probably just folklore, there was often an element of truth behind most strange stories, but I doubted if it was really as sinister as Samuel had indicated.

I stood up and smiled back at my companion.

"Well, I really have to be leaving." I bade him good-bye and walked slowly back to my car. I thought it was odd that he didn't appear to know of Ravens Deep, having lived in the area for so long, and what was all that nonsense about dark magic and curses? Could it be that Samuel was just superstitious, as some country folk were even in this day and age. Maybe, he just didn't get out that much, and Ravens Deep was well concealed. I imagined that unless you knew of the exact location, even the locals wouldn't necessarily know it existed.

I drove back to Rush Lane and to the first driveway that indicated Ravens Farm. I thought then that I should have asked Samuel about it, as farms were often better known than houses. I stopped the car and got out. I walked a little way up the driveway, which appeared to stretch into the distance, but I could see no buildings.

Maybe I should drive down and find the farmhouse.

But as I looked at the track I knew I would need an off road vehicle to navigate it, as parts of it had been so churned up that it looked un-drivable and also very steep, as my eye followed the cobbles downwards and out of sight between the hedgerows. Now I was standing here it didn't even look like a main entrance and certainly had not been used recently.

I returned to my car, and continued on to Ravens Deep. I wasn't sure if it was my imagination, but the lane seemed even longer this time.

I unloaded the groceries, and set the newly purchased mousetraps. Then I unpacked my notebooks and laid them and my research papers on the desk in the library. Tomorrow I could concentrate on their content and start to write my book. As for today, I would go outside for what remained of the afternoon.

Outside in the garden I sat down on one of the less ornate chairs that I had dragged out with me; the stone bench was just too hard to sit on for a long period of time. Having already selected a couple of old books from the library, I settled down with them. It was a perfect afternoon.

I managed to read for a little while, but found it difficult to remain idle. The state of the garden seemed to beckon me as it was in dire need of attention. I knelt down on the ground and saw that the flowers were choking under the strangled hold of the bindweed, which had attached itself to everything in sight. Despite their near suffocation, they still managed to poke their heads through the tangled undergrowth, but the garden seemed stifled; every plant was desperately competing for its space in this miniature jungle. I resolved that I would just pull a few weeds out, but before long, I was completely absorbed with the task I had set myself. The time passed quickly and I didn't notice the lengthening shadows as the sun slowly dipped behind the trees.

Lost in my own thoughts, I was suddenly aware that I was not alone; I looked up. Standing a few feet away at the garden gate was a young man, I guessed him to be in his mid twenties. Although slightly obscured by the shadows, I could see even at a distance that he had strikingly handsome features that were only slightly hidden by his long dark hair that fell lightly across one eye.

Startled, I scrambled to my feet as I tried to regain my composure.

"Hi, sorry I didn't see you," I said. At the same time I was wondering where on earth he had come from, and just how long he had been standing there?

"Good evening, I apologize if I frightened you." He spoke with a clear, articulated accent that told me he had a certain refinement and a good education.

"No, not at all," I lied, as I brushed my hands on my jeans. "I just did not expect to see anyone up here. Do you live around here?" As I took a couple of steps towards him, I saw at once that he had the most vivid green eyes, and I felt the heat of them over my skin. I tried not to blush and briefly moved my own gaze over his face, noticing that the sharp definition of his cheekbones, in his almost classical face, seemed only to make his cat like eyes more alluring. I held my hand out and smiled.

"My name's Madeline." He seemed to momentarily pause and study it before taking it briefly. "I am Darius, and I do live here." He gestured back through the woods.

Our hands must have touched for the briefest of moments. His skin was chilled, as if it had been recently plunged into cold water and I briefly glanced down. His hands were slender and perfectly formed and his fingernails long and beautifully shaped, as if manicured. Whether it was the coldness of his hands, the intensity of his eyes, or just his mere presence, I felt completely unnerved; unsure if I should be feeling frightened or thrilled. A degree of caution seemed appropriate.

"I'm staying here with a friend," I began. "I didn't realize that anyone else lived around here." I knew that I sounded flustered, his sudden appearance had that instant effect on me, but I wasn't about to let him think I was entirely alone.

A smile of amusement seemed to cross his face. I felt certain he could sense my discomfort and deception, but he kept up the charade.

"How do you, and your *friend*, like the house?" His eyes never left my own, and there was a definite emphasis on the word friend. I knew then for certain that he had seen through my deception, but I pretended not to notice.

"I love it; it's so beautiful and peaceful." I replied with confidence. "How far from here do you live?" He seemed to hesitate before answering, almost as though every answer was a well-rehearsed response.

"My home is back through the woods, but I like to walk up here. You are right, the views from here are beautiful." He continued to speak as he turned towards the moors. "The sea is very calm tonight, and you can look across to the horizon." I too looked into the distance, but in the rapidly fading light I could barely make out the dark void of sea that lay beyond the moors.

"You must have really good eyesight," I remarked cordially, and Darius turned back to me, his face expressionless.

"How long are you staying?" he asked in a tone that was almost too nonchalant. "I don't know yet," I said truthfully. Darius had undoubtedly disturbed me. Although I found him extremely attractive, I was also well aware that I was alone and for all I knew he could be dangerous. I fought to suppress my conflicting feelings and to sound unconcerned.

"Does your family come up here also?" Again amusement flickered in his eyes, but he just as casually answered.

"I live alone," he said a little dismissively. His eyes moved up to the house. "It is very dark out here, and your friend must be wondering where you are."

He knew full well that there was no-one in the house, for now it was also in complete darkness. I completely ignored his leading comment, instead I chose to be as polite as possible.

"Yes the light has almost gone, I have to go indoors as I can barely see out here."

"Goodnight Madeline," he said as he turned from me.

"It was nice meeting you," I replied cordially as he moved away and the darkness of his clothes made him quickly disappear into the obscurity of the night.

I walked inside, turned on the lights and closed the curtains. I was aware of the sensation of fluttering in my stomach and my heartbeat was faster than normal. Now I wondered just how long had Darius been watching me? So I did have a neighbour, but I found I was disturbed by that fact.

Darius was definitely intriguing. He had been polite, courteous and non-threatening, so what was it that played on my mind? I thought about the way he said my name and it made me shiver, but were those tremors of fear or anticipation? I couldn't quite decide.

I busied myself around the house for the evening, unable to get the earlier encounter out of my head. It must have been around eleven o'clock, after I had finally satisfied myself that I had closed all the windows and doors, I climbed the stairs to go to bed; excited to be sleeping in the magnificent bedroom for the first time.

Sitting down at the dressing table to brush my hair, I happened to glance up to the portrait of the girl in the white dress and as I studied the painting, my eyes found my own reflection in the mirror. I suddenly realized the recognition—she really looked a lot like me. Her hair, although arranged in an old fashioned pinned up style, was obviously long and blonde. She had eyes shaped like my own. I wondered who she was and whether she was some distant relation.

I sat bemused, brushing my hair.

All at once I had the strangest feeling that I was not completely alone. The tiny hairs on the back of my neck stood on end, and goose bumps rose over my flesh. I shivered slightly and quickly glanced over my shoulder, but the room was empty.

I undressed slowly feeling uneasy, but I knew there was no logical reason for these strange feelings and I climbed into the magnificent bed.

All the same, the sensation that I was not quite alone stayed with me and I debated whether or not I should sleep with the light on. I lay listening for any unusual noises, but all was quiet and I reassured myself that it was normal to feel a bit anxious in unfamiliar surroundings and I turned the light out. The sensation disappeared along with my apprehension; the doors were locked, the curtains drawn, no-one could possibly be watching me.

CHAPTER FIVE

Hallowed Ground

Strangely enough, I slept well. The noise of the mouse-traps springing that invaded my dreams had not disturbed my sleep.

I allowed myself to luxuriate in bed for several minutes, then reluctantly I got up and threw open the curtains and the sunlight flooded the room. I could feel that it was already warming up, but the thick stone walls of the house kept the interior comfortable and cool. I went downstairs to the kitchen and discovered that two mouse traps contained lifeless bodies.

The pantry door stood wide open. I shivered despite the warm air.

There was a distinct possibility of an immaterial presence in this house, although that notion did not disconcert me unnecessarily; it was hard to feel disturbed while standing in a warm sunlit room, and I was not about to be intimidated by that thought.

So what if the pantry door opens by itself?

In reality that wasn't a menacing force, there was probably a perfectly good reason.

"Maybe the hinges need tightening or the wood is warped," I said, convincing myself of that sensible explanation. In a house this old, was it not usual to have sensations, hear noises and the doors to open of their own accord? I wondered about the history of Ravens Deep and who had lived here in the past. If I ever saw Darius again, I made up my mind that I would ask him. Locals always knew the history of old houses and the stories of the people that had once inhabited them.

After breakfast, I sat down in the library and looked at my papers on the desk. Through my research I had traced my ancestry back to my great grandfather three times removed. With the help of Mr. Chamber's letters, I had discovered that he was John Shaw, born in 1838. He had married a girl named Maria. Mr. Chambers had not known her surname and I had been unable to discover that information myself.

At Ravens Deep there was no phone line, no internet connection. I had to rely on the research that I had previously completed in London. There I had been able to access old census records, but they were so incomplete and I had come to several dead ends. I wondered if I could get back any further into the history of my family and then again did it really matter? My curiosity for personal history had been satisfied as Mr Chambers had already given me the relevant information.

I sat thinking, knowing I had based my story on some of my own ancestry, but the main character in my book was fictional, so now I had to construct the details differently. The girl I would write about was not me. I rose from the desk and surveyed the vast array of books in front of me. I read the various titles, but it was one with no title which caught my attention. It was a very old leather bound volume, ripped and frayed as though well read over the years. The inside cover was missing, but it seemed to contain local history. I found Beaconmayes very easily and it was interesting to see pictures of the village, at a time when it had been little more than a few old cottages.

I took a seat back at the desk and carefully turned over each page. As I reached the middle of the book I found a diagram of a map showing the surrounding lands. I saw that a church was marked and roughly worked out that its location was in the middle of nearby woods. I calculated that it wouldn't be too far from here and I assumed it could be reached by car nowadays.

I looked through the entire book, but I could find no mention of Ravens Deep or Ravens Farm and this did strike me as odd. Why would a local book be comprehensive in listing all the old and historical properties in the area at that time, but leave these out? Especially when this house had obviously been here a lot longer than some other properties mentioned.

I came to the end of the book and noticed that several pages were missing from the spine. I wondered if they contained the information I was seeking, but had been removed intentionally and that thought process posed a more curious question.

"Why would someone in the past have not wanted any record of this house to exist?"

My voice interrupted the peaceful ambiance of the room and my thoughts turned back to the conversation I had with Samuel Dunklin yesterday and the fact that he had never heard of Ravens Deep.

I spent all morning searching through the library for any evidence that Ravens Deep or the farm existed on paper, but I turned up absolutely nothing and I could not help but wonder if these properties had ever been recorded.

I must admit that I was very perplexed at the mystery, but I was no closer to solving it. Instead I focused my attention on my own research notes and began to write the first chapter for my book. The next couple of hours passed quickly. I was happily absorbed with my thoughts and ideas and even happier with the progress I had made. However, I did not want to spend the whole day indoors. Eventually I laid my writing to one side, lured somewhat by the warm afternoon sunshine and I decided to explore my new surroundings.

I walked along the path that led between the hedgerows. It continued, not across the fields and moors as I had imagined, but into the trees. A well-trodden deer path, I supposed. The elevation changed as at first the path led upwards and then a steeper incline downwards, all the while keeping in line with the distant fields on the right that were dotted with sheep. I wondered if they belonged to Ravens Farm. The woods were cool and peaceful. An occasional warm breeze drifted lazily through the hanging woodlands, and emerald moss grew in wonderful abstract clumps on the boulders and trees that lined the path. I spotted a wild orchid amongst the decaying leaf mould and I left the path to take a closer look. After making my way cautiously downwards, I suddenly found myself standing on the edge of a deep chasm. I peered over the edge and found myself looking down upon the body of a dead sheep.

"Poor thing." I could not help but feel upset at my grim discovery. It had probably strayed from the field, lost its footing up here on the steep slope and fallen into the depths below. I could see how easily it could happen and was mindful that it could be just as treacherous for me and unwise to try to negotiate the terrain any further. I quickly returned to the path.

As I continued walking, my thoughts came back to Darius. Where did he live? He had indicated back through the woods. Now, I wondered where exactly. I could not imagine a cottage or house here. It was devoid of any man-made intrusion of any kind and it was easy to believe that these woods had remained this way since the beginning of time. Beautiful and unchanging, oblivious to a modern world where so many people have forgotten or even know that places like this exist.

Just the same, I couldn't help thinking about him. Darius had left a distracting impression on my mind and I had to admit that I was more that a little curious just how close he was living to Ravens Deep.

The path continued downwards getting narrower all the time and it really was not safe to stray from it, because of the steep bank on the left side and the deep ravine to the right. I assumed that if I kept walking this path would lead me all the way down to the sea.

Maybe this was an old smuggler's route.

It certainly was in the middle of nowhere, a safe haven where boats could have brought their ill gotten gains. Ironically that idea suddenly seemed to make sense. Could it be that Ravens Deep had been used as an old smuggler' haunt? Therefore its location had not been widely publicized, and the records erased to ensure the locals would not be aware of what occurred right on their very doorstep. The Exmoor coast had been notorious for smuggling in its past. Maybe that was indeed the answer to the mystery of Ravens Deep, if there was a mystery to be revealed, or perhaps I was just allowing my imagination to run riot.

Just as I began to wonder where I was, the woodlands suddenly seemed lighter and I could see a clearing in the distance. Beyond the clearing, I could definitely see the sea. So I had been right; it was a long, but direct path down to the coast.

The perfect place for smugglers!

The steep bank on my left had fallen away to reveal a sudden drop off and I found myself looking down on a stone building. A cottage? I wondered.

It was difficult to see clearly as the thickness of the overhanging trees kept it well hidden. I continued downwards and the path curved around towards the stone building.

I had been walking downhill for a considerable time; knowing that eventually I would have to walk back to Ravens Deep. The journey back would be more arduous as it would mainly be uphill, but I put that thought out of my mind for the time being and carried on down. The path curved abruptly, getting even steeper and as I turned the corner, I came face to face, not with a cottage, but a very old stone church.

A crumbling stone wall surrounded both the church and graveyard and I walked along the perimeter to find the entrance, via an iron gate. I unhooked the worn latch and the gate opened easily. The graveyard was overgrown with nettles and long grasses, but still visible were several gravestones scattered throughout and I saw that a few graves had been tended as the weeds and nettles had been removed. I felt sure that this remote church could not be in use.

Maybe relatives come here once in a while and maintain their ancestor's graves.

The only access to this church must be the way I had come, as there did not appear to be a road or path leading to anywhere else. Although I could see that it might be possible to get down to the sea through the thick undergrowth, evidently no one had tried in years.

I walked around the exterior of the ancient church. The spire appeared to be made of deal and slate. It was an early example, possibly twelfth century, and had been well preserved even though small areas of the main stone walls were now crumbling away. The porch seemed a little newer; it had a plain pointed arch made of rough red sandstone.

Underneath the porch, the south and only doorway encased a heavy old wooden door. I lifted its ancient latch and went inside. I was pleasantly surprised to find the interior in very good condition; I had expected something little better than a ruin.

Inside, the church was very cool and I felt the sudden stillness that you often get when walking into ancient buildings. The pews were still intact, as was the altar table. The font which was of a very early date, judging by its medieval depictions, stood to the back of the church, but the interior was devoid of any elaborate decoration or religious icons and from the ceiling hung a simple metal chandelier with candles that were partially burnt down.

It was certainly the smallest church I had ever visited and I figured that it could only have held a congregation of twenty five to thirty at the most. As I looked around I noticed the stone slabs on the floor were inscribed with

Latin words and numbers. I absently wondered if there was a crypt here; it just seemed too small.

The interior of the church had chilled me and there was definitely an eerie quality inside. The entire place had an atmosphere of ancient melancholy about it and I was glad to pull the door closed behind me. Instantly I felt more cheerful as the sunshine warmed my skin and I began to walk slowly around the graveyard reading the various inscriptions on the gravestones. They all seemed very old and many of the surnames were missing.

Have they just worn away or been deliberately removed?

To remove a name from a gravestone seemed such a strange thing to do these days, but I knew how superstitious people had been in the past and I imagined that it had occurred frequently. The fifteenth century churchyard cross stood straight and erect. Although relatively new, it had been mentioned in the old book that I had found in the library and it appeared to stand guard over the whole graveyard. It was roughly eleven feet tall and the plinth on which it stood gave it extra magnificence.

I remembered reading that this area had a numerous leper colony at one time. I found myself wondering just how many of those unfortunate people had been buried here. Or maybe they had never been allowed to be buried in hallowed ground, due to local superstitions of the time. I thought that it certainly would be an interesting piece of research to do as I finished looking at the graves closest to the church.

A little distance away from the main graveyard, four raised sarcophaguses were partly hidden under an old gnarled oak tree that overhung the stone wall. As I approached them I could see that one had more ornate carvings than the others, depicting vines and hunting scenes. I moved closer. Over the years the elements had decayed and weathered their stone surfaces and the moss and lichen had grown profusely over them, making it difficult to define the engravings. I walked slowly around each one, wondering who these long forgotten people were. Maybe wealthy landowners of their time, since their remains lay preserved in more ornate tombs. I studied the one closest to me and my eyes moved downwards.

My breathing became momentarily suspended as I stared in shock at the sight before me. A shiver ran through me, despite this beautiful warm summer's day and I was aware of the tiny hairs on my arms and neck standing on end.

A small bunch of honeysuckle and wild rose had been laid on the lowest plinth of the tomb. The flowers were neatly tied with a piece of grass and their petals had begun to wilt, as they had undoubtedly been there for a few hours.

It was not the fact that somebody else had visited this graveyard very recently, or left flowers on this particular tomb, but what totally caught me off guard and chilled me to the bone was the delicate carved lettering at the base.

Madeline Shaw 1818 - 1860. May She Finally Rest In Peace

CHAPTER SIX

Supernatural Discernment

Seeing my name carved out in stone was troubling to my mind. Although it was conceivable that elsewhere in the world there were various tombs with that very name.

Why shouldn't there be? My name is not that unique. But why here? Coincidence, or something else?

I stayed beside that tomb for a while, a morbid curiosity taking over my senses.

Who had she been? Why are there flowers on her tomb, when every other grave is devoid of any?

Eventually I had to console myself with the thought that I had made this journey, it wasn't as though I had been lured to this churchyard. Only I had power over my own destiny, and my inner emotions were calmed by that knowledge.

The afternoon at the graveyard seemed to pass quickly and it was getting late. I had to think about the journey back to Ravens Deep. I closed the old iron gate behind me and looked at the path I had used earlier. It really did seem to end at the church, as beyond that the stinging nettles were waist high and I had no intention of wading through them to find out if the path continued again. Instead, I retraced my footsteps back the way I had come and wondered if I would make it back before nightfall.

It did in fact take considerably more time to walk back to Ravens Deep than I had anticipated. The woodlands had grown cooler and the dappled light through the tree-top canopy was growing steadily darker. I had to stop to catch my breath several times, although I was used to walking in the city and its parks; I was definitely not used to uphill country hiking.

The sun was just setting as the woodlands began to thin out and over the hedgerows in the distance, the stone chimneys of Ravens Deep came into view. I breathed a sigh of relief; I had been anxious, and did not want to be in dark unfamiliar woods as night fell.

Within minutes the sun had disappeared, allowing my surroundings to take on a soft diffused glow. As I reached the garden gate, I heard a voice close behind me. Startled, I jumped and spun around to find Darius a few feet from me.

"I did not mean to frighten you," he began.

"Didn't you say that to me yesterday?" I replied, recovering quickly from my surprise. I smiled, relieved to see it was him, although mildly annoyed that he had again caused me some alarm. I turned towards him and took in his appearance in one casual glance. He looked pale tonight, as if unwell, which was accentuated by the shadows of darkness that had begun to loom all around us.

"Where did you come from? I didn't see you on the path," I asked indignantly. As I spoke he stepped closer to me and I was acutely aware of the magnetism that seemed to draw me to him.

"Please forgive me, I always walk up here at this time of night," he replied apologetically, "there is only one path, but I do not wish to intrude on your privacy." I realized that I may have offended him and that he may have misread my tone, so I responded quickly.

"No, really you are not ... in fact I hoped to see you again." I said as I tried to keep the eagerness out of my voice, and wanting to clear up any earlier misunderstanding.

"I desired to see you again too," he said softly, "and I did not wish you to have regret at our first encounter yesterday. I realized that may have given you some cause for concern."

He was standing so close to me now. His eyes seemed to be playing tricks with my mind, I could almost hear his unspoken words there. When he did speak, I could feel his eyes belying the other conversation that was happening in my head. He lowered his long dark eyelashes and the spell was broken.

This was madness; was I going insane?

I collected my thoughts and focused on my unspoken questions as I tried to distance myself from the part of my mind that had been working to understand this silent dialogue. I certainly had no regret in meeting Darius or seeing him again, in fact quite the opposite, but I kept these thoughts to myself.

"Yesterday, I was just a little surprised," I said smiling at him, "but I assume you have lived here for a while and so must know of the history of Ravens Deep," I hesitated for a moment, "I was hoping that you might tell me what you know?" I said meeting his gaze with my own, which only made my pulse quicken once more. I tore my eyes from him and hoped he could not sense my feelings, as I myself found them incomprehensible.

"If it is knowledge that you seek, then I will be happy to tell you what I know," he replied and he offered me his arm. Darius indicated to the stone bench.

His words and the gesture surprised me slightly, his manner seemed so charming and intriguing. I did need to sit down somewhere as my legs felt weak, from seeing Darius again? Or more realistically from the long walk. I hesitantly looked at him. I knew I should be resisting an emotional involvement, especially with someone I hardly knew.

But I didn't want to resist, I wanted to get to know him *much* better. I smiled and graciously took his arm. We walked in silence to the stone bench; I was too aware of how intoxicated I felt by his nearness and inexplicably I was lost for words.

Undaunted by my silence, Darius turned to me.

"What precisely do you want to know?"

I made myself focus on his words rather than my feelings and slowly related brief details of the chain of events that had led me to Ravens Deep, how I had found the book with the pages missing and my curious encounter with Samuel Dunklin.

"Did you tell this Samuel Dunklin where you were staying?" Darius asked pointedly, interrupting me. Slightly taken back at the question, I looked at him. His composure was unchanged, but I sensed a disapproval in his tone.

"Yes, why is that a problem?"

"You should not reveal any information about yourself or where you are staying," he replied quickly. I stared at him feeling mystified and slightly alarmed by his words.

"Why? I have a legitimate reason for being here. Or is there something else?" Darius did not speak. "Did something bad happen here?" Darius evaded my question, but he continued.

"In these parts there is still a lot of superstition, people view strangers with suspicion. There are many stories and legends that the locals still believe in." I was confused by his words and wanted to delve into exactly what he meant by legends, but there was an underlying feeling emanating from him and it seemed to say to me:

"Don't ask. You don't need to know this."

Darius seemed somewhat distracted, I was mindful of this strange feeling I was experiencing and thought it wise to continue with my earlier conversation. Perhaps he was a bit reclusive and didn't want anybody around him—even me. My thoughts came back to his earlier words and how he had desired to see me again, but I was irritated by his previous comment.

"What about you?" I challenged. "Maybe I shouldn't tell you anything either," I said giving him questioning look. Darius smiled, apparently amused by my words.

"You are very direct, Madeline," he said cordially, "but I am not superstitious, you can tell me anything," he concluded.

"Being direct is not a fault," I said defensively. "I think if you have something to say then it should be said. I don't play games with people." His eyes fixed firmly on mine.

"I can see that," he replied, and I am not being critical, but it pays to be cautious."

In my mind I knew he was right.

We sat quietly for a few minutes more and then I turned my attention back to the earlier conversation and mentioned that I had been to the church. I described the shock I had felt at seeing my own name carved on a tomb.

"It really disturbed me," I said. "Just seeing my own name written in stone was not an experience good for the soul." I laughed attempting to make light of the subject matter, but I felt deep down that I shouldn't be.

Darius had sat in silence throughout my conversation, his composure unwavering. Then I noticed a smile playing around the corners of his mouth before he finally spoke.

"Madeline Shaw was an occupant of this house at one time; it is not strange that she is buried in the local cemetery." The impact of his words shocked me.

"You mean she actually lived here ... in Ravens Deep?"

"Yes," he answered, watching me intently. "And you are as hauntingly beautiful as she was." I stared at him, bewildered. I knew I should be ecstatic at the compliment, but instead I was alarmed. I felt slightly sick in my stomach and my mind was in utter confusion as I heard myself speak.

"What do you mean? Madeline Shaw died in 1860. How do you know what she looked like?" I could feel my voice wavering.

"Madeline, you should not torment yourself," he answered casually. "I have seen old paintings, that is all I meant, but you do look like her." The uneasiness slowly subsided as it gave way to understanding.

"You mean the girl in the white dress, the portrait?" I asked, remembering the portrait on the bedroom wall.

"There were many paintings of her," he said simply.

"Do you suppose she is related to me? It cannot be just a coincidence that I look like her, have her name, and now I too live at Ravens Deep?"

Darius was staring out across the moors, he almost seemed lost in his thoughts.

"Just a coincidence," he said at last. A sudden thought struck me.

"Did she die in this house?" I ventured. I could have sworn that he looked visibly shaken for a fleeting second, but just as quickly the look was gone.

"Maybe there is a connection. Is this important to you?"

"I am a more than a little curious," I confessed, "and it would explain a couple of things that have happened in the house."

"What has happened?" Darius looked at me with renewed interest and I related the story of the mouse and the pantry door. Laughing, I told him how terrified I had been and how ridiculous I must have looked with my candlestick, but then more soberly, I told him of the presence I felt in the bedroom. "With today's revelations, I have been wondering if the first Madeline Shaw still inhabits this house."

"Do you think the presence will hurt you?" he asked, watching me closely. I thought for a moment.

"No I don't. I don't think it will hurt me. Maybe it's more a fear of the unknown that scares me." I looked at him directly. "Is there a ghost?" Darius turned towards me.

"Madeline, it will not harm you. Now that you are here, I will be forever watchful for your safety." I refused to be put off that easily.

"But you do know something," I began. He looked at me slightly bemused, before he sighed.

"You are very perceptive and I don't want you to be frightened. You should also remember that most occurrences can be explained," he remarked, but he had obviously resigned himself to tell me something. He looked at me thoughtfully.

"This house is much older than you think. It was once the site of an ancient Roman building. The main living area dates back some nine hundred years or so. Other parts were added throughout the centuries. It was also much bigger than what you see here today; a fire destroyed a great portion of it and only about half of the original structure remains. Ravens Deep has been in the same family for the last four hundred years."

"The Chambers family," I said excitedly.

"Yes," he agreed, suddenly hesitant. He continued slowly and I got the distinct impression he was choosing his words carefully.

"Chambers was not always the name, that is only a modern adaptation. The family name started out as Chamberlayne, and down through the centuries it got misspelled, in time it became Chambers. Madeline Shaw did die here, but so did many other people. Ravens Deep has a long and colourful history."

I visibly shivered, not from Darius's words, but because nightfall had come. We were sitting wrapped in a shroud of darkness and the stone bench on which we sat was slowly draining all the heat from my body.

"You are cold," he observed. "You should go into the house." I stood up reluctantly, but having fallen under Darius's charming influence, I did not want to leave him right now.

"Will you come in with me?" I boldly asked. He smiled at me.

"No, I have to go." But then he added, "besides, your friend might not like you bringing strangers into the house." I hesitated before answering, I had forgotten the lie that I had told him. He obviously hadn't.

"What I told you yesterday," I began, "was not entirely true. There is no friend, I was just being cautious."

"Very wise of you," he said standing up, "but I suspected as much," he concluded cordially. He stood very close to me now and was at least a foot taller, which meant that I had to look up to him, and now I could feel my heart racing. There was chemistry, a connection between us. It was in the way he looked at me and I was sure he felt it too. He reached forward and took my hand in his from which I instantly recoiled. His touch was like ice!

"You must come in," I insisted. "You are freezing!" "No," he said quickly. He seemed momentarily agitated. "No, I have just been sitting too long on a cold stone bench." It was as if he had read the words out of my mind; exactly my previous thoughts.

His bewitching green gaze met my own and he took my hand again. I forgot in that instant how cold his skin felt, and I realised that it was probably quite normal; it was mine that was on fire. The kiss was the merest of caresses on the back of my hand; it was like a cool breeze had danced seductively over my skin, and it took my breath away. It was the simplest of gestures, but it was one of the most romantic moments in my life. Without releasing me, he brushed a strand of hair gently away from my face with his other hand.

"Sleep well Madeline," he said before fixing me with a smouldering look that sent a shiver through my entire body, before he released my hand and turned from me. Seizing the moment I had to ask.

"Darius, when will I see you again?"

"Nightfall tomorrow," he replied simply as he stepped back from me. I turned and unlocked the door to Ravens Deep and then I looked back to him again.

He had gone.

There was no sound or movement; he had completely disappeared into the darkness. I blinked in disbelief, how could be have vanished into thin air with no sound? Darius's rapid departure confounded my understanding completely.

I let myself into the dark house, turned on the lights and felt instantly warmer, although that feeling of warmth was mixed with confusion. How could he possibly see where he was going? It was pitch black out there. Why nightfall? I should have arranged to meet him in the morning, but maybe he had to work.

It suddenly dawned on me that I still had no clue as to who he really was. Why hadn't I at least asked exactly where he lived or what job he did? But all the mundane things seemed to fly from my mind when I was with him. All the questions I wanted to ask to were still unanswered. Where exactly did he go after leaving here? There was no house through the woods; if there was, it was an invisible one.

I also questioned myself, my words and actions. Was I foolish inviting a complete stranger into the house? But when I was with him he didn't feel like a stranger, he felt familiar and I was perplexed by my lack of caution when I was around him. I knew that my confusion was also based on the fact that I was enchanted by him. He made my heart race, my pulse quicken and my attraction to him was so strong that it was quite disconcerting. He had woken up feelings that lay dormant within me, and I would have never believed that anyone could have had that effect upon me. I thought about that kiss. I was in turmoil, wrestling with my thoughts and emotions, replaying in my head everything Darius had said.

I wanted to be with him, even now, but a voice in my head or an underlying feeling that I couldn't place, nagged at me from the very depths of my being.

I was certain that his skin had been unnaturally chilled, and he had mysteriously disappeared into the night.

Was I really imagining these things? But then his words played on my mind.

"It will not harm you." Not he, or she, but *it*. Implying that *it* was something supernatural.

What had he meant? He hadn't really told me much at all and he had smartly avoided my questions about ghosts, something I had not realized until now.

A sudden chilling thought entered my mind.

Was Darius, in fact, a ghost?

CHAPTER SEVEN

In the village—Samuel's Story

Samuel Dunklin had not thought about his grandfather's stories for years. Now, sitting alone in the darkness of his living room, he forced himself to remember once more. The pretty young girl he had met in the park yesterday had unnerved him. He didn't know why, but there had been something about her, those eyes; they had been quite beguiling. He switched on the table lamp that at once illuminated the small living room and cast a warm, honey coloured light across the room. Samuel stood and walked through to his bedroom.

He turned on the main light and the room was instantly bathed in brightness. He blinked, allowing his eyes to adjust before he knelt down on the worn carpet and felt under the bed. His hands searched for a moment before they rested on a familiar object. He retrieved the old red suitcase that was torn and tattered from years of misuse. After placing it gently on the bed, he pushed open the worn latch.

Samuel lifted the lid and the case spewed forth old papers, documents and letters; they were the memories of his life and the lives of his ancestors. He picked each one up in turn and examined them. He hadn't looked at many of these in a very long time and smiled to himself as he remembered the various bits of information contained in the papers. He suddenly winced at the pain he felt in his arthritic wrist joint and was forced to rest his arm for a few minutes. He sat upon the bed to examine the papers again, but it wasn't the old papers he was looking for, he was searching for something more specific. That young girl had sparked something deep in his memory, he hadn't opened this case for decades and hoped he still had it.

After searching for a few more minutes, he reached down to the bottom of the case and suddenly caught sight of the old leather journal that had been his grandfather's. He pulled it out and opened the old book. It had a distinct musty smell to it, mixed with the familiar odour of aged leather. He remembered vaguely some of the contents of this journal and if he remembered correctly, there were notes on various occupants of the village, the curse and other related strange tales.

He wondered now what he really believed. His grandfather had believed in a terrible curse. A terrible fate that befell anyone venturing into the woods at night. Did he really believe that too?

He thought back to his own childhood and the warnings he had received from his parents. They had warned him against playing in the woodlands next to the moors. In fact, all the children in the village had believed a witch or demon resided within them; they had all grown up in the shadow of that story, but as far as he could remember, not one of them had ever seen anything. But that young girl ... what was her name? ... Madeline, such a pretty name. Maybe she had been right.

Leprosy had been rife in these parts; the living conditions had been appalling for those people back then and

Beaconmayes had never been a big village, so if a handful of people had died close together, it may have been construed as an evil force or a curse. Maybe it was nothing more than an old wives tale.

Samuel was beginning to find the bed too uncomfortable to sit on; he turned out the bedroom light and took the journal through to his living room. The room felt cosier now, the small fire in the grate giving off a comforting warmth that at once made him feel more cheerful. The stone walls of the cottage glowed in the firelight, and even they seemed to radiate a sense of comfort despite their appearance of being weathered and tired. Just like him, he thought to himself.

He took a seat close to the fireside, the fabric on the chair worn with use, but the vintage roses on the material made him smile. His eyes moved across to the chair's twin, sitting empty now across from him. Once, that had been his wife Agnes's favourite chair. If he concentrated hard he could still see her sitting there, her head bent over some needlework in her lap. Many years had passed since Agnes's death. Now, as on so many other nights he was alone with only his memories for company.

His thoughts jogged back to the present time. He absently thumbed through the pages of the journal and his eyes came to rest on a name: *Madeline Shaw.*

Didn't the girl say her name was Shaw?

Suddenly he felt more alert and he continued reading, unable to find any other information of any use; except for the fact that she had lived in these parts and had died in 1860. Too long ago, there could not be a connection to the girl he had met yesterday. He thought back to his conversation with her, she had mentioned a house. Turning the pages once more he happened upon a notation made by his grandfather.

Grandpa Joe told me today of a cursed house and an old church hidden deep in the woods. I got scared when he told me people that enter the church or house do not always stay dead. Mam told Grandpa off for scaring me.

Samuel Dunklin audibly swallowed at that last statement; he realized that he was reading his own grandfather's childish writings, at a time when he could have been no more than nine or ten years old. Archaic stories that had been handed down to his grandfather.

Rubbish, he told himself. *Just stories people tell to kids to keep them off private land.* Despite Samuel's own misgivings; hadn't he believed in these stories all his life too?

A sudden chill entered the room. Samuel shivered, it was getting late. He must have left the kitchen window open and even though it had been a warm day, the stone cottage seemed very cold tonight. He rose from the chair and walked to the kitchen. It was in complete darkness. As he stepped over the threshold, his eyes widened as they brought into focus a large black shape. He blinked. Was his mind playing tricks? The shape appeared motionless and static. Then he thought the shape moved towards him and he seemed unable to tear his gaze from it, in shock he took a step back.

Samuel recognized death when he saw it, but he felt powerless to resist. In that instant, a searing pain tore through his chest and resonated all the way down his left arm. He opened his mouth to speak, but no words would form. Instead he emitted a strangled gurgle, before falling to the floor still clutching his chest.

Samuel felt his life draining out of him and he could only watch with horror as the shadow moved lower, before enshrouding him completely.

CHAPTER EIGHT

An Archaic Tale

Maybe I was being melodramatic and reading too much in to what had occurred. Ghosts didn't kiss you. Did they? I stepped onto the staircase, and was aware of an insistent tapping coming from above.

Surely not more mice.

With apprehension mounting, I continued up the stairs. The noise seemed to be coming from the second smaller bedroom. Cautiously, I opened the door and saw the dark shadows of the ivy branches knocking against the window; the source of the noise.

Darius was right, most happenings could be explained.

I walked to the window and looked out into the darkness. In the distance the moonlight shimmered on the sea and the trees were bending and swaying ferociously. Within the last few minutes, the wuthering winds that blow across the moors had gained in their intensity. They made an eerie whistling sound as they blustered around the ancient stone walls and chimneys.

Some time later I entered my own bedroom and I felt those prickles on the back of my neck. That presence again; I half expected to see a shadow or an apparition, tonight was the perfect setting for a gothic horror story.

Wild winds, an unearthly presence, an ancient house and a girl alone—very cliché. I smiled despite the tension I was feeling.

As I brushed my hair, I stared up at the portrait of the girl. She was beautiful and hauntingly so. Darius had been right. It was in the eyes, there was a mesmerizing sadness there. *Am I really so like her?*

A sudden thought crossed my mind. If this was Madeline's bedroom, then perhaps she was still here, walking these floors in the shadows of the night; tormented in eternity by her own demons that would not allow her to rest in peace. Maybe I should send her away. Allow her that final passage if I was capable of doing so. Closing my eyes, I said firmly:

"Madeline, go back to your grave or from wherever you came."

I turned out the light and as I got into bed the prickles disappeared; the presence had gone.

Despite the turmoil in my mind and the wind howling all around, I slept well, oblivious to the muffled snap of a mousetrap far below me.

The following day, I found myself willing the time to go faster and for nightfall to come. I busied myself with my book and was pleased with its progress, but by the late afternoon, I was getting anxious. If Darius was in truth a supernatural entity, what would I do? I was also aware of the fact, that he himself might not realize his true being.

I wondered if it was possible to be caught between two worlds. Living your life completely as only you can see it, but in reality, another part of your being entirely somewhere else, or in this case—dead!

I had an even more disturbing question, if that was at all possible, given my current thoughts. Was it incomprehensible to fall in love with a ghost? I knew sooner or later I would have to confront this strange fact. The scenario was bizarre and I reasoned that I hardly knew him. I was undoubtedly under some spell, but my silent questioning asked; why shouldn't true love, when it happens, be instantaneous, all consuming and powerful?

There was absolutely no doubt in my mind of the undeniable feeling for him, it was one I could not suppress, but a constant nagging thought plagued me, in that most people fall in love with others that are actually alive!

My mind remained in utter confusion with the knowledge that it couldn't be. It was forbidden. In all the laws of nature and the universe, how could something like this occur? I eventually stopped thinking; my mind was exhausted and I closed it to these thoughts. The evening would play itself out one way or another. As the daylight began to fade, I found myself anxiously looking at my watch.

Just exactly what time was nightfall anyway?

I sat at the desk and tried to write, but I could not concentrate. Instead, I gazed out the window every few minutes. It was already dark and although the wild winds had calmed, there was still a distant howling to be heard across the moors, from the occasional gusts of wind that whipped up from the coast and chased their way across the desolate terrain.

I suddenly saw Darius's silhouette outside the garden wall. I got up quickly and straightened any visible creases in my dress. I opened the front door to find him standing in the porch. His dark hair fell across his face and a subtle smile hovered around his mouth.

I smiled back softly; my earlier feelings of what was right and wrong in the universe flew from my mind, all I felt was happiness that he was here.

"For you," he said presenting me with a bunch of flowers. "They are beautiful are they not?" I stared at the flowers and it was with a small amount of difficulty that I did not gasp. A bunch of honeysuckle and wild roses tied with grass.

I accepted them and tried to remain nonchalant.

"Yes," I murmured. "Thank you, I will put them in some water." I tried to collect my thoughts and rationalize; why would Darius have put flowers on Madeline's tomb, and why would he give me the same flowers?

We walked through to the kitchen and I avoided his eyes, because when I looked at him I was very aware of the overwhelming urge to draw closer to him. I turned towards the sink, occupying myself with the flowers and tried to remain casual.

"Did you go to the church yesterday?" I asked quietly. I could feel him close to me. He was standing directly behind me. I prepared myself emotionally and turned around to face him. He was standing unbearably close now. Given my suspicions, I couldn't let this get out of hand.

"Why do you want to know?" he asked, looking curiously at me. I took a deep breath.

"These flowers are the same as the flowers on Madeline's tomb yesterday." I searched his face for some clue, but he coolly turned from me.

"Yes, I sometimes put flowers on the various graves, out of respect for the past I suppose. These happen to be my favourite flowers; they grow wild in the hedgerows." I was relieved; at least it was an answer I could live with. I turned back to the flowers.

"I am not sure if there are any vases, maybe a glass will do. I think there are some in the pantry. Would you ..." but before I could continue Darius had opened one of the high cupboards to reveal two glass vases. He selected a vase and held it out to me.

The realization hit me; he knew this house; he knew where things were kept better than me. He was obviously aware something had disturbed me. "Madeline, what is wrong?" he asked with faint concern. He moved towards me and I took a step back. I tried to keep the accusation out of my voice, but I spoke directly. "Darius, how did you know where that vase was? How did you know the exact cupboard to look in?" The silence between us was deafening.

"I used to come here as a child. Nothing's changed, everything is as it once was," he said simply.

"So you knew the family?" I felt myself relaxing, nothing sinister after all.

"Yes," he said handing me the vase. "It was a long time ago, but being in this house again ..." he paused briefly. "I remember it like no time has passed," he finally concluded.

I put the flowers in water and offered him a glass of wine. To my amazement he accepted. I wondered, could ghosts drink? Taking the wine he walked to the doorway.

"Would you mind if I looked in the library? It used to be my favourite room," he added casually.

"Of course, go though," I replied agreeably, "I will just finish here and join you."

I finished with my arrangement and walked through to the library. I was surprised to find Darius sitting at the desk reading a page of my manuscript. I thought now, I should have put it away before he arrived.

"Please, don't read that, it's really rough," I said half embarrassed. Darius ignored my objection and continued reading. "You write with great sentient. A quality most people do not possess. There is an intensity and understanding in your words. This is the book you told me about?" he indicated to the manuscript in front of him.

"Yes it is, or it will be," I corrected myself. "I have only just started and I still have a long way to go."

"You never told me about the content of the book," Darius remarked.

"Well," I said walking to the desk, "my heroine will discover that she has connections back to royal lineage. She uncovers a murderous past that calls into question the birthright of monarchs that are on the throne today. She will discover her own ancestry remains linked in more ways than she knows with her present."

"I would like to read this book when it is complete," Darius said, putting the manuscript down. "You will have my very first copy," I said shyly.

"Your heroine, is she based on you?"

"At first she was, but now, I find I can have more creative license with her if she is entirely fictitious. That is why I needed to come to a remote place like this, to create and to be inspired without any distractions of modern or city life."

"Am I a distraction?" he asked inquisitively without taking his eyes from mine. Again the air was filled with that intense magnetism, an underlying current of electricity that seemed to resonate between us. I felt my skin become suddenly warm and it was with great effort that my voice remained even in tone.

"Yes you are, but a good one I hope." I felt very self conscious of the words I had just spoken. I could now feel my face burning as Darius's eyes gazed hypnotically into mine. I frantically searched for a distraction and I raised my wine glass.

"To my book and to actually finishing it." I smiled at him. He too raised his glass.

"To you and your book," he said smiling. I took a large gulp of wine and promptly started choking. Darius was at my side in an instant.

"I'm fine," I said half spluttering, "really I am." I composed myself quickly and laughingly observed: "Maybe it's an omen, that I may choke to death before I ever finish my book."

"Don't joke about such things," he remarked and wore a genuine look of concern. I was touched by the sincerity in his voice. "Don't worry," I reassured him, "I really am fine." I turned and indicated back through the doorway. "Shall we go through to the living room?"

Taking our wine glasses, we sat on the sofa in front of the fireplace. I was certain that being in such close proximity to him, he would be able to hear my heart racing. He reached out and surprised me by taking my hand in his. A mixture of feelings swept through me, especially as his hand was warm tonight and I was happily aware of the thought racing through my mind.

He isn't deathly cold tonight, real warm blood flows through his veins just like mine. He is alive, he is real!

My earlier inhibitions melted as his other hand stroked the bare skin on my arm. It was the merest of caresses, but it set me on fire. With the briefest of looks, a few words and the lightest touch, Darius had broken through any barriers I might have built, and any previous thoughts of caution I may have had disappeared in that instant.

"You are very beautiful," he said seductively and I found myself lost in his vivid green gaze. I knew, I was totally succumbing to whatever magic he was weaving around me.

"I have dreamed of this moment," he continued in earnest. "In all these years I have never met anyone like you, but it is a twisted fate that has brought you to me now."

"What do you mean?" I asked trying to understand his words. He sighed, leant back and gazed up at the ceiling.

"Madeline there is so much that you don't know about me," he stated sombrely.

I thought to myself that it couldn't be any worse than all my imaginings put together, but I sensed his sudden solemn demeanour and responded accordingly.

"Darius, whatever it is you can tell me when you're ready. I only need to know you are here with me now and are not going to suddenly disappear." Darius raised his head and turned to me with a slightly puzzled look. I noticed for the first time vulnerability in his eyes; a look that that I had not seen before.

"I am not going anywhere," he assured me.

"Although ... I have been wondering what it is you do and where you go," I asked, but I saw his hesitant look and I quickly added, "You know it doesn't matter. You don't have to tell me."

I wished I had not said anything. It must have seemed that one minute I was telling him he didn't have to tell me anything, and the next, questioning him about his life.

Darius seemed to be thinking about my words.

"You are curious, that is understandable. I live close by, but I also spend time and have a house in the city." He paused briefly, "as for what I do. ... I am a historian for a museum." There was hesitation in the way he said those words, almost as though he had never spoken them out loud before. I watched him, fascinated. I had known he would do something intriguing, I could not somehow have pictured him doing anything else.

"Do you specialize in any particular subject? I am not entirely sure what a historian does," I said hoping I didn't sound too ignorant. Seeing my interest he continued.

"I search for interesting objects to add to various collections and when an artefact is retrieved or purchased, I make sure all the information on that object is factually and historically correct."

"That sounds really interesting," I said as I placed my wine glass on the table.

"It has its moments," he continued, "but most of the time it is tedious and repetitive research. Searching endlessly through old libraries and archives. I can spend weeks and months tracking down cultural treasures and the documents that belong to them."

"But surely it's fascinating to discover artefacts that the majority of people don't even know exist. Isn't it?" I questioned.

"Yes it is," he said agreeably. "So few people even take the time to learn about ancient cultures or objects of art, let alone become interested in them. I have spent endless hours in old libraries and have acquired rare book collections. Books can tell us so much about the past."

I listened to his words and his sentiment, which was so much like my own and I began to feel that this was the moment in my life I had waited for. To have met someone who cared about the things I did. Someone who shared a fascination with ancient history and cultures. I was eager to acknowledge his words and I nodded in agreement.

"I know, the real tragedy of our world today is people lack the ability to research things properly. I love old and rare books. The feeling that you are holding some old forgotten treasure of literature. Modern computers cannot compete with that and people seem to be losing the ability to even pick up a book let alone buy one." Darius was staring at me as if what I had said either fascinated or amused him. Seeing his look I paused.

"Sorry," I said hoping I was not rambling. "But it is tragic that everyone expects to be able to press a few buttons and the answers magically come to them. I truly think reading is becoming a lost art form." Darius was smiling at me now.

"You are right of course, but one thing I do know is that you cannot stop progress. You have to move with it or get left behind. It is inevitable though, that some of us long for a simpler way of life. People are preoccupied with how much they can cram into their lives these days, that in fact, they hasten the approach to their own demise," he said almost wistfully. "However some people still get it right; they still appreciate the true art forms and even today in this modern world, a pace of life can be found to suit your own liking, especially here." His eyes held mine captive for a few seconds.

"I know," I said in total agreement with him. "It's so relaxing and tranquil, almost like a different world." Darius nodded in understanding. I thought for a moment.

"You know the books in this house are very old and some of them very rare. You are welcome to look through them, if you need to do some research closer to home," I offered.

"I would like to do that," he remarked smiling. I thought then that he had a beautiful smile, his whole face seemed to radiate attractiveness; it wasn't a full smile for just a hint of what could only be perfect white teeth were visible. But when I looked at Darius I could often see nothing other than his alluring eyes enticing me further and I knew I could lose myself in those eyes and almost forget how sensual his lips were.

"Of course you probably know London has some great libraries," I said, trying to keep my focus on the current conversation. "I have often spent entire afternoons absorbed in old books, especially when the weather is bad."

"Do you miss being in London?" Darius asked, and I considered for a moment.

"No I don't, it's so different down here. You feel this is how life is supposed to be, not fighting your way through traffic, or jostling for space on the underground. This is much better. Although, it will probably take me a little while to get used to living in such an old house, especially one that may have other unseen occupants."

"Are you frightened to be alone in this house?" he asked suddenly.

Taken aback by his sudden directness, I paused for a moment thinking about the question. "No I am not, although," I paused for a few seconds, "I don't think I am entirely alone. Does that sound paranoid?"

"Not at all, I think you are courageous to stay alone in this ancient house," he replied sincerely.

"What do you know of this house, Darius? Being a historian, you must have done some research. Will you tell me?" Darius leant back and closed his eyes.

"It all happened so long ago," he said quietly.

"But I am living here now, don't you think I should be aware of what has happened here?" I reasoned.

I saw him smile at my words.

"You are very persuasive," he said at last. "I will tell you, but I must begin at the very beginning and it could take a while," he said opening his eyes and looking at me.

"Well, I am not going anywhere," I replied. Still holding my hand Darius began.

"The man who once owned this house was Theophilus Shaw, born around 1788, although to everyone he was known as Theo."

"Shaw," I repeated. "A relation to me?"

"If he was, he would have been your great grandfather about seven generations back," Darius figured. "But I should begin this story a long time before his birth. It will give you an insight into his own corruption."

As Darius continued speaking, I felt myself draw closer to him, as if pulled by some unknown force. His voice became sultry and addictive and my mind was transported back in time.

"In England, early in the seventeenth century during the reign of Queen Elizabeth I, ships were chartered under her command, to purchase the finest quality Indian opium and transport it back to England. I cannot recall from my own historical knowledge how much opium came into the country before that, but after that period it became widely used for medicinal purposes.

Around the year 1680, a well known english apothecary by the name of Thomas Sydenham introduced a compound he had made up of opium, herbs and sherry wine. This compound was a revelation of the time, it became known as Sydenham's Laudanum and was guaranteed to cure numerous ailments. It made the opium trade into England a viable business enterprise.

By 1793, the British East India Company, a well known trading company at that time, established a monopoly on the opium trade. Theo's father Philip had worked with the British East India Company and had earned a well-established reputation within that industry. He successfully managed the dangerous task of getting large quantities of opium into England.

By then the demand had increased substantially not only for medicinal uses, but increasingly for recreational ones. Philip had built up many contacts, and driven by his ambition formed his own company. That business mainly consisted of smuggling opium out of both India and Turkey. He brought it via the Bristol Channel and Exmoor, here to Ravens Deep, the centre for his business. He took legitimate business away from his former employer and set up his own black market enterprise. For years he maintained a monopoly on this portion of the smuggling trade.

I am sure you know that the Exmoor coast is famous for its smuggling history, but most people think of tobacco and other contraband from the American Colonies. The opium trade was guarded well and Philip bribed and threatened many politicians and officials when his business was in full force, but you didn't engage in that type of activity without making dangerous enemies.

Philip was not unaware of the risks of his business, and his growing son Theo was exposed to all the depredation that went with the lifestyle. Ravens Deep became a notorious opium den. Many a famous word was written by poets or authors of that time staying here whilst in an opium haze. This house became a hangout for many rich, easily corruptible young gentlemen.

Philip had an acquaintance by the name of John Aston, an American from New York, who was notorious himself for smuggling opium to China, but with the problematic opium wars in China taking their toll, John Aston left the Chinese opium trade and sold solely to England. Philip trusted John and several business transactions passed between them. Over the years that followed vast amounts of money passed between these two men.

By the time Theo was a grown man, he was eaten up with jealousy of the relationship his father had formed with John. Theo believed John took more than his fair share of the profits. In time Theo manipulated John from any connection with his father's business, but by doing so he made an enemy of his father. Theo was greedy and selfish. He had learned from his father how much profit could be made in the black market trade and he was eager to gain all the profits for himself.

By the time Theo was thirty, he was a dangerous force in his own right. Philip disappeared one night and then weeks later his decomposing body was found floating in the Bristol Channel. It was not a surprise. Hushed stories circulated that Theo had committed the murder. Theo inherited everything from his father and that made him the most powerful influence in these parts; whatever anyone thought, they kept it to themselves.

Philip had been corrupt, but Theo made that corruption appear mild. He worked intently to rid himself of any rivals in the trade, lest he should meet the same fate as his father.

Not only would Theo murder, but he maimed, kidnapped and tortured rivals, seeing them as a conceivable threat to him and his business. He even travelled with armed personal servants and a huge array of weaponry.

By the year 1830, the British dependency on opium and its demand was at an all time high. I believe that year, some twenty two thousand pounds of opium found its way into England from Turkey and India and it would be nearly forty eight years before Britain passed the Opium Act to reduce the consumption of opium. In the meantime Theo had free rein and a booming business.

There was also another side of life that fascinated Theo. An even darker side. He was a true believer in the occult; it is said he partook in strange and disturbing ceremonies, even gaining the loyalty of corrupt priests of the day. Local people were terrified by the sounds they heard coming from the woodlands in the middle of the night. So it is no wonder fantastic and strange writings appeared connected with this house. In turn, the dark stories got passed down from generation to generation and they have become the myth and lore of legends.

When Theo was in his early thirties, a merchant coming ashore sought counsel with him. A matter regarding a cargo lost to pirates. Theo was convinced that the merchant was lying and had already sold the cargo to a rival. As Theo was about to slit the unfortunate merchant's throat, a gold locket the merchant wore around his neck opened, revealing a picture of a young girl. Theo seized the locket and demanded to know the identity of the girl. The terrified merchant, in fear of his life, revealed that she was his daughter.

Theo was mesmerized by the girl in the locket and he struck a bargain with the merchant: his life and the lives of the rest of his family in return for the girl. The merchant had no choice and he obeyed.

Her name was Anna and she was very beautiful with her jet black hair and striking eyes. Theo and Anna were married quickly, much to the girl's horror. The ceremony took place at the church you found in the woods and it was presided over by a corrupt priest, whose loyalty lay with Theo.

Theo did not treat Anna well. She was a little better than a servant to him. But a year after the marriage she gave birth to twins; a boy and a girl, James and Madeline. As time went on, Theo turned even more violent, fuelled by his own illicit drug use and opium addiction. When the children were about four years old, Theo, became so enraged one night that he threw Anna down the staircase and left for the city.

Anna was knocked unconscious and badly bruised; she survived, but feared that both her and her children's lives were in terrible danger. The very next day she made a journey to a county far away in the north, where she left her children with a distant cousin. She knew they stood a better chance of anonymity if she did not remain with them as she believed Theo would track her down.

She left a large sum money for them, stolen from Theo's desk and thought it was probable that he would kill her when he discovered what she had done, or even worse; force her to tell him where the children were. Anna would not allow him the satisfaction of that certainty and took a huge opium overdose. She was found dead in her garden." Darius turned to look at me.

"It was this garden, here at Ravens Deep." I suddenly shivered as my mind returned to the present time.

"So does Anna haunt this house?" I asked.

"Well maybe the garden," he smiled, looking amused. Darius stared into the fireplace and continued. "As far as I know, James and Madeline had a happy childhood far away from their father. But he had obviously not forgotten about them and for several years searched in vain for them. Anna had been a clever woman. She hid them well and the distant cousin she left them with remained loyal to Anna's memory and her wards.

Theo did find them though many years later. I do not know how he finally managed it. I believe, a great deal of money was involved. Someone, somewhere was probably bribed or blackmailed. James had already married a girl, called Eva. They had a young son, John." "John Shaw," I repeated, "that would be my great, great, great, grandfather. I said slowly. "So I am related."

"Yes," Darius agreed, "it would appear so." He continued, "However, James would have nothing to do with this father, being of a good moral character himself and he had well connected friends. Theo. quickly realized that James was not someone to be manipulated easily. So he went looking for his daughter Madeline instead.

Before James could send word and warn her of the impending danger, Theo found Madeline, kidnapped her and brought her here to Ravens Deep.

Madeline, was not as well connected as her brother. She had been working as a seamstress in a private house and was engaged to John Chamberlayne, the son of the house. When John learned that his fiancée had been taken, he tracked Madeline down to Ravens Deep and confronted Theo.

By all accounts, Theo placed a terrible curse on John and his family. Whatever it was that happened here, John fled in such fright that he fell from his horse and suffered a severe blow to the head. He was discovered bruised and bloody two days later in the woods close to his home. He had survived, but only just."

I gasped, "How awful." "Yes," Darius agreed. "It truly was a tragedy, for Madeline was heartbroken. But she was strong, she realized quickly that she would never be free of Theo or the horrors that may lie ahead for her. Then three days later, Theo fell ill. Madeline refused to let anyone near him. The seemingly dutiful daughter nursed her dying father for two days and nights. On the third day Theo was dead. The cause appeared to be an opium overdose.

There was speculation that she had poisoned him, but nothing could be proven. He was already an opium addict. Her brother James with his good connections quickly silenced any talk of foul play and James and Madeline took care of all the funeral details. They did not allow anyone near the body. Theo was buried in an unmarked grave, lest anyone ever tried to exhume the remains.

Madeline and John married and they had two children, but that blow to John's head was more serious than anyone imagined. For three years he suffered headaches and some days had to be confined to his bed, from the pain in his head. He died when his children were two and three. Both children were sickly children and Madeline believed that her father's curse was indeed taking vengeance."

"What happened to them?" I asked. Darius became quiet before continuing slowly.

"They grew up here, but I do not know any more. Madeline lived for a while, we can tell that from her tomb."

"What a sad story," I said. "It's amazing to think how one person can ruin the lives of so many." I paused for a moment. "Do you believe in curses?" Darius looked at me strangely.

"I think there are things that cannot be explained," he said quietly seemingly lost in his own thoughts. "It all happened such a long time ago, I can barely remember." He gave me a very strange feeling when he said those words, but then, as if forgetting himself he quickly added, "I heard the stories when I was very young."

"Who told you these stories?" I asked intrigued.

"I knew Mr. Chambers when he lived in this house," he replied hesitantly.

"So if Madeline murdered Theo. in this house, he could be the presence and not a good one at that?" I summarized, feeling suddenly chilled even though the air was warm.

"I shouldn't worry about that," Darius said lightening the mood. "Theo is long gone, exorcised by the various occupants of this house." Darius looked at the old French clock on the mantelpiece; it was close to midnight.

"I should go, it is late. It would like to see you tomorrow night," he said giving me a questioning look.

"I want to see you too," I said demurely, and then I paused.

It was now or never. I had to ask the question playing on my mind.

"I was wondering, do you ever go out during the day? I only see you at night." Darius turned and he looked at me, as if he were gauging my reaction to his next words.

"I do avoid the daylight; I have a condition called porphyria. I am allergic to the sun," he said in explanation. "It causes a severe reaction in my blood, even in low levels of sunlight."

"How terrible," I began, "I was beginning to let my imagination get the better of me, believing that you may be a ghost," I concluded cordially. Darius gave me a curious look before replying.

"There are worse things than being dead, Madeline." I felt a little unnerved and not sure how to take that remark. I wasn't sure if he was serious or joking and I decided to ignore his last words.

"So what does that really mean? That you can never go out at all during the day? What about when it's overcast?" I felt saddened by the thought that he could never know the beauty of the world around him in the sunlight.

"No, during the day even low levels of light can cause my skin to blister. Do not look concerned Madeline, I have adapted to live my life to deal with my condition." I looked down at his hand, his perfect white skin. I could not imagine it disfigured with blisters.

Darius stood up and I followed. Drawing my hand to his lips he said, "Maybe one day, you will know all my secrets."

"When you are ready to tell me, Darius, I will be here," I answered and wished he wouldn't leave. As we reached the front door he turned to me and smiled.

"Until tomorrow, Madeline." Releasing my hand he disappeared into the blackness of the night.

CHAPTER NINE

First Lamentation

Darius's tale was replaying in my head as I set the mouse-traps for the night. I thought absently that these mice were either getting smarter, or I was setting the traps incorrectly. Each morning all four traps were sprung, but there was never a body to be found. Then again the thought did cross my mind:

If there was a ghost, maybe it was causing the traps to spring.

In my bedroom, the familiar presence was apparent.

I was slowly growing accustomed to the unearthly feeling that came and went, but tonight, more than any other, I was chilled by it.

I shouldn't have been so insistent that Darius tell me the stories of Ravens Deep.

Now, I felt scared and haunted.

I lay in bed with thoughts of opium and murder going through my mind and wondered if Theo had been murdered in this very bed. Uneasiness swept through me, but logically I told myself that I had slept here peacefully on previous nights and tonight I was allowing my imagination to take control. I reassured myself that everything Darius had told me had happened over a century ago.

This is probably a different bed anyway.

But in the back of my mind, I knew, this furniture was just as ancient as the house.

I fell into an uneasy sleep where I was tormented by disturbing dreams. Tortured corpses rose up to haunt me and somewhere amongst it all Darius figured greatly. I suddenly awoke from my nightmare, aware that my heart was beating fast. A combination of my disturbing dream and a sound from below. A muffled snap and then another.

Those damned mice!

I eventually fell into another fitful sleep and I didn't remember anymore until I was aware of sunlight pouring into the room. The curtains were open; I had forgotten to close them the night before and I sleepily looked around me. It was hard to believe anything evil could have ever taken place here. In the light of day Ravens Deep was as beautiful and tranquil as ever and outside it was promising to be another perfect day with not a single cloud in the sky.

A little later I walked outside, dismissing my previous thought of continuing with my book because the garden lured me into its rambling and secluded corners, where I delighted in the discovery of an old-fashioned rose bush. The sweet fragrance enticed me further and I felt dismay that it was almost hidden from view, I worked to free the rose from the long tendrils of ivy, then I decided to clear the tangled weeds from the base of the stone walls. Maybe, I would discover how the mice were getting inside. Besides, Mr. Chambers had been kind enough to loan me his house; the least I could do was maintain the garden a little.

Previously I had noticed a small structure in the back garden, similar to a potting shed. I made my way to it and opened the door. It was virtually empty apart from a few rusty old tools.

These will have to do.

Enthusiastically, I cleared the tallest weeds away from the foundations, pruning back the overgrown roses and working my way steadily round to the side of the house. The ivy had climbed the entire stone wall and I cleared the weeds from underneath and started to trim the ivy back. It had grown clinging to everything in sight and cascaded downwards to form a thick curtain. After trimming years of growth, I found myself staring at a wooden wall. I pulled aside the curtain of ivy to reveal, not a wall, but a solid wooden door. I was astonished at my discovery.

What is a door doing in the side of a chimney breast?

My eyes moved upwards and I wondered if it were a surviving remnant that connected the current house to the part that had been destroyed many years ago. I saw a black metal keyhole with matching latch which I attempted to lift, but it was well and truly locked; solid and impossible to move. I allowed the ivy to swing back into its original position and stood back, speculating exactly what was behind the door?

The library wall should be on the other side.

I judged the distance from where I stood to the window and realized that there could be a room; a cellar perhaps, or maybe a staircase or a secret passage. I cast my gaze over the entire wall and I could see that the bedroom where I slept was located directly above the library.

I was intrigued about what lay behind that door and I went to the library to look. Apart from the actual chimney breast, bookcases lined the entire wall. There was no way to tell if a hollow space was hidden behind the cases.

I was disappointed that I would not be able to discover any hidden passage from this room, so I made my way upstairs to my bedroom. I took up position at the wall that ran behind the dressing table and I began to knock gently. A constant solid sound emanated back at me until I reached behind the dressing table, where it changed to a soft hollow sound. I stepped back.

Is it a hidden room or just attic space?

My eyes found the small recess in the wall, which I supposed had held a candle many years ago. I examined it again, this time more closely, but just as before, there was complete darkness. It was most likely just attic space. I could not see or feel any evidence of a bricked up doorway and I ran my hands lightly over the wallpaper to be certain, but there was nothing to reveal that there had ever been a way through.

The wardrobe stood in front of part of this wall, but it was so heavy and appeared to be firmly fixed in place. I couldn't even move it an inch and I concluded that if there had been a way through it could have been behind this wardrobe, but it was unlikely I would ever know for sure. Just another perplexing mystery at Ravens Deep; it seemed just as I solved one thing, another came along to intrigue me.

I resolved to ask Darius about the door, maybe he knew the explanation. I put the tools back in the potting shed and left the garden to its own devices.

I needed to go into the village and buy some supplies. In recent days I had been so preoccupied with my writing, Darius, and the mysteries of Ravens Deep that I had thought about little else, even food.

I really should take better care of myself and eat a proper meal.

Leaving Ravens Deep, it seemed as though the lane had grown narrower still, as my car was once again enshrouded by the hedgerows. As I passed the driveway to Ravens Farm, a white shape lying motionless to the side of the cobbles caught my attention. I stopped the car and got out. I walked closer and saw that it was a dead sheep. I wondered why the farmer had left it here. It did appear to have a small amount of dried blood soiling its white coat, which suggested that it had been attacked by something. But what? A fox maybe? That was the second dead sheep in as many days.

"These things happen," I told myself. "All part of country life."

After all, this sheep was probably destined for some-one's dinner plate anyway.

Trying in vain to make myself feel better about the discovery, I knew there was nothing I could do and returned to my car, determined to dislodge the image from my mind and think about more pleasant things.

I continued on to the village of Beaconmayes and was mildly surprised at the amount of traffic. I wondered if it was market day or if some local event was happening. It took several minutes to find a space to even stop, but I eventually parked the car and walked to the small grocery store. After selecting several items I placed them on the counter and smiled warmly at the woman who was packing my groceries into a plastic bag.

"Is there something happening in the village today?" I inquired. "There seems to be a considerable amount of traffic around."

"That'll be the funeral procession, quite a turn out too." She spoke with a thick West Country accent. "That'll be ten pounds and twenty-two pence please."

"Oh, who died?" I asked. My question was more out of politeness than interest, since I didn't know anyone here.

"Samuel Dunklin." The woman held out her hand for the money I had been counting, but I stopped counting and froze. An odd shiver ran through me.

"You mean the old man Samuel Dunklin?" I asked.

"There was only one that I know of. He'll be missed, one of me regulars he was. Did you know him?" she inquired.

"No ..." I hesitated. "Well yes, I met him only a couple of days ago. What happened to him?" I asked still reeling from the shock. The woman handed the bag of groceries to me.

"I am not really sure, he died sort of ... sudden like."

"And they are burying him already?" I asked incredulously.

"Yes," she continued, "I think it's the family. Some people are heartless. Want to burn him up before he's even properly cold," she concluded, shaking her head.

"They are allowed to do that? What about an inquest?" She looked at me knowingly.

"They don't much bother with things like that out here, too remote. Unless it was a murder of course. We pretty much take care of our own out here."

I took my bag of groceries and left the shop in stunned silence, wondering what year I was living in. I knew this place was remote, but this was positively behind the times.

Samuel Dunklin had been fine when I had spoken to him, he hadn't seemed sick or really that old, come to think of it. I was also very much aware that he had been the only person I had so much as spoken to since arriving on Exmoor, apart from Darius of course.

Now Samuel was dead.

I did not feel like going back to Ravens Deep so soon. Instead I drove through the village with Samuel in my thoughts. As I drove passed the old Beaconmayes church, I could see the congregation of people milling around the graveyard and I felt deeply saddened by the sight. In a few days I would go and pay my final respects to him. I was sure his ashes would remain in that churchyard.

As I reached the end of the village, I noticed a sign-post: Selman Point. The sign brought to mind Samuel's recommendation. Now, out of respect and sadness for the man who was gone so suddenly, I turned the car towards the sign.

Samuel had been right, the winding road up to Selman Point was beautiful and scenic. A short distance from the top the road ended, but a large patch of gravel provided a parking place for my car. I continued on foot for maybe a quarter of a mile, it was actually further than I had first thought, but the walk was worth it, as the scenery was breathtaking when I finally reached the summit.

It did indeed feel like I was on top of the world. It was a clear day and I could see for miles. To the left, I looked down upon the village of Beaconmayes and across the moors. To the right, down across the rugged cliff face to the sea.

I wondered if it was possible to see Ravens Deep from here, but as I scanned the distant woodland I could see no indication of any building. I spent a tranquil hour sitting on the grass, contemplating the events that had occurred since my arrival on Exmoor; the sadness I felt at today's turn of events and of course Darius, who was never far from my thoughts at any time.

It was hard to imagine that I had only known him for such a short while. He seemed so familiar to me. The way he spoke, the way I felt when I was with him, I couldn't remember a time when I had felt happier. He was so unlike any other man I had ever met. I was drawn to him and his irresistible charm, he was a being like no other, but that thought continued to play on my mind, for I had a strange feeling of not understanding some elementary part of him. I dismissed my confused notions and wondered if Darius had ever come up here. I wished he could see the beautiful landscape in front of me. Witness it as I did; bathed in warm sunshine.

I finally left Selman Point and drove slowly back down the winding road, and back through the village. The traffic had all but disappeared and Beaconmayes had regained the air of a sleepy country village once more.

I returned to Ravens Deep and unloaded my groceries from the car. I walked through to the kitchen. The pantry door stood wide open. By now, I was half expecting it. I looked down and saw that all four mousetraps had sprung, but there was not a single mouse body anywhere. I didn't know why I even bothered setting them. After all, I hadn't seen any more mice. I picked them up and put them in the cupboard under the kitchen sink.

I continued working on my book for the rest of the afternoon and wondered what time Darius would arrive. At least, I knew he wouldn't be here before sunset. I thought about his illness. Had it developed? Or had he been born with it? He would tell me when he was ready I was certain. I thought to myself that it must be a difficult life; not to be able to go out in the sunshine. I could not imagine living in perpetual darkness. It was no wonder he was so pale; his skin was never exposed to daylight.

Was that why he appeared so dark and mysterious? But that did not matter to me. I could deal with that and we would work around his illness. What did matter was being with him. Anxiously I looked at the clock, acknowledging that there were only a couple more hours of daylight left and how empty my world now felt when he wasn't in it. Did he feel that way about me?

Darius arrived at precisely eight-thirty and as he entered the hallway he brushed my lips with the lightest of kisses.

"Good evening Madeline" I was slightly taken aback, but I managed to respond.

"Hello Darius, come in." That was a moot point, as he was already in. My inner voice told me to tell him how I felt, to tell him how this strange magnetism was compelling me to him, but my voice of reason told me to wait, let him make the first move.

Just as before I poured out two glasses of wine and set them on the table by the sofa. We sat down together.

"You look tired," he observed studying me.

"I didn't have a very good night," I confessed. "I must admit the story you told me was a little disturbing."

"It is my fault, I shouldn't have told you," he began.

"No, you were right to tell me. I needed to know. Sometimes it's better to know the truth, so you can move on from it."

"Maybe you are right," he said thinking. "But some-times there is danger in knowing too much and the truth can be too painful and too unbearable."

"What do you mean?" I said looking at him curiously. He seemed slightly agitated and I wondered why.

"I don't mean anything. Are you happy here Madeline?" he said. The agitation seemed to disappear as he regained his normal composure.

"Yes, I am." I took a deep breath, plucking up the courage to utter the next words. "I am happiest here with you, Darius." He smiled softly at me and took my hand in his.

"I am happiest here with you also." He pulled me close to him and I laid my head on his shoulder. I could feel an overwhelming sense of being drawn into a state of complete security. It was as though there was an invisible force field surrounding our entire beings. As he rested his head against mine, I took his hand in my own. The slender fingers and long glass-like nails fascinated me, I had never seen hands like his. They were beyond perfect, with not a blemish or mark of any kind.

The evening wore on and we sat unmoving, making small talk about the house and garden. All the while, I desperately wished that this evening would never end.

I began to tell him about my day and how I had found the strange door. I felt the slightest reaction in him and I lifted my head. His expression was unreadable.

"What is it Darius?" I turned so that his eyes met mine.

"There is nothing behind that door," he said quickly.

"How do you know that?" I asked slightly bewildered by his reaction.

"I too, found that door when I was a child. It is what remained of an entrance to the part of the house that burned down. It was bricked up years ago and the door locked for good."

I was about to tell him of the hollow wall I had found, but thought better of it. For some unknown reason when I mentioned that door, it had disturbed him. I wasn't sure what to make of it. Instead, I told him about my day and my discovery of another dead sheep.

"Who owns the farm?" I said at last.

"The farmhouse is derelict, no-one has lived there for many years. Those sheep live in fields that are rented by some distant farm. Sometimes a rogue wild dog will kill them."

"There are wild dogs here?" I asked shocked. "I have never heard that before."

"Animals die, Madeline, it is part of the world we live in. What else did you do today?" I was slightly taken aback by his tone and wondered if he was deliberately trying to change the subject? I sensed that it would be unwise to pursue the topic any further.

"Well … I went into the village," I began cautiously. "I discovered that Samuel Dunklin died. Do you remember the man I told you about?" I continued without waiting for his reply, "I couldn't believe it, I only spoke to him a couple of days ago and they are burying him already without an inquest!" Darius suddenly turned and regarded me with the strangest expression.

"They are burying him?" he asked pointedly as his eyes narrowed briefly.

"Yes I know, can you believe it?" Seeing the look on this face I suddenly was aware he was not listening to me. "What is it Darius?" Darius regained his former composure.

"They normally cremate people here," he said, distracted for a moment. "Oh yes," I said casually, "that's what I meant." Darius visibly relaxed. "Why don't they bury them then?" I asked, realizing I was missing the point.

"Probably local superstition," he replied, completely back to his former self now.

"But what's the significance?"

"You don't need to hear more superstitious stories, otherwise you will have another bad night," he answered a little dismissively, but then he smiled at me.

"You are probably right," I agreed with him. The atmosphere had completely lightened, although I felt it would be wise to change the subject. "How was your day? Did you work today?" He considered for a moment.

"Yes, I have been researching something."

"Are you working on anything interesting right now?" I asked.

"A piece of Egyptian jewellery that I acquired recently," he replied, "believed to be over two thousand years old. In fact, I will need to leave for the city tonight. I will be away for two nights."

A feeling of panic swept through me, two nights without Darius was more than I could bear. "Surely, you don't need to be away that long?"

"London is a great distance from here," he replied slightly amused by my reaction.

"London? I thought you worked in a local city." Darius smiled.

"Why would you think that? London is the best city for research, the libraries stay open late into the evening and I have connections in the city that allow me access after dark to search archives and records," he concluded.

"How do you get there?" I asked. It had suddenly struck me, as to how he actually got anywhere. As if expecting this question, he readily replied.

"There is a shortcut to Beaconmayes from here and I have a car in the village. I know you think that I am behind the times out here in this remote place, but even I have learned to do modern things—like learn to drive." There was definite sarcasm in his tone.

"I'm sorry Darius I don't think that at all. I know I have an inquisitive mind, I was just curious that's all." He pulled me closer to him.

"Don't worry Madeline, I will be back before you know it."

CHAPTER TEN

A Bitter Chill

Later that evening as I reached the top of the staircase, I felt the full impact of the fact that Darius had left Exmoor. I felt inexplicably alone and unhappy. A sudden loud snap from the vicinity of the kitchen halted my progress and in alarm I turned and ran back down the stairs.

One of the mousetraps had sprung. I stared at it in complete horror.

I put those traps away earlier. Didn't I?

Was I losing my mind? Or now that Darius was gone, was the ghost playing tricks on me? Darius's previous words came back to me now:

"*Now you are here, I will be forever watchful for your safety.*"

But Darius wasn't here, I was alone. Maybe the ghost, presence or whatever entity that shared this house with me realized that. I tried to calm down and think rationally.

"It's not real," I reassured myself.

I could have taken those mousetraps out of the cupboard and not remembered doing so. I felt tearful. *What is wrong with me?*

Was it because Darius had left? Was his nearness really having so much of an effect on me, so much so, that it was slowly driving me insane?

Darius will be back soon and we will be together once more.

I was comforted by that thought. I left the mousetraps on the floor and went up to bed.

Let the ghost have its fun!

Ravens Deep seemed emptier and quieter, the stone walls colder and the darkness outside more foreboding. The following two evenings were endless and I counted the hours until I would see Darius again. During this time the presence in my bedroom was not apparent, but the entity in the kitchen seemed more agitated than usual. Now it was not content with opening and closing the pantry door, for other cupboards had taken to opening and closing by themselves. The kitchen tap had managed to turn itself on and the mousetraps continued to spring even when they hadn't been set. I knew I should be deeply disturbed by these events, but in truth it was reassuring that I wasn't entirely alone in my world right now.

True to his word Darius did return after two nights and I was ecstatic at his presence once more.

And so began the curious relationship between us. Over the days and weeks that followed I would see him nightly. Our embraces were but the lightest of kisses, the briefest of moments. I felt like he understood me completely, and in turn I was totally absorbed by his every word and action.

But, there was an underlying darkness in him that wasn't easily observed and although he had mastered the art of keeping his emotions disguised, there were several occasions when I saw a disturbing change in his persona.

He would alter from being relaxed and attentive, to cold and dark in the course of a few minutes. Every relationship has its ups and downs, the emotional highs and lows, but with Darius I witnessed bizarre and strange extremes of his personality and at such times his coldness felt unbearable, but this unseen demon that tormented him could disappear just as quickly as it came and things would be back to normal for a while. What hurt me most were the times that he would leave me abruptly and not return until the following evening.

A part of me desperately wanted to know what lay hidden in the depths of his soul, but another part was happy for him to reveal to me only what he wished, for I was well aware that there could be something terrifying there.

Now, I wondered as on so many other occasions what our relationship was destined for. I knew that Darius had a dark secret, one that he wished to conceal from me and although I was scared of just how awful it might be, I was certain in my love for him; I would have forgiven him anything. Dark secrets aside, I did want more from him than he was prepared to give. I was willing to give everything to him, my mind, body and soul if that was what it took. Darius would hold my hand, caress my skin and entwine my hair in his fingers as though he were fascinated by it, but there was something sinister about the way he withdrew from me if I did get too close.

It reminded me of a courtship of long ago; stolen kisses and caresses in the briefest moments of solitude in an age old society. Stolen looks across a room where the other occupants were blissfully unaware of a certain chemistry between two lovers, but we were not lovers, there was no society or other occupants. There was just

Darius and myself and I longed for more; I craved a complete relationship with him.

By this time I knew that I couldn't exist without him in my life and I thought he had the same feelings about me. I could deal with his illness, maybe that was why he held back from me. Perhaps he did not wish to entangle me in his life of darkness, and I knew that apart from his occasional visits into the city, he didn't see anyone here on Exmoor. In fact he led a very remote and reclusive life.

My own life had changed, I could no longer concentrate for long periods of time and I found myself willing the days to pass quickly so that nightfall would come, and with it Darius. I was vaguely aware that my own appearance had changed. I had lost weight from not eating properly, but I never seemed to get hungry anymore. The relationship I had with Darius was all consuming. Nothing else seemed to matter. It was as though I had lived my life looking through a veil, but since meeting Darius that veil had lifted and my eyes were well and truly open. He made me feel that life was worth living and the world was really an exciting place to be in, especially here at Ravens Deep.

I had spent many hours in Darius's company and I knew the stories that he told were guarded; maybe he had not wanted to frighten me, alone in this old house. As much as I tried to dismiss them, I was still aware of my earlier suspicions: that he belonged to another place, another time and that thought seemed absurd; a notion straight out of a science fiction movie. But there was a part of me that had to face the fact, something was not quite right! I thought back to our first night together at Ravens Deep.

I did not see him take a single sip of wine, but the wine did disappear.

Now I had come to think of it, I could not recall him ever drinking anything since, but maybe this was all in my head. I made up my mind that tonight I would confront Darius with my feelings. He would have to respond to me and acknowledge how he felt about me, for better or worse, I simply had to know.

It was early afternoon and I had tried to work on my book, but today like so many days before, after picking it up I laid it to one side. I really didn't feel that well and spent the rest of the afternoon lying on the sofa with an old Victorian novel from the library.

By eight-thirty in the evening there was the usual knock on the door. I had the strange sensation of butterflies in my stomach when I stood to answer it. Darius entered, instantly bewitching me once again with his usual charm.

"Good evening Madeline," he said leaning forward and kissing me lightly.

"Hello Darius," I said casually, "I think the weather is cooling down at last."

"Yes," he answered, "it is a little cooler out tonight."

We walked into the living room and sat down together on the sofa as usual.

It suddenly occurred to me that we did this routine every night: I would hand him a glass of wine and he would pretend to drink it. We would talk and he would reveal to me another tale, appealing to the senses of my mind, some hours later he would kiss me briefly and leave. Occasionally he would leave for the city and predictably return two nights later and the routine would begin again.

All these thoughts ran through my head in detail and I must have become quite absorbed as I was suddenly aware that Darius had spoken my name. His voice abruptly pulled me from my considerations.

"Sorry, I was miles away," I said meeting his eyes with my own.

"I had asked if you were feeling well," he repeated. "You look very pale."

"Yes, I am fine," I replied a little too quickly. He was studying me and I could feel his eyes burning into mine and my skin suddenly felt extremely warm. I stood up and moved to a different seat; away from Darius. I saw in his eyes that my actions surprised him, I lowered my eyes and stared at the fabric of the sofa as I hesitantly began to speak.

"Darius, I need to talk to you," I began. "What is it Madeline?" Darius was leaning forward now. I glanced at him briefly.

"Please let me speak and don't say anything until I have finished. This is really difficult for me."

"Very well," he sat back. "Go ahead." I took a deep breath.

"From the moment I first met you and each day since, I have felt a certain connection between us. A force compelling me to be with you. All these weeks it has been growing stronger and now I am in a place of no return." I paused briefly and still refused to meet his eyes in case I faltered. I could feel my skin getting hotter by the moment, but I continued.

"You ask about my days ... my days are filled with constant thoughts of you. I once said that I did not wish to know everything about you, but now, I don't care what you've done or what you are, I only know I cannot exist without you and that I want to be with you all the time."

I quickly glanced up at him. His eyes seemed to have developed an intense emerald hue. I sat staring at him, and caught up in my own emotion, I willed him to speak, to say something, anything, but he remained silent. Taking the initiative, I got up and went to him. I knelt on the floor and took his cold hands in my own.

"Darius, tell me you feel the same. Tell me I have not imagined this connection and that this chemistry that exists between us is real," I pleaded.

For a moment I did not recognize the man that sat in front of me; I could almost feel his pain. I saw the emotional conflict within his eyes and it warned me that a wicked inclination tormented his mind and at this moment it was struggling to surface.

The atmosphere in the room was tense, almost sinister and I was on edge waiting for his reaction acutely aware of the darkness building within him, as my mind tried to decipher an unspoken dialogue that I had witnessed before and something, somewhere within myself told me to be afraid and a bitter chill passed through my body.

Regardless of these strange perceptions, my gaze never wavered from his. Then I witnessed gentleness behind the darkness and my apprehension dissolved. He finally spoke softly; holding me spellbound with his eyes.

"Madeline, from the moment I first saw you, I have desired to be by your side. You have opened my eyes to living again. I see what delights you, and I feel the passion within you, but you have also made me aware of how empty my life is. How dark and tragic it has become and how dark I could make yours."

"But Darius," I interrupted, feeling confused by his words. "It is not empty, you have me and together we can work out any problem that exists."

Suddenly he pulled me to him and his lips were covering mine. He kissed me fiercely and I responded with passion; but it was a kiss unlike any other. His chilled lips sent a slight shiver through me and I felt a hunger in him. A longing that equally excited and terrified me. He finally released me and held me slightly away from him.

"Forgive me," he said. The look of horror that I saw in his eyes confused my every emotion.

"There is nothing to forgive," I said breathlessly as I tried to ignore his look. "Darius, stay with me tonight, don't leave me." The look changed into one of incredulity.

"No, I cannot ... I can't be with you right now."

"What do you mean?" I began. Darius rose from the sofa and brushed me aside. "I have to leave," he said urgently.

"But you've only just got here." I had a terrible feeling that I had misread the situation, but I tried to remain calm, despite being upset and confused by his reaction. "Darius please tell me what's wrong? ... I have to know. Or I can come with you and ..."

"No Madeline," he said abruptly, "where I go you cannot follow."

Darius went to the front door and without a backward glance silently disappeared into the shadows of the night. I was distraught.

What had I done? Why was this happening and where exactly was he going?

I sank down to the floor with the tears running down my face; in his kiss I knew that he loved me.

How could he possibly make my life any darker? It was in darkness without him.

CHAPTER ELEVEN

Opium Dreams

I awoke the next morning in a daze. I had suffered an extremely disturbed night, during which my sleep had been fitful and nightmarish.

Now, I felt barely alive. My skin was on fire, but I was thoroughly chilled. It felt as though all my energy had been drained from my body.

My thoughts were of Darius and his reaction to what I had said. I failed to understand why he had left so abruptly, especially when I had plucked up the courage to tell him my innermost feelings. If he really didn't want me then why had he kissed me with such passion? I felt sick to my stomach; this situation was worse than when my mother had died, I felt lonely and empty and as if nothing would ever be right with the world again.

I drifted unhappily through the rest of the day. I continued to feel weak and needed to eat something as I had hardly eaten for days now and I wondered what was wrong with me. Was it the house that was slowly driving me insane or was it Darius? Maybe I was just delirious. I searched the pantry. There were a few tins of various foods, but as I read their labels, I realized I couldn't face any of them. I settled instead for some dry crackers, which I hoped would take away the feeling of nausea.

I managed to force down a few crackers and then, I rushed to the sink where I was violently sick. I raised my hand to my forehead; it felt hot with fever and my head was feeling strangely detached from the rest of my body. I decided that perhaps it was best to make some tea instead. Minutes later I lay down on the sofa sipping my tea and that was where I remained for most of the day.

I experienced a feeling of floating out of my own body and a strange sensation of nothing being real anymore; all the while, the voices in my head replayed the events of the night before. I wondered if Darius would come tonight, or maybe he would just leave me here and ignore my existence completely. Chaos and confusion spun around my troubled mind.

I was unsure how I managed to stumble to the door and open it when the familiar knock came in the evening. In my disoriented mind I was happy only in the knowledge that Darius had come, although I felt strangely light-headed as my eyes focused on him for a moment before I fell.

I remembered no more—only blackness.

I had no recollection of how he carried me to my bed and laid me gently on it, or how he sat by my side all night applying cold compresses to my forehead. When I woke, after the strangest of dreams, Darius was sitting beside me holding my hand.

"Go back to sleep, I am here and I will not leave you," he had said and I had fallen into a deep sleep.

Darius remained true to his word, whenever I awoke over the next few days he was always attentive by my side. The heavy curtains were kept drawn and the room appeared dark, so I was unaware if I woke during the daylight hours. I dreamt of food and water passing down my throat, along with some strange brown liquid. Everything appeared to happen in a distant haze, but I must have eaten the food and drunk the fluid; because I survived.

When I had collapsed into Darius's arms I was suffering from a severe fever and early symptoms of malnutrition. Much later I would realize that Darius had saved my life. Now, I opened my eyes and my head seemed clearer. I slowly sat up, feeling enormous gratitude towards Darius as he had obviously stayed with me, although I was slightly disconcerted as I didn't remember undressing myself. I pushed my childish thoughts of modesty away; I wouldn't have expected him to put me to bed fully clothed.

There was a large medical book I recognized from the library, lying open on my bed. Darius later told me he had devoutly read it from cover to cover to understand the cause for my rapid decline. I felt as if I had been asleep for a very long time and the effects of my sickness were disappearing fast; my mind felt clear and I was stronger than before. I began to wonder if Darius was in the house, when right on cue, the bedroom door opened and he entered carrying a tray of food; instantly he smiled at me.

"Madeline, you are awake."

"Yes," I said sitting up. "I still feel a bit shaky."

"You should eat something," he said, laying the tray on the bed.

"How long have I been in bed?" I said ignoring the food, but responding to his smile with my own.

"Four days." He saw my look of surprise and continued, "don't worry, you were not alone. I stayed with you most of the time," he said as he sat down on the bed.

"What happened to me? I really cannot recall … anything," I asked hesitantly. Darius related the details of what had occurred and his conclusion from reading the medical book. He paused for a moment and then asked, "When was the last time you ate anything before that night?"

"I cannot remember," I answered truthfully.

"So were you deliberately trying to harm yourself?" he asked pointedly. I was shocked by his question and I just sat staring at him as I was unable to fully understand what he was asking me.

"I wasn't trying to hurt myself," I replied slightly indignant. Darius looked at me rather oddly and seeing the look on his face I asked, "why would I do that?" I searched his face for some clue, but found nothing.

"Perhaps being here in this house; being with me has clouded your judgment," he replied. "Perhaps your coming here was a mistake," he said almost to himself. I felt scared that he was leading up to something. I sat up so that my eyes were level with his.

"Are you going to leave me?" I asked anxiously.

"No, I won't leave you. I want you to get well again." He spoke the words softly. I felt quietened by his assurance and my earlier fears subsided. On the bedside table I saw a strange looking bottle and a large vial of brown fluid.

"What is that?" I said pointing to the contents. Darius considered for a moment.

"It helped you get better," he replied casually.

"But what is it?" I asked, thinking that must have been the strange brown liquid I was aware of in my dreams.

"A tincture of opium." Darius saw my look of horror and smiled. "Don't distress yourself, I didn't give you enough to hurt you, only to help you sleep. I know how dangerous it can be, but I also know how to safely administer it," he concluded as he tried to reassure me.

I felt a little unnerved. I knew only too well how easy it was to poison someone with the incorrect dose, but I reminded myself that I trusted him completely and was confident in his ability to have given me the correct amount.

Over the next two nights Darius came and went as usual and by the second evening I felt completely recovered and sat waiting for Darius to arrive. I heard the front door open and rose from the sofa as he entered the room.

"I am glad you are up and feeling better," he said cordially.

"I do feel much better," I said moving close to him. I leaned up and kissed him on the cheek. "Thank you for being here Darius." He moved abruptly away.

"Madeline, I have to talk to you, come and sit down with me."

This was it; the moment I had dreaded. He would tell me that he didn't love me and it had all been a mistake. I had a lump in the back of my throat and my legs felt suddenly weak again, but I sat next to him without protest. He turned to me and I saw a sudden distracting coldness in his eyes.

"Madeline, I want you to leave Ravens Deep tomorrow, you are not safe here." I certainly had not expected him to say that and I was completely taken aback.

"From whom," I began, but Darius silenced me with a deliberate penetrating stare.

"If you really love me then you must leave. The last few days have shown me that if anything were to happen to you, I would forever exist in misery." I thought he was being a little over dramatic and with the tension that had built within me in the last few minutes, I began to get irritated.

"Why? … because I got sick? People get sick all the time, but I'm fine now, I survived because of you," I said defensively.

"No, not because you got sick, but because there is real danger here for you. This house is truly cursed. You must leave," he repeated patiently. I allowed the amusement to creep into my voice; I knew he had to be joking.

"Don't be silly Darius. A few creaks and mice are not much of a curse." He stood up abruptly, pulling me with him. His grip was tight on my wrist and his nails were digging into my flesh. I saw anger in his eyes and felt the sting of the venom in his words.

"I am not asking you to leave Madeline, I am telling you," he said angrily. "Look what has happened to you. You almost died—isn't that proof enough?" He hesitated for a moment. "I thought you would be safe, I thought I could keep you safe, but I cannot for I am the reason you are sick, my presence distorts your reality."

"No," I protested. "You give my life meaning, Darius," I choked out the words bewildered by his statement. Darius's eyes narrowed quickly and his next words came out cold and clear.

"Do you want to die?"

Shocked by the intensity of the way he spoke, his aggression and the pain pulsating through my wrist, I stared at him in horror. He was trying to frighten me and succeeding, but I wasn't about to back down that easily. Instead of allowing my own anger to surface I tried to calm down and changed my tone.

"Then come with me Darius; come away with me." I softly pleaded with him.

"Don't you see? I am as cursed as this house," he snapped. I saw a disturbing darkness in his eyes and my fright increased. In desperation I tried to figure out what I could say to appease him and appeal to his gentler side.

"Is it because of your illness? We can find a good doctor that can help you. You know your illness has no bearing on how I feel about you."

"There is no doctor that can cure me," he said quietly. Then he spoke with such intensity that I found myself shaking with fright, as I watched the strange darkness grow into its own terrifying entity within his eyes.

"You *will* leave this house by tomorrow. The presence you feel is real, you are not imagining it. It is evil and it will cause your destruction." I found my voice, but unsteadily.

"But Darius, I love you and I know you love me. Why are you doing this and saying this to me?" I cried as I refused to comprehend his words. We stared at each other for several moments, I was trying desperately to understand the reasoning behind his words, but my own frustration and temper was beginning to rise. "Tell me that you don't love me then." I had meant to sound calm, but my voice betrayed me completely. Darius narrowed his eyes slightly before he coldly voiced the deepest cut to my rapidly breaking heart.

"Madeline, I do not want to ever see you again!" I let out a gasp of pain, from the physical pain of my wrist and the emotional sting of his last words. Darius looked down at my wrist still gripped in his nails and he released it. I was only vaguely aware of the deep marks he had left in my skin, and I felt the relief of the pressure from his tight grip, but was still reeling from his remark.

"You will leave, Madeline, or I will make you!" he concluded icily, and turned to walk towards the door.

Regardless of the consequences, I stepped in front of him. I was fearful of what he would do as the shadows of darkness seemed to surround him and I could see the terrifying rage in his eyes that still refused to be quietened. I comprehended the disturbing thought that he was very capable of actually killing me and that perceived threat hung menacingly in the air, but I just couldn't let him leave me like this.

"No Darius... I will not go until you tell me why... I cannot live the rest of my life not knowing the truth. I need to know." I emphasised the point before trying to summon the courage to speak again.

"Do I mean anything to you?" I could feel my voice wavering, but I could not stop. "All the evenings we have shared, all the moments we've spent together, what were they? A figment of my imagination?" Darius stood motionless.

"Madeline," he said at last, "don't do this, I cannot reveal this to you. You must go," he replied softening his tone a little. "I do not want to see hatred in your eyes when you look at me; it's only a matter of time, I know I would find it there. I do not want to endure remembering that. It is better for us both if you leave now."

"I would never hate you," I said in surprise. "I would do anything to remain by your side. I promise I will never hate you and I would never break my promise to you."

Darius considered for a moment.

"If that is so, then promise me you will leave here before tomorrow evening," he said calmly.

That was not what I had wanted him to say and I started to protest, but his threatening demeanour once again possessed him.

"Madeline, your promise?" he demanded. Tears were freely flowing down my face now.

"I promise," I said miserably, looking at him through my blurred vision. Darius's hand briefly touched my wet face and he brushed by me as he walked out the door. I stood motionless for a few seconds, before the bewilderment subsided slightly and I ran after him, but I found myself staring into a void of total darkness. He had gone.

"Darius please ... please come back. I love you ... come back to me," I cried choking back the tears; but there was silence.

CHAPTER TWELVE

Darius's Vision

Darius moved silently through the garden and quickly unlocked the ancient wooden door. He paused for a moment and then stepped softly onto the staircase. Effortlessly he moved upwards, acutely aware that her aura lingered with him still as he entered the dark chamber. He sat heavily upon an ancient chair; alone again in his own domain he waited patiently for her to appear in his vision. The walls seemed to enclose around him as he felt the constant burden of being entombed and trapped in his own underworld.

Time had always passed slowly, but this night the passing of time was unbearable. A beam of light suddenly emanated from a recess in the wall, sending a small amount of light to his chamber. Darius hesitantly leant forward a little, his eyes fixed in an unwavering gaze; the better to see through to the room beyond.

She entered the room and he felt haunted by her image again as he committed to memory every last detail: her hair, her skin and those green eyes to match his own. He sees that she is crying and distraught and Darius feels what he perceives to remain of his heart—break.

He watches as she pulls a suitcase from under the bed and starts to throw clothes into it, then she gathers items from the bedside table and throws them in as well; everything is strewn together in a jumbled mess.

Darius feels her grief intensely, knowing only too well that he is the cause of her extreme suffering. He acknowledges again that this situation should have never happened, for he is not supposed to be capable of love, only devastation and ruin, but how could he have known that she would have awakened feelings in him that he thought no longer existed. It was a mistake to have made himself known to her, for now he will be falling forever, listening only to the agonizing voices in his head that remind him constantly of the pointlessness of his existence.

She finishes with her suitcase and throws herself down on the unmade bed. Her whole body is wracked with grief and he wants with every ounce of his being to go to her, to hold and comfort her, to caress that silky hair and smooth skin, but he also wants to go to her and possess her; a dark, dangerous possession that he will not allow—he must resist.

Several agonizing minutes pass before she stands up and moves across the room. She is so close to him now and sits down at the dressing table, her beautiful green eyes are red from distress and Darius sees her visibly shiver and she quickly looks over her shoulder.

He knows that she has sensed his presence again.

She turns back and takes one last look at her reflection, before rising to go and pick up the suitcase. The next moment the light has been extinguished and the chamber darkens; she has gone.

Darius is suddenly aware and surprised by the wetness on his hands; fallen tears? He didn't think that was possible anymore and he knows that this vision alone could destroy him entirely, for now he has sent her away, what shall his life become? Surrounded only by the shadows of the night, he shall have nothing but regret and remorse. Without her, his life is meaningless; his being nothing more than a tortured and tormented dark prince watching his beloved for the very last time and tonight, more than any other, Darius feels himself fading into the darkness of the damned.

CHAPTER THIRTEEN

Back to London

It was early when I left Ravens Deep. The haze of the morning mist filled the air and the pre-dawn eerie silence that haunted the house was apparent; everything seemed cold and foreboding.

In my turmoil I had thrown my books and papers into a bag, not caring if they got destroyed in the process and then I struggled to the car with my suitcase and possessions. My tears were falling freely down my face, my vision was blurred and my heart was broken. Ravens Deep held no more magic for me; no more enchantment. My enchanter was gone, or at least he didn't want me anymore.

I slowly drove away and regretfully glanced back at the house before it disappeared, for the last time, behind the hedgerows. It had held such promise and hope and now I could not understand why it had ended like this. Why did this whole experience seem unreal?

I knew I had to go back to London, back to the desolate and lonely place that city life now seemed to be. I had found what my life had been missing; in Ravens Deep and with Darius, but it had been abruptly ripped away from me and I was still reeling from that shock.

During the entire journey back to London I replayed the events of the past few months in my head and tried to figure out exactly what it was that had disturbed me about this whole experience, but nothing that made any sense came into my thoughts.

The traffic was light and I made good progress, but it was with a heavy heart that I left the wild moors far behind and entered into the urban life of London.

Had there always been this much traffic and noise in London?

Everything seemed more frantic than I had remembered. I eventually pulled into the street beneath my flat and looked up to my small balcony. I searched for some spark, something that would tell me that I belonged here, but I felt nothing save emptiness through the constant drizzle that had begun shortly after leaving Exmoor. How appropriate I thought, even the weather had turned on me.

My life had been colourful and wondrous, but now, here alone and far away from Ravens Deep and Darius, it was grey and dismal.

I slowly walked up the flight of stairs dragging my suitcase after me, I felt exhausted, not just physically tired, but emotionally drained. I didn't think I would ever feel normal again and I was not sure if I even wanted to. How could I possibly live a normal life again knowing that I was still very much in love with Darius.

Maybe I should have defied him.

But in truth he had frightened me intensely, and I had made him a promise; he knew I would have promised him anything, although now in the cold light of day I was more terrified of never seeing him again. I reached the top of the stairs and let myself into my flat. I looked around the silent and forlorn space.

Was everything always so grey in these rooms?

Perhaps I had not noticed before or my eyes had been shut to the mundane and the sheer drudgery of everyday life. Darius had opened my eyes and made me see everything differently. I left the suitcase on the floor and lay down on my bed allowing my mind to succumb to an all consuming numbness.

I couldn't cry anymore; there were no tears left.

In the days that followed, I tried in vain to infiltrate back into the world I had once known. The mundane routine of getting up and attempting to get through each day with a degree of normality depressed me no end, because inside I was screaming.

My thoughts haunted me and my dreams were confused and frightening. I felt distraught and my feelings of distress soon became mixed with a feeling of anger.

How could he have done this to me?

Then on the third evening back in London, my doorbell rang.

My heart almost stopped. I hoped with every ounce of my being that it was Darius and it felt as though I practically flew down the stairs in my eagerness to open the door.

Not Darius, but Charlie stood before me.

"Madeline, where the hell have you been?"

It wasn't really a question, more of an accusation. I tried to hide the disappointment in my voice as I hastily responded.

"Hello Charlie, you know I was in the West Country," I said feeling extremely irritated.

Why couldn't this have been Darius?

"How the hell do I know that? You take off without a word to anyone, for all I know you could have been abducted," he snapped at me. I stared at him, he seemed really angry.

What was he talking about? I wasn't in the mood for this; I didn't have to explain myself to anyone, especially to him.

"Charlie just go, I'll call you in a few days. I haven't been well and I need to sleep." I felt extremely agitated and wanted him to leave now, but he remained standing in the doorway looking at me almost as if he were seeing me for the first time.

"Madeline," he said in a calmer tone, "I've been really worried; no-one knew where you were. If you are sick … I should stay with you."

"No," I said at once. "I really need to be alone. Just go, Charlie. I'm fine, I will call you." I closed the door amid his protest. I knew I had to end this relationship with Charlie once and for all. I just didn't have the strength for any sort of emotional confrontation with him; not in my fragile state of mind.

Strange though, I was sure that I had told him where I was going, but the plain fact was I hadn't even thought of him for weeks and seeing him again now had surprised and shocked me.

Just goes to show that we shouldn't be together.

I endured another restless, tortured night and the next morning I went downstairs to the communal foyer to collect my mail. I picked up the few letters waiting for me on the doormat. Initially I did not pay much attention to them as my lack of interest in everything around me was becoming stronger. I walked back to my flat and quickly glanced at the contents in my hand. They appeared to be the regular sort of mail: bills and junk, and I casually discarded them on my side table. In doing so, one envelope caught my eye. It looked familiar; it was the finest quality stationery adorned with beautiful handwriting that had been penned in ink. I instantly seized it, scattering all the others over the floor, and tore it open. Two sheets of paper were inside, one of which fluttered to the floor. I quickly scooped it up and unfolded its single crease.

I was staring at an ancestral family tree; but not just any tree. I saw my own name and realized—this was my own family tree. I was fascinated to read the names of my ancestors going back several generations, but it was when I read the name Theophilus Shaw near the top of the page, I audibly swallowed as the realization hit me that I was *his* direct descendent. Somehow that was a fact I had not realized before and that knowledge brought to the fore-front of my mind the tale that Darius had related.

I continued studying the page and even though I had been shocked by that revelation, there was far bigger shock to come. One name jumped out at me above all others and I stared at it with unbelieving eyes, before I read the death date underneath.

My breathing shallowed and my pulse quickened along with my heart and I fought to calm myself. I leaned against the wall as I felt my legs would surely buckle under me at any moment. I remembered the other sheet of paper that I still held in my trembling hands and unfolded it slowly.

My already dry throat became parched and my trembling increased on account of the words contained within the letter. At first I was unable to fully comprehend the magnitude of those words, then shock and horror hit me simultaneously with full force. I sank to the floor unable to stand any longer. Obsessively I read the letter many times, the revelations spinning around my head and I did not move for what seemed like hours.

I must have got up at some point, but had no recollection of doing so. I believed I eventually put the letter in the wooden box along with the many others from before. I moved into the bedroom in a dream-like state. I still had not opened my suitcase and it stood on the floor. Now, I tipped its contents out. My actions had no reason, I just needed to do something. My mind was somewhere else and my thoughts were irrational.

What should I do?

I sat unmoving in front of the pile of clothes and cosmetics, my eyes were seeing, but they did not register anything. Then, very slowly they came to focus on a glass vial of brown liquid. I picked it up and stared at it. Somewhere in my mind Darius's voice came to me. It told me that this would help me. I knew I needed help. I couldn't take this burden and it suddenly made sense. It was the sign that I had unconsciously looked for and now it was so clear to me what I must do.

Did Darius put it there? He knew I couldn't live with this knowledge or without him.

I lay down upon the bed with the vial clutched in my hand. I pulled out the stopper and after a brief moment, I drank the contents and then I closed my eyes and my mind to the outside world.

CHAPTER FOURTEEN

The Letter

I could hear muffled noises; my head felt strange, my stomach hurt and nausea swept over me. I opened my eyes and tried to focus on the dark shape that was closest to me. Slowly my vision sharpened.

"Charlie, what are you doing here?" I said in surprise. I was in a white room, and there was a humming noise coming from some sort of monitor close to me. "What happened?" I asked as I unsteadily sat up feeling dazed and confused.

"You are in hospital," Charlie replied quietly. I stared at him in shock.

How in the world did this happen?

"How did I get here?" I asked feeling confused. Exactly what had happened after I lay down on the bed? I didn't remember anything, only a peaceful darkness. "Did I have an accident?" I pressed, looking at Charlie to give me an explanation. He sighed softly.

"I came back to the flat in the morning because I was worried about you." He paused for a moment. "Your neighbour downstairs let me in, but when I got to your door I heard a noise. It sounded as if you had fallen, and when you wouldn't answer the door, I broke in." Charlie saw my look of shock and quickly added, "I'll get the door fixed for you tomorrow, I just haven't had the time yet. After I got in, I found you on the floor unconscious. I think you fell from the bed when I knocked on the door. You were bleeding from the broken glass in your hand, so I called an ambulance and here you are ..." his voice trailed off. He wore a strange expression, one that I did not recognize.

"How long have you been using drugs, Madeline?" It was an accusation and I stared at him, not fully understanding his words.

"What are you talking about?" My head hurt and I couldn't believe what Charlie had just accused me of. Why would he think that? He turned reproachfully to me.

"They found enough heroin in your bloodstream to have killed you. Don't pretend you don't know what I am talking about," he remarked bitterly.

It was suddenly clear. Darius had given me several doses of opium and combined with what I had taken, any blood test would have shown positive for a substantial amount of morphine in my bloodstream as opium and heroin both contained morphine. It must appear like I was a drug addict, but I couldn't tell Charlie the truth. I couldn't betray Darius. I didn't know how to account for the opium without going into details, so I chose to ignore Charlie's last question and ask one of my own.

"What hospital am I in?"

"St. Julienne's," Charlie replied angrily.

"But ... that's a psychiatric hospital," I said feeling uneasier by the minute.

"What do you expect when you try to kill yourself?" he snapped back at me.

"What?" I couldn't believe what Charlie was saying. "No, I wasn't trying to do that, you have got it wrong!" I slowly and reluctantly told him the story of Ravens Deep and how I had been sick. I told him that the medication I had been given may have contained morphine and that a neighbour had assisted me, but I did not mention Darius's name. Charlie didn't need to know everything. Charlie listened to me in silence, but I could see the disbelief in his eyes as he narrowed them slightly and I realized that he probably thought I was unstable. "How long have I been here?" I said with sudden urgency.

"Two days," Charlie replied watching me suspiciously, as though I might do something unpredictable. Seeing his look I calmed myself and remained quiet. It was Charlie who finally broke the silence.

"I have spoken to the doctor; he wants to keep you here for a while. They feel you could be suffering from some sort of drug induced breakdown ..."

I didn't hear Charlie's next words; I was starting to feel panicked. They couldn't keep me here against my will. Could they? I suddenly remembered the letters and in anguish I looked at Charlie.

"Please do something for me. This is really important, you need to return to my flat and get my mother's wooden box. It contains some letters. Please bring it to me, I really have to have it." I saw a look of reluctance.

"I should stay here with you," he said. "Charlie, please. Please do this for me," I smiled at him hoping to appeal to his sympathetic senses. I could tell he was shocked and angry with me, but he finally agreed. He left me alone a little later with my thoughts.

I did lock the box and reseal those letters. Didn't I?

I didn't think Charlie would read them, he would respect my privacy; he was that type of person. I couldn't risk anyone reading those letters and I was extremely worried as now the door to my flat was broken, anyone could walk in there if they so wished. The thought had also crossed my mind that those letters may be useful in proving to the doctors that I wasn't delusional. They obviously would have their doubts when they heard how I came to have so much morphine in my bloodstream. At the very least, I could prove where I had been for the past few months, but I would have to be careful, no-one could ever be allowed to read that last letter.

I had to leave hospital; maybe Darius would change his mind and come looking for me. A few days ago I had desperately wished he would, but now that very wish was mixed with terror from the fact that he might. I felt bewildered at the situation I now found myself in and from the shock I had received and I lay back thinking. Had I intended to kill myself? I didn't think so. I thought I was doing the right thing. After all Darius had saved my life when he had given me the opium to help me sleep and get better. I knew now that I had obviously taken too much.

With nothing to do apart from lie quietly in the hospital bed, I had time to think rationally and calmly and now I knew the truth, all the previous months made sense. I searched the very depths of my soul and found that regardless of what Darius was or the words he had written—I wanted to see him again.

At first that very thought had terrified me, but I couldn't forget all the hours we had spent together. My love for him was still there and I knew that we shared a deep connection that defied all reason, but I realized he was also afraid and because of that fear he had sent me away. My own previous fears subsided.

Charlie returned a little later and as he entered the room, I eagerly looked at this hands. But they were empty.

"Where is the box and the letters?" I asked. He sat down by the bed. "Madeline there were no letters. The box was empty," he said and I saw the disturbed look that passed briefly across his face.

"Empty, how could that be?" I was confused and thought back to recall exactly what I had done with those letters. I knew I had put them in the box; there was no doubt in my mind. I sat in stunned silence. Charlie interrupted my thoughts.

"Madeline, I telephoned Beaconmayes Post office," he said slowly, "they told me that there was no such house as Ravens Deep," he paused for a moment. "In all their years of business they have never delivered mail to any such address."

"Well why would they?" I retorted bitterly. "No-one has lived there for decades."

I was still trying to figure out what had happened to my letters. The only plausible explanation was that Darius must have come and taken them. He must have realized that they were a terrible threat to him, but did he come to find me also? Did he believe that I was also a threat to him? Or had he realized that we were meant to be together?

A doctor had entered the room and was now talking to Charlie in a hushed voice. He turned to me.

"Hello Madeline, I am Doctor Matthews."

"I need to leave doctor. When can I go home?" I replied instantly.

"Well, it's like this, Madeline," he said pulling up a chair, "we really would like to keep you in for a while and run some tests."

"No!" I said at once, "I want to leave."

"When we are certain that you pose no further risk to yourself, you may leave. In the meantime I want to keep you in for observations. You are very pale and well below a healthy weight, and in good conscience I cannot discharge you until I feel you are well again." He wrote something on my chart and went to speak to the nurse, then turned back to me.

"I will check on you tomorrow," he said smiling at me before he left the room. "Why Charlie," I said looking at him nervously. "Why do they want to keep me here? I am not a danger to myself. What tests are they talking about?" Charlie sat quietly. "Charlie tell me, I have to know," I said now feeling scared. Charlie looked at me with an expression of concern, then he dropped his gaze and hesitated before replying.

"The doctor thinks you may have suffered some sort of mental breakdown and developed an alternative personality," he said meeting my gaze with his own. "One part of you may be totally unaware of what your other persona is doing. It could be caused by the stress of losing your parents so suddenly and compounded by your drug use, and you are also showing symptoms of anorexia."

"What are you saying? That I am insane?" I glared at him realizing the implication of his words, I was furious and upset.

"Get out Charlie; I am as sane as you. Get out now." I had raised my voice and a nurse instantly hurried into the room.

"I think you should leave," she said looking at Charlie. "You are upsetting Miss Shaw and she needs to rest." Charlie left abruptly without a word, slamming the door as he went. "How are you feeling?" The nurse took my wrist and checked the bandage.

"What happened to my wrist?" I asked, not having noticed it before.

"Don't you remember?" she asked, releasing my arm gently.

"No I don't or I wouldn't be asking, would I?" I replied in my most sarcastic tone.

"Calm down Madeline, we think that you tried to cut your wrist when you took the overdose." I must have looked blank for she emphasized, "When you tried to kill yourself." Satisfied that I comprehended her words and was not in any immediate danger, she walked out of the door. I sat up with a feeling of growing confusion.

I looked down at my wrist and undid the bandage. My skin was covered with bruises and deep welts from where Darius had gripped my wrist—I did remember.

I sat there alone and started to think about what had happened to me since returning to London. What did they know? The doctor, the nurse, even Charlie. I would get out of here, they couldn't commit me. They had to let me leave after a few tests and observations. I would leave soon and Darius would find me. Despite the contents of the letter he would realize, just as I had, that we were meant to be together.

He can no longer exist in this world without me, anymore than I can without him. I will wait until I hear his voice and gaze into those eyes that will compel me to him. He is out there somewhere, but not close enough yet. In the meantime, even though the paper may be gone, his last written words remain imprinted in my heart and etched in my mind for all eternity; where I alone can see them.

27 Parson Place
London, SW3

My Dearest Madeline,

I choose to write this letter to you because now that you have gone, your words haunt me still: "It is better to know the truth so you may move on from it." If this allows you to move on with your life, then I am compelled to reveal the truth of my existence. I know in your love for me, or maybe after consideration, that love will turn to hate, you will keep your promise and never return.

Why did I lure you to Ravens Deep? I believe the answer is curiosity and because of the striking resemblance to your namesake buried in the churchyard. After all these years I selfishly longed for someone to amuse me, someone that was more extraordinary than anyone else and I certainly found all those things and more in you, but it was the more that I hadn't bargained for.

You awoke feelings and desires which I believed to have died longer ago than I care to recall. You will always be my beloved, my one and only true love, but my soul has been damned and I refuse to allow that fact to destroy your life.

In our time together I was aware of the horror of what I could do. In my enchantment over you I clouded your rational thoughts and judgment, and despite my best efforts you suffered anyway. I watched over you whilst you slept in my belief that I could keep you safe, but in reality I knew you needed a life far from me to keep you truly safe. I can no longer allow you to live your life that way or bring you the torment of my life and my existence. I want a better existence for you.

I reveal to you now in trusted safe-keeping that I am immortal, an eternal creature of the night, one who walks the earth only in the shadows. My lust for blood is my torture and my nightmare, but it allows my existence. You know I have learnt restraint and far from me you are forever safe. My life is darkness and infinite misery, but my happiness will be the knowledge that you have light in your life and can find peace; whereas I can never.

It is with great sadness that I send this letter, for I know it must be the very last correspondence between us, but I have completed your family tree and at least you will understand why the first Madeline Shaw was so special to me.

You are the very last living descendant in my family line and my wish for you is to forget what has occurred and continue to move forward with your life.

Darius Chamberlayne, a.k.a. Mr. Chambers

Ancestral Tree

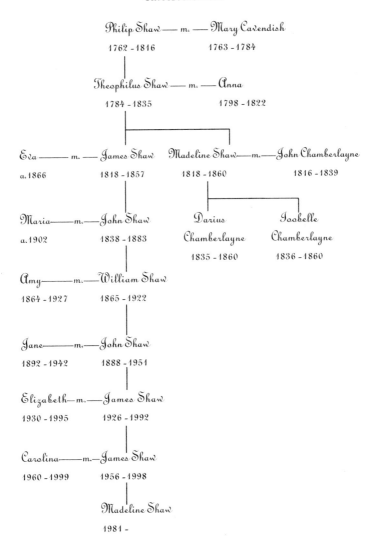

Philip Shaw — m. — Mary Cavendish
1762 –1816   1763 –1784

Theophilus Shaw — m. — Anna
1784 – 1835   1798 – 1822

Eva — m. — James Shaw   Madeline Shaw — m. — John Chamberlayne
a. 1866   1818 – 1857   1818 – 1860   1816 – 1839

Maria — m. — John Shaw   Darius   Isobelle
a. 1902   1838 – 1883   Chamberlayne   Chamberlayne
       1835 – 1860   1836 – 1860

Amy — m. — William Shaw
1864 – 1927   1865 – 1922

Jane — m. — John Shaw
1892 – 1942   1888 – 1951

Elizabeth — m. — James Shaw
1930 – 1995   1926 – 1992

Carolina — m. — James Shaw
1960 – 1999   1956 – 1998

Madeline Shaw
1981 –

CHAPTER FIFTEEN

London, Eighteen Months Later

I am still waiting; the time passes in agonizing slow motion. My life seems to drift from day to endless day with no relief in sight from my unhappiness.

It had been fourteen months since my release from St. Julienne's psychiatric hospital where the numerous tests had proved inconclusive. The doctors had satisfied themselves that I really posed no serious threat to myself and had reached the conclusion that I had probably suffered some sort of breakdown. My time in hospital had not been all bad; now I was back up to a sensible weight and at least I looked healthier.

But I returned to my empty world; to a life that held no hope or promise. I had waited, and hoped, beyond all hope that Darius would come, but he had not. Without my letters I had nothing, except my memories and the odd scar on my wrist that refused to heal properly; a constant reminder of him. I had secured another job and picked up with my writing again, but my creativity was lost and my passion gone. Charlie had stayed in my life for a while, but even he could not cope with my coldness towards him, my depressing moods and my unwilling-ness to discuss their cause.

Charlie had been the one who finally broke off our relationship. He probably knew that I didn't love him and now I was well again he had a clear conscience about leaving me. It had not even upset me. To me Charlie had become like a comfortable old chair that sits in a corner for years until it is time to replace it, then once it is gone, you cannot remember why you held onto it for so long. It was not important to me what Charlie felt, if he was sad or heartbroken. My only thoughts were of what I had lost.

I had tried hard to forget. I had resolved to put Darius and Ravens Deep out of my mind, but as much as I tried, he was always there. He haunted both my dreams and my waking hours, he was in the very depths of my being and my longing to see him again was utterly consuming me.

When I wasn't working I spent my afternoons and evenings visiting museums, especially the ones that stayed open late into the evening. All the while, I hoped to catch a glimpse or to feel his presence; something that would indicate to me that he was close by. If he ever did see me then he never allowed himself to be seen.

I researched the numerous museums and their employees, even befriending several curators as I tried to obtain information regarding their various historians, but not one of them seemed to know of a historian named Chambers or Chamberlayne.

I parked my car outside these different museums and sat silently with my eyes fixed firmly on the darkness of the back entrances and alleyways, which always seemed obscured with curious shadows. I watched any movements with anticipation, but night after night I had been disappointed as all my endless vigils had turned up nothing.

The weeks had turned into months and I was despairing at ever seeing Darius again. Yet, there were times when I could have sworn he was close to me. It was a feeling, a sixth sense, but whenever I looked into the darkness my eyes found nothing.

Sometimes in my flat I would sit at my desk next to the window and on occasion something would make me look up. I would find myself staring endlessly into the shadows of the night, but all I saw were the iron railings, and the branches of the trees swaying softly in the breeze. Those railings marked the boundary to the little square across the road from where I lived. They threw distorted shadows across the pavement and I would strain my eyes to take in every tree and shrub. However, nothing would appear out of the ordinary and much to my dismay no dark shapes shifted or moved unnaturally. Maybe in my longing for Darius, I was actually imagining that he was close.

Today marked the two year anniversary of that first fateful meeting in the garden at Ravens Deep. Perhaps because of that very fact, my mood was darker than ever. I knew I couldn't wait forever and if he refused to come to me, then I must be the one to find him.

I was certainly afraid of the implications of that decision and very aware of what he was capable of. I wondered about his reaction if I did break my promise to him, and then I questioned my sanity. Even to my own mind it was dubious. But I had endlessly reasoned the possibilities of what I should do and in all that reasoning I could come to only one conclusion. If

I did nothing I would spend my life languishing in despair and regret until I died, or I could take charge of myself and go back to Ravens Deep and to a life with Darius.

I did not know how his existence was possible and even though he had stepped from the pages of a horror novel and entered my life, the plain fact was that he was real; he did exist. Every rational thought seemed irrelevant, the only thing I knew for certain was I had an undeniable connection to him and my entire being ached for him. His words came back to haunt me now, just like on so many other occasions.

"Do you want to die?"

I didn't know the answer, but I felt as though I was slowly dying inside. What was the point of living without him? I had lived at Ravens Deep by his side, although I had not been aware at the time. Why couldn't I go back to that? And if I did return to him, would I condemn myself to a hell of my own making? But hell is where I felt I was living right now.

I knew Darius might actually kill me and although that thought frightened me, I reasoned that it was better to die by his hand than to waste all the years ahead of me, growing old with only pain and regret in my heart. I would watch my skin shrivel and turn grey and know all the while that he was still as young and perfect as he had always been.

I convinced myself of what I should do and I sat down to write the letter that I would deliver to the London address that I had memorized from the past. Sooner or later he would come to London, he always did.

August 12th
My Dearest Darius,

I only can hope beyond all hope that this letter finds you, since I have no other way of contacting you. Enough time has passed since we parted for me to be certain that I do not want to exist in this world anymore without you. The horror of your existence pales into insignificance when it is compared to the terrifying thought of never seeing you again. I know you are capable of love behind that darkness.

Forgive me for breaking my promise. I am compelled to return to Ravens Deep. I will remain in London for two weeks, enough time for you to receive this letter and know of my intention.

I know we can be together and our love for each other will make us both strong. I did find my destiny at Ravens Deep, it is to be with you.

Forever Yours, Madeline

I re-read the letter, it seemed so brief. I wanted to say so much to him, but I needed to say it to him in person, not formally written in a letter. I wished to tell him how much I longed to see him again and tell him of my agonizing need to be with him that would not cease. But when I wrote down the words, it sounded too desperate and I didn't want him to interpret it that way. When I finally got to speak to him I would be calm and logical and he would realize that I absolutely meant every word.

I sealed the envelope and addressed it to Mr. Chambers, 27 Parson Place, London SW3. Then I pulled out a map of London's West End. Rush hour traffic would already have built up and I knew I had to leave immediately, or else I would be sitting in a traffic jam for the next hour. London wasn't the easiest city to drive through at this time of day.

I wasn't sure why I had not made this trip to Parson Place before now. I had always assumed he was either at Ravens Deep or the museum, but this address was the only way I had to contact him, besides, it was my best hope.

I drove through the city streets and checked my map several times. The traffic was very slow moving and it was almost 7.50pm before I reached my destination. I scanned the various street signs and on my right I found the one I had been searching for and turned my car into Parson Place. At once I saw dozens of grandiose old Victorian houses that lined both sides of the street. I parked the car next to the kerb and stepped out. I walked along the street and peered through the various iron railings to read the house numbers.

Suddenly I saw it—number twenty seven.

The butterflies fluttered through my stomach and my legs felt strangely weak as I gazed up at the house. It did look large and imposing, but not necessarily sinister. The tall black railings and gate led through to stone steps that led up to a solid door. Steps also led downwards giving access to a lower basement below street level. I leaned over the railing, it looked dark and uninviting. I looked up again and noticed that black grates covered all the windows, making them inaccessible to burglars.

Darius obviously has to be cautious in the city.

But these grates did not particularly look out of place, as several others houses had similar type grates that covered their windows.

I walked up the stone steps and I could feel myself shaking. My butterflies had multiplied. I glanced down at my watch; it was still too early. If he was at home, he would not answer before the sun went down. I walked back to where I had parked and moved my car further up the street, positioning it to give me a clear view of the house and then I waited.

My eyes never moved from the doorway, but I was extremely aware of the sun moving lower in the sky. By nine thirty five the sun had set; this long summer's day had seemed endless, even now I could still make out the sun's faint glow on the horizon.

Now, I could feel the apprehension mounting inside me. I walked back to the door and lifted the heavy brass door knocker. I knocked on the door as loud and hard as I could.

This would wake even the dead!

As my tension mounted once more, I glanced down at my hands which were shaking uncontrollably from the anticipation of seeing Darius again, mixed with the knowledge that he might be very angry. I suddenly felt chilled. A chilling presence? Or was I just caught up in the anxiety of the moment? I listened carefully, there was nothing but silence from within. Was Darius really here and was he watching me? I somehow found my voice.

"Please open the door Darius," I said softly. I was not certain if there was anyone to hear my pleas. I must have stood there for twenty minutes or more, hoping that the door would open, but I eventually realized I was not going to get a response. I looked down at the polished brass letterbox and quickly pushed my letter through.

It was done.

I went back to my car and waited for any sign of life, for the door to open, for him to appear, but there was no movement. I still could not shake the feeling that he was watching me from inside the house, but after an hour, I acknowledged that if he was here, he was not going to make an appearance. He obviously wasn't going to make this easy for me, but maybe he wasn't here. He could be at the museum or maybe at Ravens Deep. I drove slowly back to my flat thankful that the roads were clearer than before.

What now? I knew I had to put my next plan of returning to Ravens Deep into action. My letter had said two weeks, that would give him the time to read it and he knew where to find me if he so wished. If he didn't find me, then I fully intended to find him and I reassured myself that he wouldn't be able to stay angry with me forever.

CHAPTER SIXTEEN

The Return

The following two weeks were the longest of my life. Each night I waited patiently for a perception of his closeness, a voice to come to me out of the darkness of the night or a knock at my door. I soon grew tired of the constant waiting and watching as I sat by my window night after night and nothing happened. Then I was forced to face each morning with the persistent gnawing emptiness that I felt inside.

Did I really expect Darius to come to me? Deep down I believe I did and I refused to be disheartened by the fact that I had heard no word, nor seen any sign. I had to suppose that he had read the letter by now, and knew of my intentions.

The fact that he had not made any contact did disturb me, but I convinced myself that he also could be unsure of how to proceed. Perhaps deep down he longed to see me again and wished that I might return to Ravens Deep. He would find that truth difficult to comprehend.

I ensured everything was in order before I left. I packed most of my clothes and personal possessions, a few groceries and other items that I thought I may need. I cast a farewell glance over the flat and hoped it would be many months before I had to walk though this door again. I left London early to miss the heaviest traffic and ensure that I arrived on Exmoor during the daylight hours. I needed to prepare myself mentally to face Darius again, and time to figure out the actual words I would speak, after so many months apart.

I wondered how I would feel when I laid eyes upon him again. I had a clear picture in my mind, but now I knew how dangerous he could be and was acutely aware that I was entangling myself into a potentially deadly situation. Despite all my feelings of apprehension, the excitement was building at the very thought of being with him again and that in itself was a bittersweet emotion; he might not be as pleased to see me. My previous thoughts came back to haunt me; possibly he could be *very* angry, and my stomach tied itself in a knot for a few moments before I firmly relegated that thought to the very back of my mind. I knew I could do nothing to change his reaction to my decision. In lots of ways I felt better than I had in months, my mind seemed clearer and I had direction and for better or worse, I was following it.

Several miles outside of London I let out a sigh of relief. Now, I could almost feel the wilds of the moors and Ravens Deep beckoning to me, calling me back. With each mile that passed that pull grew stronger. Was Darius calling to me? It was where I belonged; in my heart I knew it and this time I wouldn't leave, no matter what occurred.

The drive was long, but the thought of seeing Darius at the end of it kept my thoughts occupied for most of the journey. As I drove across the wild landscape my feelings of elation were once again mixed with apprehension, but the beauty of the landscape all around me and the calling I felt, whether it was imagined or not, inspired me to continue.

It seemed that even the grey clouds overhead had parted to reveal rays of bright sunshine lighting the landscape and the way forward. The swirling mists that were often so apparent had lifted enough to reveal the grey and blue tones of the sea. It was an omen; even the landscape was calling me back.

I eventually passed through Beaconmayes and as I read the village sign my earlier feelings of apprehension grew stronger.

Am I doing the right thing?

I was aware of those ever present butterflies beginning to tie themselves into tighter knots within my stomach. My common sense told me to turn around and go back to London, but my heart and every part of me that longed for him whispered unrelenting in my ear and bade me continue. Deep down I already knew that there was nothing on this earth that could make me turn around now, especially having come this far not only in distance, but in emotional strength. I was compelled to return to Ravens Deep and to Darius. I could no more resist him at this present time than I could have done two years ago.

Several minutes later I turned from the main road and swung the car into Rush Lane. I noticed that the shrubs and trees had grown significantly in my absence. The hedges had encroached further onto the lane and long vines had twined themselves further around the trees, as they stifled their unsuspecting victims with their long tendril clutches. A large dangling branch obscured my immediate vision beyond its curtain of foliage. I negotiated my car around the branch and as I drove past I felt it heavily brush the top of my car. I looked into my rear view mirror and it swung back into its original hanging position. My vision suddenly focused immediately forward and I just had time to slam on the brakes and bring my car to an abrupt stop.

The metal farm gate that once had stood open and pushed back into the hedgerow was now firmly closed.

I got out of the car and saw that a relatively new, heavy chain and padlock secured it in place. I lifted the padlock and pulled on it, but it remained well and truly locked. A lump formed in my throat and tears sprung to the back of my eyes, but I firmly refused to let them fall.

"You'll have to do better than this Darius," I said to nothing in particular.

I pulled the car up to the gate, as near as it could possibly go without actually touching it and I removed essential items and only what I could easily carry. I locked the car, climbed over the gate and began walking to Ravens Deep.

Darius must have got my letter, he knew I would be here. Did he really think a padlocked gate would deter me?

Rush Lane was long enough in a car, on foot it seemed endless. Now, I was very thankful for my decision to leave early in the morning and arrive in the daylight. The bags I carried seemed to be getting heavier by the minute and I regretted trying to carry so much with me. After twenty minutes or so, I finally came to the driveway that led to Ravens Farm. The familiarity of it made me quicken my pace; it wasn't far now. Several minutes later I rounded the corner and Ravens Deep stood before me in all its magnificence. I felt relieved not only to finally be here, but also at discovering that it was just as beautiful as I had remembered.

I pushed open the front gate and put my bags down. Nothing had changed, it was all as it once was. I walked to the porch, but there was no key. I had known that this wouldn't be an open invitation, but standing in the porch I suddenly felt reluctant. I gripped the door handle and silently prayed that it would open, but it refused to move—it was locked.

I wondered why Darius was trying to send a clear message for me to stay away, but he had refused to contact me in person to tell me that. He knew I would return and maybe his padlocked gates and locked doors were by way of a half-hearted protest on his part. Whatever he tried to do I refused to be intimidated, after all, I was here now and he would have to deal with that reality.

I walked around the outside of the house in hope that I might find an open window, or one that I could force open and after completing a full circle, I found myself in front of the ivy curtain. I pulled the thick curtain aside to reveal the hidden door that I had found so many months ago. I lifted the latch, but predictably it was locked.

Was Darius was behind this door? If so could he sense my presence?

I let the ivy swing back into place and moved away debating whether I should wait in the garden until nightfall, or just break into the house. I decided that I did not want to wait around in the garden, especially as it got dark; I needed to take control of this situation and be prepared for what would arise later. Breaking into houses looked so simple in movies, but in reality I found it impossible. Nothing would move even an inch and

I soon discovered that my only option was to break a window; the downstairs bathroom seemed the smallest and easiest to repair or to board up.

I should have brought tools.

Then I remembered my basic tool kit in the car, but the idea of walking all the way back to the car did not appeal to me right now; instead I looked around for something else, a rock maybe, but there were none to be found.

Then I remembered the potting shed and made my way to it through the nettles and weeds. Once inside, I found the same old tools I had used long ago and in the dim light I could also see an old metal garden rake and that seemed like a good implement to break glass. Seizing the rake, I made my way back to the doomed window. I aimed the rake at the window, closed my eyes, and then with all my strength I struck it hard into the glass. The shattering sound of glass breaking was a shock—I had done it. A mixture of relief and horror swept over me. What would Darius's reaction be when he found out?

I knew only too well that the scenario was getting worse by the minute, for I had gone against my promise and his warnings and now to top it all, I had damaged part of his house. I did feel anxious that he would be angry.

"What other choice did he leave me?" I reasoned with myself trying to justify my actions. I knocked the remaining broken fragments out of the frame and removed any jagged edges with the rake and pulled myself up and through the window. I edged through and eased myself down to half balance on the sink and bathtub. I moved with extreme caution, unsure that the sink would support my weight, but it didn't move, then I lowered myself onto the bathroom floor.

Once inside I realized everything was as I remembered; just as I had left it. I opened all the curtains and ran upstairs to what had been my bedroom. I surveyed the room before me. The bed was now re-made with its original linens, but apart from that nothing had changed. My eyes at were at once drawn to the recess at the side of the dressing table and to the strange black window that I had wondered about all those months ago. What exactly lay on the other side? Was Darius beyond, watching me even now? I could feel nothing, no presence, no ghostly being, but Ravens Deep had always seemed like a benign place during the day.

Perhaps he is sleeping. Did he sleep?

I checked the house from top to bottom and noticed that even in the library every book was in its correct place. I busied myself with boarding up the bathroom window feeling slightly concerned that there was no evidence Darius had even been in the house since I had left all those months ago.

Nightfall came and I nervously paced around the living room waiting for the inevitable to happen. I sat down several times with a book, but I could not sit still for long. The long evening passed into the dead of night and that steadily progressed into the early hours of the morning. All the while I waited nervously for Darius to appear, but he did not.

Has Darius left Ravens Deep for good? Logically my thoughts told me that this was his house and he would return. He would know I was here and I would wait forever if that is what it took.

But he had forever, I did not.

I pushed that thought away, I was tired from hours of anxious waiting and eventually I fell asleep. It was some time later that a sudden noise woke me. My thoughts instantly flew to Darius, but the room was empty. The noise was coming from the kitchen. I cautiously entered the kitchen and my eyes immediately rested on the pantry door—it stood open.

At least the ghost was still here!

Here we go again.

I suddenly wondered if the ghost made itself apparent when Darius was close. I ran up the stairs and into the bedroom.

What can I feel? A presence?

I couldn't feel anything. There really was nothing here and I started to believe Darius was not at Ravens Deep. My belief became stronger as days and nights passed and he did not appear.

During this time I made several trips back to my car and to the village for groceries. I had to leave Ravens Deep via the back door, at least that still had a key. I had looked for the key to the front door, but it was missing. There was no doubt in my mind that Darius had it in his possession. The days merged into weeks and constant thoughts nagged at me.

Where was he? How long would he stay away?

I realized that I had been back at Ravens Deep for almost three weeks, and they had been the loneliest three weeks I had ever spent. I wondered what I should do if he did not return, but a voice deep within me told me he had to return here; he had to return to me.

Each night I anticipated his appearance before enduring bitter disappointment when he did not come. I felt lonely without him, but not truly alone. Strange occurrences took place at Ravens Deep; the pantry door still opened and closed itself on a regular basis, but other things happened too. I had not noticed them before, or perhaps my focus had been so much on the mousetraps and Darius that I had noticed little else. I would put a coffee cup on the table, only to find that it moved to a different location or its contents would be dripping down the side of the table as though knocked over. Paperwork would rearrange itself or an item would suddenly fall from a shelf of its own accord. But as I became accustomed to these happenings, I found them to be a kind of reassurance in my uncertain world right now. Confirmation that there were indeed other forces to be reckoned with. The ghost it seemed did not wish me harm. Maybe, like me, it was lonely in its eternity.

Another day slowly passed. I couldn't remember what day of the week it was anymore, every day seemed to merge into the next. That did not matter to me, although I had been careful to keep myself healthy and eat on a regular basis, as I knew I had to be strong to confront Darius, I couldn't afford to be weak and sickly.

Again the thoughts crossed my mind; where was he and why had he not returned? Was he watching me now? Did he know I was even here? But the endless questions remained unanswered.

The sun had already set as I selected a book from the library and sat curled on the chair absorbed with its contents. The table light cast a warm glow across the whole room illuminating the pages in front of me.

Suddenly I experienced the strangest feeling, a perception of something about to happen. The prickles that started at the base of my neck ran all the way down my spine and I shivered inwardly. All my senses were on full alert as my ears picked up the faintest of noises at the front door—a key in the lock.

I felt my already rapid heart beat increase and my eyes remained fixed intently on the doorway to the hall. I felt my throat go dry and my stomach clenched into a tight knot sending a wave of nausea through my entire body, but I could not move—I was paralyzed with fear.

The door opened quickly and Darius entered. He looked taller than I remembered, and shrouded in the darkness of the hallway, strangely sinister. I tried to speak but no words would form. We remained staring at each other across the room, my eyes locked with his in defiance, but his very presence now frightened me and unstoppable chilling thoughts from horror stories filtered through my mind. I pushed them away and concentrated on trying to steady my nerves, but my pulse raced frantically and the tension that had built in the air was electric.

Darius finally broke the silence.

"Why do you continue to defy me, Madeline?" His voice was cold and the way he looked at me with his intense, darkly disturbing gaze chilled me completely, but then the paralysis released me and I stood up with my eyes firmly fixed on him. Somehow I found my voice.

"You know why ... I cannot live my life without you." My words were barely there and my voice sounded frightened even to my own ears, but I knew I had to be strong and I couldn't let him intimidate me. I took a deep breath and glared back at him as I tried to ignore the familiar urge to go to him for his eyes, although ferocious and damning, held me captive, but I remained motionless as the shadows of the night still clung to him.

Instead he swiftly and silently drew closer to me and I was horrified and chilled by his laugh, for it was the first time I had ever witnessed it, and it exposed his perfectly formed teeth. His eyes were glittering dangerously, as he asked in a mocking tone.

"Even now do you not realize what I am?" Startled by the suddenness of the question and the sight before me I was too frightened to respond, but undaunted by my silence he continued.

"Why did you come back here and break your promise to me? I am already damned to eternal hell. Why do you wish to see me tortured so?"

Getting over my initial shock, I retorted shakily, "Why do you wish to torture me so? You may be living in an eternal hell, but I am living in an earthly one. You cannot send me from you ... and your torture is of your own making." My statement seemed to startle him, for I saw a fleeting look of surprise, and my voice gained confidence as I continued.

"If you want to kill me then you know I am powerless to prevent it, but you can also allow me to live and to stay with you. It worked once; you delighted in being with me once." Darius stared at me with a dark incredulous look in his eyes.

"I have never wanted to kill you," he said quietly. "You are but the lamb and I the wolf, how long before instinct takes over and the inevitable happens?" Meeting his stare straight on I looked into his eyes, my fear disappeared and it was replaced by a feeling of calmness for I felt that he wasn't about to kill me just yet.

"Darius, you were mortal once, you must remember what it is to love and to feel pain," I reminded him gently. "How were you able to be with me night after night without harming me? You controlled yourself then, so what has changed? You saved my life once: what part of you did that, if not the mortal part?" I demanded, hoping to appeal to any remaining mortal senses. He stood in silence for a few moments and when he finally spoke the coldness in his voice was not so chilling anymore.

"Because once I had found you, I did not want to ever let you go," he replied, "but you cannot live here knowing what I am. Your life will be in constant danger and you will know the horror of what could happen to you sooner or later." He hesitated before continuing.

"Why is that so difficult for you to understand?" He raised his voice as he concluded, "Knowing the truth should horrify you, you should fear me, not seek me out!"

The effect of his words was largely wasted because I had been prepared for all the possible reasons for me not to remain here and I responded to him instantly. My voice was steady now and it rose to meet his own.

"You presume to know too much about me Darius," I said defensively. "Don't you think I have tormented myself, knowing that you are immortal and the implications of that fact, but how can I fear you when my love for you overwhelms that fear?"

My confidence in my own words grew stronger as I continued, "I know the horror of what you are and how you live, but even with that knowledge do you really think I can exist away from you?" I paused for a moment gauging his reaction; it was unreadable. "My life has no meaning without you and all the gates, padlocks and locked doors will not keep me from you," I concluded, feeling a sudden surge of relief to have finally said those words to him.

It was the first time I had ever seen Darius's normally cool composure disturbed and he sat down on the sofa with his head in his hands.

"Madeline, you ask too much of me!"

I saw the hesitance and vulnerability in him and it empowered me to continue.

"I ask only what I know you to be capable of," I said quickly, "mortal and immortal have no relevance here at Ravens Deep. I know I can make your life full once more and I believe that you can control your hunger when you are with me, just as you did before. With you I can live my life and with me you will have a life," I paused for breath before I continued softly.

"I really can take away your darkness and bring you light if you let me, but you cannot send me from you—I will only return."

He looked up at me with his bewitching green gaze and I wished at that moment that I could read his thoughts. He seemed to be digesting the words I had just spoken and thinking about them in detail, then he finally appeared to come to a decision and stood up.

I remained motionless for several moments, anticipating what was yet to happen, but then I noticed the darkness cease to enshroud him and he looked calm and composed. I confidently moved much closer to him and as I looked deeper into his beautiful eyes, I saw they no longer held any trace of fierceness. I closed my eyes and kissed him on the lips, to which he responded gently and after a moment he held me firmly back from him.

"I have missed you Madeline," he said before encircling me with his arms.

CHAPTER SEVENTEEN

Desires of the Flesh

If I had any doubts about returning to Ravens Deep they were soundly pushed to the back of my mind in the moments that followed. Darius released me from his embrace and his long fingers intertwined with mine. He brought my hand to his lips and kissed it softly. We stood in silence for a few moments more before he spoke.

"Madeline, I can no longer be content to leave you each night. You are correct in the words that you speak, part of my torture is of my own making because I want more from you. I hunger for all of you and your very presence fuels my deepest desire to possess you, but that very desire puts you at risk." His gaze made me tremble and I softly responded to his words.

"I did not return here just to endlessly hold your hand; I too want all of you, Darius. You have a strong mind and you have learnt control and restraint. I truly believe in your love for me I will be safe." I paused for a moment. "Do you hunger for my blood or for the mortal that I am?" I asked breathlessly as his smouldering look sent waves of longing over me.

"It is your being that sets me on fire, not your blood," he replied as his fingers stroked my hair.

"Then am I not safe enough?" I replied hesitantly, distracted by his continuing seductive touch. He drew me closer to him still as he seemed to construct a firm decision in his mind.

"I will keep you safe," he said firmly and picked me up in his arms. Our kiss lingered as he effortlessly moved up the stairs and to the bedroom, before setting me down to face him. The anticipation of his touch was unbearable and I could wait no longer, even if I would be damned because of it. His silky hair fell across my face as he bent his head again and I entwined my fingers in its long strands and pulled him close.

His deep kiss inflamed my already simmering passion and I felt the intensity and desire build within him, rivalling my own. With ease he lowered the straps of my top from my shoulders, before my clothes seemed to fall away under his expert guidance. I shivered slightly from the exposure of my bare skin to the air and then again, from the way he kissed me and his seductive caress down the length of my body. My own fingers found the buttons on his shirt and with trembling hands I slowly undid them, exposing the perfect whiteness of his flesh. We kissed again and as our lips parted I looked up at him with sudden hesitation.

"Can we do this Darius?" I asked breathlessly. A faint smile touched his lips as he understood my real question.

"I cannot infect you this way; you have to be bitten." Seeing my subtle look of concern he continued, "I do not have a need for blood right now. It is my desire for you that consumes me tonight." He took my hand and placed its palm on his bare chest.

"Do you feel that I am warm? Trust me; I will do whatever it takes to keep you safe." His skin was not only warm, it was positively hot and my mind felt quietened.

"I do trust you Darius. I trust you with my life," I said as I encircled my arms around his neck. With my own quickening pulse and the urgency I felt build within him, I responded to his tantalizing seduction and throwing all caution to the wind, I answered him with my own wanton desire.

His lean body fitted perfectly with the slenderness of mine and we fell to the bed with our limbs entwined in a passionate embrace. I wanted him desperately and in his arms I felt reckless as all fears and doubts were firmly chased away. His body pressed into mine and we joined together in a frenzy of carnal desires of the flesh. My body trembled beneath his touch and my nerves were electrified under his kisses that bound me tightly in his love.

I could feel the intense fire that burned within him and as I pressed my lips to his throat, waves of ecstasy washed over me before I simply melted in his arms as his dominant strength beckoned me, unrelenting until I surrendered my mind, body and soul to that dark desire.

I was beyond caring what the consequences of our actions might be. Now, we were part of one another; joined as one. He was my demonic lover and I was his to take possession of, as I succumbed to his every wish and desire.

Some time later with our passion spent I lay back in his arms unmoving, the minutes passed and I shifted so that I was able to see his face again. His long eyelashes swept downwards softly touching his cheek. I lightly ran my fingers over the smooth skin of his body marvelling at its perfection and beauty; he was so exquisite and I was enchanted with him all over again.

I felt him move slightly and I looked up; he was watching me and smiled faintly before leaning up and sliding his hand sensually down my back, his kiss danced lightly over my skin causing my body to tremble once more. His eyes lingered for a moment on mine before he pulled me firmly back into his arms.

"In all these endless years I realize it is you that I have been waiting for. Now you are mine, you belong to me and I will never let you go." He spoke with such vehemence that I was briefly startled, but in silent acknowledgement I closed my eyes, aware of the undeniable feelings of love that flowed from my heart and I fell asleep, secure in his arms.

I awoke alone a few hours later. The tousled bed-clothes and the faint scratch marks on my skin were the only evidence of the night before.

CHAPTER EIGHTEEN

The Hidden Chamber

Now, life at Ravens Deep marked a new beginning for us, and although we were aware of the dangerous complications of our relationship, we entered into this uncertain undertaking completely.

We took each obstacle as it presented itself; after all, Darius did have to fulfil his need for blood—his hunger. But now he rarely came to me when his skin was chilled; in the evenings he was always warm. I knew the full horror of his existence and no longer questioned the shadows that sometimes surrounded him.

I never asked how or whom and he never spoke of it either. It was something he had to do to exist. Why torment myself with the details? Although I had been initially torn apart by my own conflicting emotions; the horror of his existence versus my undying love for him, in time I came to accept that it was the way it had to be.

My days became shorter and my nights longer. During those nights we talked in detail about our months apart and Darius told me that he had watched me on several occasions in London, but had been resigned never to reveal himself. He confessed that he had been in Parson Place on the night I delivered the letter and he described how he had watched me waiting patiently in my car. I knew then that my senses must be very in tune with his, to enable me to sense his presence.

Looking back, I knew I had sensed him then and on other nights too. It seemed to me that regardless of mortality, destiny had determined that we would find one another and, however unconventional this relationship was, there was no denying the fact that some other force or supernatural energy was at work.

Each night he enchanted me once more and I knew that I delighted him again. We were observant of our unspoken connection, in which we needed no words, oblivious to the world outside and unconcerned by the morality of our situation or unknown fate. The only importance was our persevering devotion, and caught up in our emotions of the intimate moments we shared, nothing else mattered. Every day just before dawn, he would leave me alone and return to the chamber where he spent his days. I found comfort knowing that he was still at Ravens Deep with me and only a wall kept us apart during the daylight hours.

We were mortal and immortal sharing an existence; a relationship. We knew that we had to be careful and Darius proved he had control, he mostly suppressed the underlying instinct that threatened to destroy my mortal life. That underlying fear was real and occasionally his inner demon did rise up and take possession and had to be quickly subdued, but I remained confident in my love and trust that Darius would continue to retain control.

We were content in the fact that not everything in this world is easily explained or understood and in that knowledge we both knew we had chosen to find happiness wherever we could, even if that happiness did not conform to normal convention.

After the first few intoxicating nights with Darius, when my mind could not concentrate on a single thing but him, I slowly became accustomed to this all consuming, passionate love affair and began to take notice of the world around me again. With Darius in my life this world remained magical; I relegated the dark side of his life to a hidden place in the remotest corner of my mind and concentrated instead on the light.

Tonight I requested that I be shown the hidden chamber where Darius slept. Darius had obliged and led me by candlelight under the ivy curtain and through the wooden door. We walked up the flight of steep wooden stairs and I found myself standing in a small stone-walled room. By the light of the candle I instantly recognized the recess in the wall that looked through to the bedroom beyond. The chamber was small, only enough room for an old chair, a few feet of empty space and a long polished wooden box that lay on the floor.

The coffin where Darius slept by day.

The sight of the coffin and the reality of its purpose disturbed me intensely. That one item brought home to me the horror of Darius's existence and although it was not open, the shock of actually seeing it suddenly made me feel entombed myself. Darius did not protest when I pushed past him and ran down the stairs into the darkness of the night. The cool breeze allowed me to breathe normally again and to regain my composure.

"Madeline?" his voice was behind me, I turned to look at him.

"I just couldn't stay in there, I'm sorry," I answered his unspoken question.

"I shouldn't have taken you in there, the reality must be hard to bear," he said looking concerned.

"I wanted to know," I readily replied. "I'm cold, let's go into the house." In truth it wasn't the cold breeze that had chilled me.

A little later we sat wrapped in our own shroud of love and understanding. I was relieved to be out of the chamber and tried to dislodge from my mind the image of the coffin. Instead I focused on something else.

"I have the glass you needed to repair the window, I picked it up today. Can you really fix it?" I said enquiringly.

"Yes, I will do it now," he answered as he rose from my side. I had finally confessed to him that I had broken the window and to my relief he had been undisturbed by the fact. He had merely said: "I really did under-estimate your determination to remain here, didn't I?"

Darius had unlocked the gate and I had brought my car up to the house. He had instructed me to buy the glass needed and now to my amazement he repaired the window.

Darius never failed to surprise me at the things he knew or could do. When questioned, he had simply replied: "When you are as old as I am, you learn to do many things." It always made me feel strange when he made comments like that, for it forced me to acknowledge that he was approximately a hundred and sixty eight years old compared to my twenty two years, and yet he still looked his immortal age of twenty five. I tried not to dwell on that fact often; it was too disturbing.

Later that same evening as I sat on the sofa, he laid his head on my lap and closed his eyes. I absently played with his hair, coiling it around my fingers as I gazed at him with a mixture of sublime adoration and curiosity. Suddenly he opened his eyes and looked questionably into mine.

"What is troubling your mind, Madeline?" I stared at him in shock.

Could he read my thoughts? "Can you read my mind?" I hesitantly asked with caution. "Sometimes your thoughts become clear to me, other times they do not. I know something disturbs you tonight." He paused for a moment. "The chamber? Is that the cause of your distress?" he asked inquisitively.

"Maybe," I hesitated, "but it is more than that. It made me think about you and your life before." Darius sat up and turned to lean against the back of the sofa, I turned to him. "Darius, tell me how it happened. How you became un-dead."

Darius's eyes found mine again and voices in my head were apparent, but almost unrecognizable. In fact I couldn't hear them, I just knew what they said:

"Don't ask me, the memory is still too painful!"

I could see him struggling with an internal conflict, the memories and thoughts of long ago were terrorizing him as he fought to conjure up the past. I took his hand in mine and squeezed in reassurance.

Despite his obvious agony he began.

CHAPTER NINETEEN

1860

"The year was 1860. I had grown up at Ravens Deep along with my sister Isobelle and my mother Madeline; my father had died when I was a small child. We had three servants; a cook, my mother's personal maid and a stable boy.

One evening in late spring I was returning home, having been away for two weeks in London on business. The journey had taken several days, travelling on horseback and staying at various coaching inns along the way. On this particular evening I was very tired, and anxious to be home." I smiled at Darius.

"Do you know, I could almost picture you on a black stallion with your cloak flying in the cold wild winds, racing across the moors as a daring highwayman." His smile met my own.

"That is one crime I have never been guilty of," he replied cordially before continuing with his story. "As I approached our property on Exmoor, I took my usual shortcut through the woodlands to the church. I intended to pay my respects to my father who lay buried there.

When he had died, my mother had his remains buried in a specially designed sarcophagus. She had

commissioned stonemasons to work it until they satisfied her wishes with the depictions, then she had the
sarcophagus positioned in its final resting place.

My mother without fail would walk to the churchyard at
least twice a week. She would tend the area around the
tomb and lay fresh flowers, her favourites being honeysuckle and wild rose. That evening as I approached the
church the sun had already set and it was rapidly getting
dark. I remembered thinking I should take care that my
horse did not stumble in the darkness of the woods, and
wished I could have ridden a little faster, so that I arrived
whilst there was still enough daylight.

I arrived at the church, but as I dismounted from my
horse, my attention was caught by an image that made
my blood run cold. Lying on the ground outside the
open church door was the body of Father Talus, the local priest. I was horrified by his appearance, for I had
never seen anybody so deathly white, and the light of a
full moon made his appearance even more ghostly. Of
course I did not comprehend the reason for his strange
white pallor, it was only later I realized that his body
had been entirely drained of blood. I knelt beside him
and noticed an old book still clutched in his hands. At
first glance I assumed it to be an old Bible, but as I gently released it from his grip, horror struck me with grim
reality as I realized I held in my hands a grimoire—A
Book of Shadows.

I remained by the body and as I turned each page I
was sickened at the content of this evil book. It had been
composed from the writings of various priests and I
deduced that it had originated in Italy. Over the centuries
notes had been added by its various owners including the

final entries, Father Talus's own handwritten notes. I remember sitting unmoving, paralyzed by fear as I read page after page and tried to decipher what indeed it all meant, before I discovered what Father Talus had done before his life had abruptly ended. I still remember that vice like grip of horror as I read his neat handwriting printed in black ink before my very eyes. The implication of my discovery was too terrifying for me to fully understand straight away, so I remained for a time reading by the moonlight on that terrible night."

Darius paused. He had a very distant look in his eyes and I thought I should comfort him, but I could not find the right words. I remained silent and took his hand in mine. That action brought him back to the reality of the moment and he looked down at my hand in his, and then continued slowly.

"I once told you about Theophilus Shaw who had died several years before, and only James and Madeline, my uncle and mother," he emphasized their relationship to make it clear to me of whom he was talking. "Only they had dealt with the body and burial and the location of the unmarked grave. They had trusted only one other; the priest, Father Talus. But unbeknown to James or Madeline, Father Talus's loyalties had always lain with Theo. I discovered later that Father Talus and Theo, had attended numerous occult ceremonies that took place here in our very own woods. They blatantly used black magic to supposedly conjure up evil entities to give them power over the simple country folk, whom were already fervently superstitious."

"How … what did they conjure up?" I said incoherently in a tense voice. Darius shrugged and shook his head.

"Who knows what they really got up to?" he replied, "I never found any evidence that the ceremonies actually did conjure anything at all. I have to believe that Theo was insane. If he had been a poor man he surely would have been locked away in an asylum and left to rot, but he was rich, and with his money and power came the faithful followers. The disciples who will carry out anything that may be required of them, regardless of the consequences. So when by unknown means this book came into the possession of Father Talus, he acquired the secret that had been handed down through the ages; the knowledge of how to resurrect the dead!"

I felt the hairs stand up on the back of my neck at that statement. Darius sensed my feelings.

"Do you want me to continue?" he asked concernedly.

"Yes, absolutely," I answered quickly.

"I don't want to give you nightmares," he said with a slight smile.

"You will be here to chase my nightmares away," I said confidently." Darius's smile faded as he continued.

"By the priest's reckoning, what better person to resurrect than Theophilus Shaw himself. He believed Theo would make him immortal in return and give him the gift of eternity for his loyalty. Father Talus believed he and Theo would endure an eternal reign of terror, unstoppable in all the acts of horror they could dream up together.

However, Father Talus's plan went horribly wrong. He did manage to resurrect him, but Theo, who had been one of the completely un-dead, woke with such an insatiable hunger that he drained the priest of every drop of his blood, in fact killing him.

In his haste to resurrect Theo, Father Talus had failed to read the warnings within the writings of people that had gone before him. I have studied the grimoire in detail and there were many accounts and forewarnings of the terrible risks and consequences to anyone who would choose to follow that dark path. That night the grimoire had also been within Theo's grasp, but like me he had probably thought it was a Bible and he had left it with the body. The reality did not sink in straight away, but as I read, it revealed to me the horrifying detail of the life's work of evil men. Not only did it give detailed accounts on how to resurrect the dead; it described how to make certain the dead remained in their graves. As frightened as I was that night, that notation was the one I paid careful attention to. It revealed that the only true way to ensure death is by fire, for once the body has become ashes, the soul can never live again.

My greatest fear was that the priest might not be entirely dead. I believed back then that he would change into a hideous walking corpse or some other terrible fiend," Darius said with a hint of a smile, "so I burned his body, right there and then in front of the church.

A little later I approached Ravens Deep, but my mind was in turmoil from what I had witnessed, the contents of the grimoire in my possession, and the act I had been forced to commit in the churchyard. I was barely aware that something was terribly wrong when I entered the house. Calling out to my mother, I walked up the stairs when suddenly I heard a noise coming from her room. It was an unearthly noise that made me shake with fear. I ran up the rest of the stairs and burst into my mother's room. The scene that met my eyes was one of the most unimaginable horror. For the man who could only have been Theophilus Shaw was standing over the dead body of my sister Isobelle and as I entered the room, he released the lifeless body of my mother and she too fell to the ground. Her blood still staining his lips.

The rage inside me was unstoppable and with one movement I pulled my father's sword from the wall, which my mother kept in her bedroom, and lunged at him. I cannot remember how many times I drove that sword through him. He had an unearthly strength and despite the terrible wounds I was inflicting upon him, he resisted fiercely. He fought me like the demon he had become. There was such intensity in the way he refused to weaken, regardless of what I was doing. His hands gripped my throat and as his terrifying eyes met my own, I was horrified by my own awareness that I was trying to kill my own dead grandfather! We finally fell to the floor and before he gained total control, I somehow summoned the strength to push him from me and gain an advantageous position. I aimed the sword once more and adrenaline or fear must have given me the strength for one final blow, as I brought the sword down with force—I decapitated him.

My mother and sister were dead. I was distraught, but I was aware of the awful situation that could unfold if I didn't act fast, for I was uncertain of how much time I had before Theo might spring to life in front of me. I was all too aware of the contents of the grimoire and the frightening reality that Theo may still be un-dead. Even worse still, I was not certain if my mother and sister would befall the same fate. Not knowing what else to do, I took the oil lamp and tipped its contents over all of their bodies. The fire spread quickly and engulfed the room in flames. I managed to escape just before the ceiling fell in, and made my way back down the stairs and out of the house. I think I collapsed in the garden overcome with grief, exhaustion and the effects of the smoke. The servants, who had been in the other part of the house, came running carrying buckets of water. The stable boy rode to alert the tenants at Ravens Farm and together they put the flames out, but not before the fire had destroyed a large portion of the house.

The next morning I stood amongst the ashes, still dazed by my grief and the shock I had experienced, I remember absently bringing my hand to my neck and the horror I felt as I discovered two puncture wounds. Caught up in my rage and the intensity of the fight the night before, I had no idea I had been bitten."

Darius paused. I could see the memories greatly pained him still, and I squeezed his hand to give him reassurance and encouragement to continue. I myself was unable to speak at that moment.

"I was the only remaining infected one," he said at last. "The only one, soon to become un-dead. The infection spread slowly, despite what you think; it does not happen instantly. Instead it takes over your being like a creeping poison through your bloodstream; a venom that slowly pulsates its way with every beat of your dying heart. I knew I had to act fast, I knew I was damned, although I did not know how much time I had left. In the week that followed, I arranged for three more sarcophaguses to complete the four in the churchyard that remain now. One each for my mother and sister, to be placed next to my father's that was already there, and the fourth for me, for when and if I did die to enable me to lie in eternal rest with my family. Obviously the fourth remains empty for now," he remarked dryly, looking at me.

"Theo's remains or what was left of them were re-buried in his grave. Ashes at last, he can never be resurrected. My mother's and sister's ashes were placed in their respective tombs." Darius paused for a few moments, his words made the atmosphere seem very sombre and I felt great sadness and horror for him at what had occurred in his life. Darius, sensing my melancholy, smiled softly at me and his next words were spoken in a more cordial tone.

"My mother had been wealthy and owned not only Ravens Deep and the farm but all the surrounding lands. Not only inherited from my grandfather Theo, but my father John who had been a man of substantial means. I also owned properties in London, one of which I eventually turned into my museum.

The portion of Ravens Deep that was destroyed was levelled to the ground and then I salvaged the existing wall to have the chamber built where I now sleep. The foundations of the part of the house which burnt are concealed beneath the undergrowth that has grown up over the years. Now, there is only the memory of them in my mind.

I inherited everything, the house, farm and surrounding lands. The property in London I already owned and the museum is a private one. In recent years it has had the facade of a rare bookstore, and operated by loyal people that I pay extremely well to take care of business matters." Seeing the look on my face he added, "They do not know. They think I have the illness I once told you about, so they understand I cannot have too much contact with them, and it explains why all my business transactions are conducted in the hours of darkness. I believe they think of me as some eccentric, reclusive collector, but the family has been loyal and I have never wished them harm.

Many years later I purchased the house in Parson Place, another safe haven for me when I spend time in the city. Existing amongst the living is a constant reminder of the dangers that surround you. That was especially apparent in my early days, when my hunger drove me to be there."

As I watched Darius I noticed a slight change in his demeanour and a distinctly sinister edge to his voice. "It is easier to find prey in a big city where no one pays too much attention to a few corpses here and there, especially when they are found well decomposed or have been in the Thames for long enough to not be suspicious."

I had remained entranced, deeply saddened and horrified by his story, shocked into silence throughout most of its content, but now I could contain myself no longer.

"Why do you come back here? When surely it must be harder for you to exist?" I asked at last. Darius considered for a moment before answering.

"I find peace here, not true peace, but it quietens my soul. I truly belong here and the need for blood, my hunger, does not control me as it once did. Once it was all consuming and all powerful, but now I have learnt control," he said looking at me. "I have come to believe that being un-dead gets easier with time. At first it is a terrifying, tormenting demon inside that you have no control over, but to survive you must be able to live amongst the mortals without drawing unwanted attention. Perhaps now that I am older I do not need to feed as much—not even every night. Any blood will do. Being with you I have gone through enough animals to keep my skin warm and appear more mortal to you." Darius sighed. "Feeding is in fact of little consequence in the scheme of things, the worse thing is the endless time. Until you have eternity you do not realize how long and tedious it can be," he remarked wistfully.

"I have to fill my waking hours with more than feeding and now that is not so demanding, it is even more important to me. In the past I have looked for many distractions, something or someone to spark my interest." He hesitated for a moment. "What I have told you in the past is true, I have travelled extensively and collecting for my museum became a huge source of my interest. I travelled to acquire rare artefacts or a rare book for the bookstore, but in modern times travelling can be very dangerous especially in strange cities so I do not travel so much anymore."

"Is that why you decided to complete your ancestry?" I questioned. Darius looked at me thoughtfully before answering.

"I suppose curiosity and boredom made me decide to complete it in recent years. I decided to find out if any relatives did indeed exist as I believed they must. I had obviously seen my uncle James before I became immortal and I had told him a story of sorts about what had occurred at Ravens Deep. I convinced him that the place was cursed and so was I, and made him promise he would of never return, for I knew I would be forced to kill him. Thankfully he kept his word and never did. Whatever he thought had happened to me, he did not wish to involve his own family; I never saw him again.

I vaguely followed the births and deaths of the family down through the generations who were an obvious interest to me as they were my distant descendants."

As I watched Darius I was suddenly curious myself about this ancestry.

"So why me?" I asked directly. "Why was I lured to Ravens Deep out of all the others?" Darius leaned back thinking.

"The advert had been running for a couple of years in the magazine. Perhaps it was a frivolous thing to have done, but it fuelled my curiosity to see who would actually respond to it. Whilst in London I had learned of your father's death and then a year later your mother's. Her obituary had your name on it; Madeline Shaw. I was curious about you. I wanted to see what my last descendant looked like, especially because she shared my own mother's name. Several people had responded to the advert over the years. As you can imagine there have been several James Shaws, but no real connections. It was you above all others who captivated me from the first moment I saw you, and when I saw the resemblance to my mother, I knew I had to meet you."
I smiled at him.

"That evening in the garden when you scared me?" I remarked, remembering. Darius hesitated.

"No, I first saw you in London. Who do you think left the magazine for you to find?" I looked at him, shocked. Of course he would have seen me before I even came to Exmoor; all the pieces in this strange puzzle suddenly seemed to come together. The revelation spun around my head for a few seconds.

"But how did you know I would even pick it up?" I said, referring to the magazine.

"Because I had observed you on many occasions, leaving the hotel in the evening with various papers and magazines. In fact it wasn't the first one left for you, but I knew it was just a matter of time before you would take one home with you."

My mind was spinning; it all had been an elaborate plan to lure me to Ravens Deep. I was not sure if I should be feeling upset about that or not. I didn't know what to feel; how could I be angry with him when he was my life now? Suddenly things started to make sense.

"Darius, did you take the letters from my flat when I went back to London?"

"Yes," he said quietly. "I knew you had kept them all. I had watched you from the street. I watched you sit by your window and put them all into a wooden box."

"Did you know I took an overdose of opium in London?" He looked at me, startled.

"You wished to kill yourself because of me?" he asked incredulously.

"I don't know, my mind was in turmoil at that time," I said thinking back. "I knew I couldn't go on without you. When I read the contents of your letter, I was lost … confused. I knew deep down despite your letter I didn't want a life without you and in the emotional state I was in, I imagined I would never see you again. Maybe subconsciously I did try to kill myself, but Charlie found me and took me to hospital," I said remembering.

"Yes … the boyfriend," Darius said slowly, watching me. He hesitated before speaking.

"I was in London by then and I sensed something was wrong. I felt that you were in danger, but the time of day would not permit me to come to you. By the time I could get there you had already gone. I discovered the door to your flat had been broken and I was able to walk in and take the letters easily." He paused again.

"The boyfriend," I noticed Darius refused to say Charlie's name, "came back a while later and looked in the box." His eyes narrowed briefly.

As he spoke the next words he observed my reaction as if to gauge my response. "I was in two minds whether to kill him that night but I realized that he may lead me to you, so I watched and waited and followed him to the hospital. Once I found you, I decided to allow him to live, for you needed someone with you. Over the next few months I observed you nightly. When you returned to the flat, I left for Ravens Deep and apart from my usual excursion into the city and the occasional vigil under your window I did not dare to try and see you. When I read your letter telling me you were coming back here, I was in turmoil. I knew with every instinct that I should not allow you to come here, and I should stop you from returning. I believed at my absence, you would realize your quest was hopeless and return to London, but I misjudged your determination and ... you know the rest. But in truth there was also a part of me that wished you to return."

I was still digesting his previous words. I glared at him, was he deliberately trying to upset me? "You were going to kill Charlie?" I asked quietly.

"Of course, it is the nature of what I am Madeline," he answered a little dismissively. "He could have been a threat, besides I didn't want to think of you with *him*." The casual way he said the words made me suddenly angry. Although I didn't want to be with Charlie, the fact that Darius might have killed him because of me angered me greatly. Without thinking I snapped at him.

"You know, you remind me of Theo. It's the sort of attitude I imagine he would have had." Quite shocked at my own remark, I instantly regretted my choice of words and I wished I had not spoken them as Darius's anger was apparent.

"You are his descendant too!" His eyes were blazing and darkly menacing. "If I am such a monster what does that make you? For wanting to live your life with one." His voice was aggressive and threatening as he continued. "I gave you the opportunity to be free of me and you choose not to, yet still you persist in torment-ing me!"

I was reeling from the sting in his words and a mixture of fear and shock swept over me. Unable to respond I stood up and turned from him. I walked to the fireplace with my back to him and tried to fight back the tears that threatened to fall at any moment.

My thoughts were of Charlie and the relief that he was still alive, but then my thoughts flew to Samuel Dunklin. Did Darius kill Samuel? I realized that because I had spoken of Ravens Deep that day in the park, it was I who had probably sealed his fate.

"Yes, I did." Darius's voice was like ice and there was something like satisfaction in his tone. "I can hear your thoughts clearly, Madeline." I turned to find him stand-ing close behind me and his eyes betrayed the rage he was feeling.

"You have to accept that I cannot expose myself or this house," he said darkly. The tears ran down my face as I couldn't control my emotion no longer.

"I know," I said sadly. "I'm sorry Darius." I brought my hand to his hair and let it run through my fingers. "I do accept what you are. You are right, I am Theo's descendant also and I would be just as ruthless if anything were to threaten your existence. I do not mean to torment you, but you cannot talk of killing people I know and expect me not to react." As Darius continued to look at me, a strange dark expression seemed to pass across his face.

"You know that you break my heart, Madeline, but do not try and hurt me with your words. If you anger me that is when you are most at risk from me. You will do well to remember that." In his most disturbing gaze I found the sincerity of those words.

"I know," I said at last, feeling suddenly threatened by his closeness to me and the words he had just uttered. I looked for a distraction.

"Is that why you were so concerned that he was cremated? Samuel?" I asked quietly brushing away my tears. Darius turned from me.

"Everybody has been cremated in this area for generations. When the terrible things happened here, I made it known that the only way to rid the moors of this curse was to ensure any dead bodies were burnt." His previous menacing tone seemed to calm.

"The stories and folklore started with me, nowadays no-one can remember how and why they began and the stories have been handed down from generation to generation. Now there is no one left alive to make any correct assumptions anymore. It is good that the stories live on and that it remains so." I relaxed somewhat as his earlier ferociousness was not so apparent. I tried to clarify his words in my mind and I reiterated, "Only by being bitten can you become infected, but if you are drained of all your blood you are dead anyway?"

"Yes," he said looking at me. "Why is this important?"

"I was just thinking that it didn't really matter if Samuel Dunklin was not cremated." "It's best that the tradition remains," he said simply.

"How long after you were bitten did you truly become immortal?" I said gently trying to understand all the details and I sat down once again. Darius sat close beside me. All the tension between us had gone and was replaced by his irresistible charm once more.

"With me it took just under two weeks. At first any food I tried to eat sickened me, then bright lights, especially sunlight, made my skin tingle and my eyes extremely sensitive. I felt as though I was truly dying and my mind was tormented. I would see things move but they had not. I had disturbing hallucinations, as I would see people I knew to be dead cross my path as I walked, and just when I could stand the agony and torment no more—I changed. Then an intense instant hunger consumed me until I was forced to partake of the blood-lust, as only that could satisfy my craving.

At first I killed indiscriminately. My servants were the first to go, then the tenants at the farm and the animals in the field. In those early days, there was not enough to sustain me here and I had to leave for the city to quench my thirst. The first year was the worst, but very slowly I began to choose my victims—the ones that wouldn't be missed; vagrants, the homeless and runaways." I shivered at the horror of it all. Darius was now much calmer and he took my hand.

"I should not tell you anymore, I can see the horror in your eyes."

"No," I protested. "I want to know, I want to know everything." Continuing on I said, "Surely there must be others? When the priest revived Theo was it luck that it worked? Or was he the first ever?" I questioned. "No, Father Talus came from Italy originally; he knew it was possible. It was just by chance that the grimoire came into his possession and with it the darkest secrets of the church," Darius answered.

"You mean the church is concealing the immortals?" I asked shocked, hardly being able to believe what he was telling me. Darius looked at me.

"I have to believe that," he said simply. "After all my years of research and travels and threatening a few priests along the way, I deciphered the strange writings in the grimoire. I came to the conclusion there is a sector hidden in the depths of the Vatican in Rome, a hidden sector that is concealed and surrounded by the religious hypocrisy of what we know as the church today. This elite few have the dark connections to the immortals, they know how to make them and they know how to kill them. After all, was it not the church who invented the ideology of the devil to scare its followers into belief?"

I was shocked at the revelation Darius had confided in me and sat horrified by the implications of what I was hearing. Everyone knew the church was corrupt, but this corruption went deeper than anyone could ever have imagined. After a moment or two the realization came into my head. "So there are others like you?"

"I have witnessed only one," he said casually. I stared at him hardly daring to ask. "Who? Where?"

"In London many years ago," he said bemused. "I saw him observing me and he watched me watching him."

"What did you say to him?" I asked. I could not imagine how strange that reality must have been. Darius smiled at me.

"We are not social creatures. We barely acknowledged each other; he was probably wondering if I was any sort of threat to him. I sensed him one more time in London and never since, but as I said that was many years ago now."

CHAPTER TWENTY

Life with an Immortal

At first I was haunted by the revelations Darius had confided to me, but before long I opened my mind to understand and accept every part of them. I had willingly committed myself to him and he had allowed me to bear witness to his true existence. With that privilege bestowed upon me, I knew that he would never let me leave him. It was not that I wanted to, but occasionally the life I had chosen to lead evoked an enduring sadness.

Our love seemed truly cursed, for how could it ever be more than the pain and horror of his existence? But despite the darkness, there were many more hours of extreme happiness and as the days turned into weeks and months, I believed that with Darius by my side and in the tranquillity of life at Ravens Deep, I could forget the horror of what his life entailed.

Whether I was truly under some enchantment, or a spell of my own making, I could never be certain. The only thing I was sure of was my love for him and besides that I refused to let anything else concern me. Darius kept much of the horror from me, protecting me from his underworld existence of perpetual shadow. I never witnessed anything or anyone being killed, when it happened it was far from my eyes or ears. It was almost like it happened in a dream, a horrific dream, but one that didn't interfere in my world too much.

We spent endless hours of darkness enshrouded together in our eternal love and I remained bewitched and entranced living my life only for him. Darius always had mesmerized me, but now it was even more so and I learned what a truly intoxicating being he was.

He told me elaborate stories of his travels, detailed accounts of how he had searched out ancient libraries and church records, in search of some fact that would reveal how his existence was possible. Apart from the scribbling of ancient monks on yellowed parchments and the grimoire, he never turned up any other evidence to support the theory that there were many others like himself. Darius believed when they existed, they would have been exposed, hunted down and fallen by the wayside over the centuries. Disheartened by his endless searching across Europe for a reason or an answer and still no closer to finding one, he had returned to England and to his beloved Ravens Deep. Back in England he had studied various writings, supposedly true stories and actual accounts of encounters with the un-dead. But all turned out to be folklore and superstitious legends that had been handed down from stories of old. With amusement in his voice he had related most were absurd; crucifixes, water, silver or garlic could not harm him, for as long as his flesh remained it could be repaired. Only fire and sunlight, which to him were the same, could destroy him completely.

Darius had endured decades and with those long years had come the education and refinement of what his life was today. I believed there was not a subject in existence that he did not have some knowledge of and listening to him was better than reading any history book; his sultry tone and descriptive storytelling made the images vividly come to life in my mind. Being well read and versed in many cultures of the world, both ancient and civilized, he would relate great love stories from ancient Persia, or the mysterious stories of curses and buried treasure from Egypt.

He told me stories of his childhood, his life as a mortal and whilst doing so he would stroke my hair or caress my skin, knowing only too well of the effect it would have upon me. I could never resist him; he was my addiction. He encouraged me to write again and with his guidance, I learned to write with a deeper feeling. He attempted to teach me to speak French and Italian, in which he was fluent, although I knew I exasperated him on several occasions. Unlike him, I did not have a natural aptitude for languages and I could never master his level of perfection, but it was good to see him smile in amusement at my disastrous efforts.

Darius had so much knowledge and I felt that I didn't know anything compared to him, but in time he very slowly educated me in the history of various cultures, the use of natural medicines and herbs and how to make and administer poisons. Something he had learned from his mother, he had said. She was a healer, but when he had shown me how to brew dangerous concoctions and related how they would induce sleep or death, information he said could be useful to me, I felt more like I was dabbling in witchcraft.

I wondered if she had been a witch, but I did not mention that thought to Darius. He was a good, competent teacher; we would spend hours in the library together poring over a book or researching some fact. Occasionally he would bring me an intriguing artefact out of the depths of the museum and he would tell me its fascinating history and from where it had originated.

Darius would still leave me every two weeks or so for the city, but then he would delight me on his return by bringing me a rare book or some ancient trinket, along with a detailed story of love or corruption that went with each object. He lavished his attention on me and most of the time I felt completely safe, not only from him, but from the world in all its entirety.

Yet there were times when I witnessed his inner conflict, the demon that he had to bring under his control. On these occasions he would leave abruptly and disappear into the night, returning only when his bloodlust had been quietened. Although I had been initially disturbed by these outbursts, in time I began to see this as just a minor inconvenience to our being together and as time passed it did not disconcert me so much.

I still had several hours to myself in the daylight and I delighted in the warm sunshine, the garden and the beauty of the countryside around me. Slowly I brought the garden back to its former glory, pruning and weeding and giving much needed attention to the neglected plants. I discovered the ancient herb bed, where Darius's mother grew many of her herbs to make her strange potions and I planted new ones in memory of her. The garden was once again a beautiful place, well cared for and loved and the only legacy I could leave at Ravens Deep.

I still needed to venture out on my own, to the village and occasionally further afield. Unlike Darius, I had to eat food and needed to participate in a normal life of sorts without him. But my excursions became less frequent and whenever I left Ravens Deep Darius's manner would change for the worse and an underlying coldness would emerge for a while. It was almost as if he wished to keep me far away from any other mortal, lest I decided to return to that world. His fears were unfounded, as nothing could have been further from my mind and I would constantly reassure him of that fact.

After many months together he found a kind of peace with his inner conflict, and I too was at peace myself. I had known that we could live this way and even Darius came to believe that it was possible for immortal and mortal to exist together in relative harmony. I knew that I fulfilled a deep need that he had longed for in his life. I gave him a reason to exist and in return Darius's significance in my world could not be overstated; he had become as fundamental to my life as the very air I breathed.

CHAPTER TWENTY ONE

A Marriage Vow

It was early evening, the sun had set an hour ago and I was sitting on the kitchen floor wiping up the tea that had been knocked from the table top. The china cup lay on its side with its contents still dripping down the table leg: it seemed that the ghost was agitated once more.

To my relief, I had learned that all the terrible things that had taken place at Ravens Deep had happened in the part of the house that no longer existed. The bedroom where I slept wasn't the master bedroom as I had first believed. It had been Isobelle's room—Darius's sister.

According to Darius nothing untoward had ever taken place in there. I knew now that the only presence I had ever felt in that room had actually belonged to Darius. I had often thought about the opulence of that room, for I imagined Madeline's bedroom must have been even more spectacular. It was sad that half of Ravens Deep had been reduced to ashes, for I imagined in its former glory it must have been a truly magnificent house.

I often thought about Madeline and wondered what she was like. The portrait that hung in my bedroom was a constant reminder that she had once inhabited this house. My resemblance to her was uncanny and I often puzzled as to why it was so strong since there were many generations between us, but I completely understood why Darius's attention had been drawn to me; it must have initially been a great shock for him to have seen me.

Caught up with my own thoughts I was barely aware when moments later Darius walked into the kitchen. I looked up at him, startled, then on seeing his puzzled look I merely said:

"The ghost." Darius's look changed into one of amusement.

"You still believe this house has a ghost?" he asked half smiling. I stood up, meeting his gaze with my own. My voice was thoughtful when I answered his question.

"I know it does. It's not apparent when you are here, but when I am alone it moves things around, opens and shuts doors and creates havoc," I said gesturing to the mess I had just cleaned up. "Especially in here and in the pantry and the mice are not strong enough to carry the china." I remarked cordially. I remained thoughtful in my gaze. "I am surprised you cannot sense it; I would have thought it would be very apparent to you."

"Maybe it is quietened by my presence," he said agreeably as he leaned against the counter. He paused and smiled. "I don't think it means you any harm. Whatever it is, it must be truly dead ... unlike me." I stood quickly and went to him.

"No it is not like you. You are real and I know it is not," I said softly. "I suppose it's quite comforting in a strange sort of way." I thought for a moment before continuing, "I believe it is the ghost of Madeline, in fact,

I am sure of it," I said decisively, making up my mind resolutely. By his expression I could tell that Darius was clearly astonished at my assumption.

"Why do you say that?" he asked clearly interested. "A reasonable explanation," I said hesitating as I hoped my words would not upset him.

"It feels female and she would be quietened by your presence—her only son." Darius considered for a moment, almost as if he was deciding whether to humour me or not.

"Just when did you come to that conclusion?" he said watching me inquisitively.

"Actually just now," I said truthfully. "It all suddenly seemed to make sense to me," I said as I continued with my explanation. "I think the things she does is just a way of telling me she is here and perhaps she thinks she can communicate through me to you. I often think about her when I am in here—knowing this was her kitchen." I paused for a brief moment, "I know she had a cook, but when you said she used to concoct her various potions I assumed she must have done it in here." Darius smiled and pulled me close to him.

"You have a very colourful imagination. Maybe that is why you fascinate me so, for I could have never come up with that scenario in all of eternity," he remarked cordially. I laughed as I took a step back from him.

"You are making fun of me," I said dryly, "I am sure *you* would have figured it out sooner or later. With all your refinement and education and it takes a simple mortal like me to point out the obvious to you."

"There is nothing simple about you," he answered amused, "but it does make sense. My mother used to spend all her spare time in the garden gathering various plants, or in the kitchen and pantry. It was in there that she did her *concocting,* away from the prying eyes of anyone that may have happened into the kitchen." He paused for a moment. "She had the gift to heal, uncommon for her time, and I know you think her a witch, but if she was she would have been a white witch; the only evil things she did were out of necessity."

"I know," I said quickly.

I should have known that Darius would have been able to read my thoughts, especially when they concerned his mother. "Had I been in her position I would probably have done the same thing," I said with sincerity. I hesitated for a few moments.

"If she did kill Theo, she would have concocted that poison in the pantry, out of sight of any servants."

"Yes, most certainly," Darius said reflectively. "That is why her soul is not at peace." There was sadness in his voice. "She killed him once, only to have him return and take her life years later, also destroying the lives of her children into the bargain," he remarked with a distant look on his face. I placed my hand gently on his arm.

"You know it's only a theory, Darius," I said softly.

"I know—a good one though. She would be quietened by my presence." I smiled at him.

"Well, that's good isn't it?" I asked cautiously, "I mean when you are here you know she is calmed."

"I suppose so," he answered distantly. I had the distinct feeling he was lost in deep thought, transported back in time to that night. I waited for his mind to return and I reflected that Darius in fact had never died, not in the true sense of the word, he had only transgressed into another being. Perhaps I was wrong to assume that he would be aware of ghosts and other entities any more than mortals.

Darius looked at me and smiled and I knew he had come back to me and the present moment.

"Come with me," he said taking my hand. "There is a full moon tonight—let's go outside."

The garden had taken on a magical quality, bathed in full moonlight. An occasional heavy cloud briefly obscured the moon causing our surroundings to plummet into darkened shadows for a few minutes, before appearing again in the luminous white radiance. In the distance the sea was smooth and as dark as black velvet; not a single ripple disturbed the surface. It was the month of October and the trees had begun to shed their leaves. A sudden cool breeze coming in from the coast whipped those dead leaves into the air where they danced for a few moments before falling silently to the ground. I shivered slightly and moved closer to Darius. He wrapped his arms around me and we stood watching the night unfold about us. I felt comforted by his presence and after a few minutes more I turned to him.

"Can we go for a walk?" He looked at me with surprise.

"Where do you want to walk to?"

"Let's walk to the church," I said making up my mind quickly.

"You could fall in the darkness," he reasoned. "The path is very narrow in places and in the dark it could be dangerous for you."

"I have a torch, besides, you will not let me fall," I replied confidently. I was curious that he seemed reluctant, but maybe he was just concerned for my safety.

Although it did suddenly occur to me that we had never left Ravens Deep or its gardens together and I wondered if that was what had made him hesitate. Whatever the reason he never spoke it out loud and he agreed to walk to the church. I saw him take some matches and put them in his pocket. He saw my curious look.

"For the candles in the church," he said as he answered my unspoken question.

We walked through the cool woodlands, surrounded by blackness and the shadows that moved constantly in the breeze. The beam from my torch gave me a small amount of light so I could at least see where I was stepping.

I looked at Darius and noticed that he paid more attention to me and where I was walking than himself. Observing this led me to a thought process that I had not imagined before.

"Can you see in the dark, Darius?" I asked.

"Yes, I see everything. It is different for me," he answered as he tried to clarify his words. "Darkness is not that dark—more like twilight, but the details are much clearer than they would be in your twilight."

It seemed so strange that we were side by side and yet our perception and view of everything around us could be so different. The rustlings of the nocturnal creatures moving amongst the undergrowth disturbed the silence of the air. My mind went back to my previous thoughts and I continued with my line of questioning.

"Can you hear better than me?" I asked now intrigued.

"Yes, I hear everything. I believe all my senses are heightened, although it has been so many years now that it feels normal to me; how it should be."

"So what about telepathy?" I pressed.

"What about it?" he replied, obviously amused by my train of thought.

"When I first met you …" I began to try and explain what I had felt. "I could have sworn that you said different words to me … words not uttered from your mouth, but from somewhere else … from your mind maybe?" Darius laughed as he considered my words.

"You know telepathy is the communication of thoughts, feelings or desires between people involving mechanisms that cannot be understood in terms of known scientific laws. I desired you and I knew that I appealed to your senses. Why is it strange that out of that you could hear my inner voice?" His words seemed to make sense to me, but I thought about the other voices I had heard.

"But I also heard things when you did not wish me to continue a particular conversation,"

"It works both ways, Madeline; it's just a thought transference. When you are very in tune with other beings, senses, or their perceptions, it is easy to master. Or maybe I can do it because I am immortal," he paused, "I do not know for certain." We had been walking a while and with Darius's guidance I had managed not to fall. As usual we talked about everything and nothing, and I had not realized how close we were to our destination. So I was surprised when the church loomed out of the darkness before us. Moments later we stood in the graveyard.

"Why did you want to come here?" Darius asked as he turned to me.

"I wanted to come here with you—I know you come here on your own," I answered casually.

Our surroundings had taken on an eerie and ghostly atmosphere that was made more apparent by the tombstones illuminated by the moonlight. Darius took my hand and we walked around the tombstones. He related the occupants of the various graves, all of whom he had once known. We finally reached the four sarcophaguses that stood underneath the oak tree. Now, they held more significance to me than before and I instantly saw the one that had more carvings and depictions than any of the others.

It was obvious to me now that it was his father, John Chamberlayne's tomb. Madeline had the time to commission this intricate work. The other three stood with only a few markings. Darius had not the time to allow the others to have been made in such elaborate detail. I turned to him.

"Which one is yours?" I said quietly. Darius seemed slightly taken aback by my words, but he pointed, indicating to me—his tomb.

"That one," he said simply. I looked at it. On the bottom was a simple letter D. I had not noticed that before on my previous excursion to the graveyard. Although the sight of the letter and the significance it represented disturbed me, I asked why there was only one letter. Darius moved closer to his tomb.

"For every hundred years I exist, I will carve the next letter in my name," he said nonplussed. I smiled at him.

"You have a long name—you must be confident that you will be around for a long time to come," I said cordially, trying to inject some humour into the sombre conversation. He sighed.

"Not necessarily." I shot him a puzzled look and I walked up to the sarcophagus. I ran my hand lightly over the rough stone and turned to look at him.

"Darius, when I die, I want to be buried here so you know I will wait for you," I said matter of factly. His eyes held mine captive for a moment, but he was clearly startled by my words.

"Madeline don't ... I don't want to think about that." I refused to be put off by his reaction and I moved close to him.

"Darius, I will die one day and when I do I want to be here. So you will know that I will be forever waiting for you," I said, suddenly caught up in the emotion of my own words. He put his arms around me and held me tightly.

"If you die—I will surely die too," he replied in barely a whisper.

We stood for a long time wrapped in each other's arms, but the breeze that blew across the graveyard was cold and before long, I was shivering. Darius released me.

"You are cold; we should go into the church."

We entered through the ancient door and I instantly felt warmer as the thick stone walls kept the cold breeze at bay. It was very dark, for within the last few moments the moonlight had become shrouded by thick cloud. The small windows did not allow much outside light to penetrate the building and I could barely see in front of me.

"Stay here," Darius instructed as he left my side and I watched his black silhouette move beneath the metal chandelier. He reached up and released the chain that bound it and lowered it slowly which enabled him to light the candles, then he secured the chandelier in place again. The church was instantly illuminated with dozens of flickering shadows that danced their way across the stone walls.

Darius took my hand again and we walked silently through the church, until we came to a stop in front of the altar with its long table. It was deathly silent, as the thick stone walls allowed no noise from the outside world. In this ancient building, in this remote place it was as though we were the only two beings in the entire world. Darius turned to me.

"If only I were mortal I would have married you in this very church." I stared at him, and caught up in the intensity of the moment I was aware that my voice trembled as I spoke.

"There is nothing in heaven or earth that can keep us apart. I have opened my mind to understand and accept your being. I would marry you, mortal or immortal, it is of no consequence and I do not need a priest or piece of paper to make a marriage vow to you."

The chill I had felt in the air disappeared and was replaced with an intense feeling of heat.As I looked at him, I was more certain of this than anything else.

"Darius, I will take you to be my husband for now and forever and nothing shall keep me from you." As he looked back at me his beautiful vivid eyes hypnotized my mind, leaving his soft sultry voice to appeal to any remaining senses. I heard him utter the next words:

"Madeline, I take you to be my beloved wife, my mortal love, for when your life is over mine shall cease also." Darius pulled me into his arms and kissed me with such intensity that it took my breath away, but I responded, clinging to him with every ounce of my being. As we stood with our bodies entwined, his chilled lips only gave me moderate cause for concern. His sensual kiss moved slowly further down to my neck and then to my throat and suddenly I felt him freeze. He released me instantly and I looked up at him in shock; his eyes belied a glowing dark intensity. I drew my breath in a half stifled gasp and stepped back from him, suddenly afraid.

He hadn't fed.

"Darius?"

"Stay here" he whispered darkly and he left me alone in the church.

I felt the warm tears running down my face and I instinctively put my hand to my neck. I knew what had happened; he had not been out for two nights and now he needed blood. Caught up in the emotions of what we had just done, the vow we had just made, he had allowed that inner instinct to take over. I realized I had come very close to being infected tonight.

Now, I thought about the words he had said to me all those months ago; that it was inevitable. Was it? No, I couldn't think like that. Darius could control it, he would control it.

Minutes passed and somewhere in the distance I heard an animal scream, the sort of terrifying noise an animal makes when it is suddenly aware of its own imminent death.

I sat down on the pew for support.

Some wedding! I thought bitterly, but I could not blame Darius and whatever poor creature had died out there tonight; it had died so that I might live.

I waited for forty minutes or so, before the church door opened. Darius silently came to me, his composure was normal and the darkness in his eyes was quietened, but he had a grave look on his face.

"Forgive me Madeline, I should not touch you when I am so cold." "There is nothing to forgive," I said taking his hand and noting that it was now warm. He looked into my eyes imploring me with his own. I felt his anguish, but I smiled reassuringly back at him.

"Madeline," he hesitated briefly. "Can you really live like this?"

"Yes, I meant those words," I readily replied. "I am just as compelled to you now as ever and it would be incomprehensible for me to imagine a life without you. Besides, I thought that you would never let me go?" he smiled at me.

"No ... I could not bear to let you go ... not now," he concluded. I glanced up at him fixing him with a determined look.

"And I am not afraid," I said as I turned and led him to the front of the church. I removed my jacket and spread it out on the alter table and then I turned and began to unbutton his clothes, avoiding his startled look.

"What are you doing?" he asked with a small amount of surprise mixed with a hint of amusement in his voice. I looked up meeting his gaze with my own.

"I thought that it was obvious," I said innocently. "We just got married didn't we? We have to consummate the marriage." "What, here?" I detected the faint shock in his voice.

"Why not?" I said provocatively, "Or do you think it inappropriate and I sinful because of it?"

"Whatever sin you think you might commit, it can be no greater than my own," he remarked as he lifted me in his arms and placed me on top of the altar table. He pressed me firmly to him and then I cast aside my own clothes, allowing the heat from his body to replace the warmth of their fabric. I pulled at his remaining clothes still in pursuit of my own desire. He did not resist, instead he responded with his own seductive touch that enticed me further. As our kiss became more passionate, I tried to ignore the faint taste of blood in his mouth. Then as I relinquished myself entirely, I completely forgot about that metallic taste of only moments before.

The ancient table groaned under our amorous passion, until we at last became still, but we remained on our impromptu marital bed, unconcerned by our surroundings, and I knew that I was bound to him body and soul; for he was now my husband.

CHAPTER TWENTY TWO

A Journey into the Night.

A month had passed since that fateful night in the church and I knew Darius would be leaving for the city any day now; it had been almost two weeks since his last trip. I was sitting in the when Darius came in; hesitantly I rose from the desk and greeted him with the question that had been playing on my mind.

"Darius, can I come to London with you?" His gaze showed no immediate expression, but shifted slowly from me and rested on the bookcases, as though he were preoccupied. He remained silent for a few moments.

"With you in the city, it could be dangerous for me," he remarked at last.

"Why?" I did not hide the surprise in my voice. Darius moved closer to me trying to find the right words to emphasize his doubts.

"I can disappear easily, dissolve into the shadows and you cannot. I have no interest in mundane things like shops and restaurants and with you needing to participate in a normal life, it could draw attention to me."

I felt slightly resentful of the fact that he thought I wanted to go shopping and not just be by his side, and

I quickly retorted, "I am not incapable of doings things on my own during the day and we don't have to be in public together. Besides, I would not draw attention to you and you forget I have lived in the city—I know how to take care of myself." I stopped talking. I could tell by his demeanour he was getting agitated, then without warning he suddenly became threatening.

"Do you want to see him, is that it?" he suddenly levelled at me.

"Who are you talking about?" I answered, bewildered by his unexpected attitude.

"*The boyfriend*," there was sarcasm as he spoke and then it became mixed with venom as he continued. "I do not want you in the city, with or without me, do not argue with me!" I stared at him in amazement, shocked at his accusation and his obvious jealous thoughts, but I knew him well enough to realize this situation could potentially get out of hand and if Darius believed I wanted to see Charlie—he would kill him! However, I was hurt by his words and disregarding his venomous manner, I angrily snapped back at him, acutely aware of my own resentment and the slight satisfaction I felt as I continued to provoke his anger.

"Don't you think you're being a bit possessive? And it's got nothing to do with anyone else. I can go to the city if I want to and you cannot stop me," I replied hotly.

He was angry now.

"You wanted this life, Madeline, here with me. You didn't want to be in the city. Remember? And I could and would stop you!" he snarled taking a step towards me, his menacing demeanour making it clear that he did not wish to continue this conversation.

I willed myself to calm down for I could feel my blood rising and my temper with it. I glared at him for a few moments and then I tried a gentler approach.

"Darius you know that I only want to be with you, I don't care about shops and I do not intend to see Charlie again, if that is what you are really concerned about." I started to feel a little calmer and I continued. "I want to be in all of your life. You have all of mine, but I feel as though I only know a part of yours." Darius's dark mood subsided a little.

"A good part, Madeline. Here at Ravens Deep is the life I want to have with you. You know there is a part you cannot have—the darkest part. I do not want to share that with you," he said in a gentler tone. "You are right, I am possessive, but now you are mine I have a right to that possessiveness."

"Darius, I know what you are and what you do. Here or in the city it makes no difference to me, but I hate it when you leave me, I feel empty without you. Do you not feel the same when you are away from me?" Darius moved closer to me, his hand moved lightly around my waist and he looked at me with a slightly anguished expression.

"I agonize over leaving you every time, but I know I must, it is how I am able to be with you. You know my hunger is less these days but it still persists. My excursions into the city allow that need to be fulfilled completely and away from you my conscience is diminished," he replied quietly.

"It makes no difference to me," I repeated, moving even closer to him and imploring him with my most endearing tone. "Please, Darius let me come, I want to see the museum and all the things you have told me of, the objects you have collected. Let me be a part of that life too." He sighed in resignation.

"You know I would not deny you anything that would make you happy." He remarked, but his expression became less gentle and his voice lowered as he spoke. "If you come with me, you will stay by my side and there will be no excursions into the city on your own." His eyes narrowed. "I do not want you seeing *anyone*," he concluded.

I was surprised by his words, but I thought that Darius probably meant Charlie when he emphasized anyone so I nodded in agreement.

"I only want to be with you, Darius," I said softly. "Madeline if you break your promise to me this time, I shall never let you leave here again!" he warned. I was startled by his sudden remark and I responded defensively. "Stop threatening me!"

"Why?" he snapped back at me coldly. "I give you life here with me and peace for what life it is and yet you persist in seeking something more. A side of me you may not care to witness. I wish you could save me from the darkness and awaken me from this torturous life, so that I could become something more than this ... this nothing that I am."

"Darius, you are not nothing," I said gently trying to sound calm although his words were beginning to frighten me. "As you exist now is the person I fell in love with, demon or angel it makes no difference. It is what it is; neither of us can change that fact." I hesitated for a moment. "You see me as a danger to you away from here, but that is not true, you must know by now that I would never betray you. I love you more than life itself; more than anything."

Darius's eyes softened and so did his tone, he put his arms tightly around my waist and pulled me closer to him.

"I do know," he said softly, "but my inner conflict is at times unbearable and my love for you is as strong as my instinct; my hunger for blood. You are not aware of the moral dilemma I face every time I take a life. Once it did not matter, but now each time I commit the act I question myself: what if this was Madeline? I am tormented by you, because of my love for you," he said sadly and I found myself distraught at his words.

"Darius, would it really end your torment or give you peace if I left you?" Even as I spoke the words I was aware of a growing sickness in my stomach at the very thought of leaving him.

"No!" he said at once. "You cannot leave me now and you know I would not let you go, I can bear any torment for you, because you saved me from the dark and let light into my life. You made it possible for me to live again and to feel alive."

"Then let me in—let me be in all of your life," I demanded gently. He considered for a moment before he spoke.

"I travel to London tonight and you can come if you keep your promise." He bent his head to kiss me and I responded unable to resist.

"I will keep my promise Darius," I murmured softly.

❧

Quickly I packed a small bag with essential items and some food and drink, as I knew Darius would have nothing at the museum and he probably would not let me out of his sight. I hurried in case he should change his mind and decide that I shouldn't go with him after all, but he was totally calm and seemed resigned to the fact that I would accompany him tonight. I rushed about gathering my things together and wondered about his sudden rages. I thought about the words I had spoken earlier. At times I did feel as though I was living with a demon and an angel as both beings could be apparent to me within a matter of minutes. It seemed to me that being un-dead was a constant conflict of good and evil. For within the good there was love, peace and beauty, but on the other side was a dark, possessive, jealously and of course, death. Darius didn't often show the latter to me, but when he did it was powerful and all consuming. I thought absently: I really should try not to invoke his rage too much for my own sake.

It was a bittersweet emotion as we locked the door to Ravens Deep. It really was home and I was sad to leave even for a short time. However, the brief sadness was replaced with the excitement of going to the city for a few days with Darius and to see all the things in the museum that he had talked about so often. I wondered how long it would take us to walk to his car, as Beaconmayes was four miles away and it was dark. We closed the garden gate, but instead of leading me along the woodland path, where I imagined the shortcut existed, Darius headed through the hedge in the opposite direction.

"Where are we going?" I asked. Taking my hand he pulled me after him.

"To the farm," he replied. "I had to mislead you before," he smiled, "it was for your own good. You will see," he said mysteriously. We worked our way down the rough path for several minutes and then we were suddenly standing before an old derelict farmhouse. Even through the darkness I could see that it must have been a sizable house at one time. To the side of the ruined house stood a large barn in seemingly good condition. I could see a gravel road ran behind the farm and disappeared into the trees. Darius turned to me and I detected the amusement in his voice.

"Did you really think that I would walk four miles every time I needed to get to my car?" I ignored his amusement.

"Where does it lead to?" I asked.

"It continues for about a mile, before meeting up with the main road. This road runs out and becomes grass as it rounds a corner that conceals it completely from view. There is a gate and an electrified fence that is connected between the trees. To any casual onlooker it looks like a foreboding entrance into an overgrown field. I had the electricity run up here decades ago and I connected it to the house." Seeing my look of astonishment, he remarked, "I have told you that in eternity you have the time to learn all sorts of skills."

"But wasn't that incredibly dangerous?" I asked still amazed by this revelation. Darius laughed at me.

"Maybe, but what's the worst thing that could have happened to me? It couldn't kill me, unless I erupted in flames," he remarked dryly.

We reached the front of the barn and Darius unlocked the padlock and threw open the double doors. There before me stood Darius's car. I stood in awe, stunned by its age old elegance and style. The paint-work shone even in the darkness and shadows of the barn. It was the colour of midnight and it gave me the feeling of having both a sinister and regal quality. I could just imagine a car like this prowling through the desolate moors in the dead of night, hauntingly beautiful and ghostly. Its image evoked another time—an archaic era. A car like this would have a history.

"What is it?" I asked as I turned to Darius.

"A 1939 Rolls Royce Wraith," he said, watching my reaction to his obvious beloved possession. He walked to my side.

"I don't think I have ever seen a car like this before, only perhaps in a movie," I said as Darius opened the passenger door for me.

"There were only 491 produced and many of them are owned by collectors. I have owned this one from new." He looked at me and remarked, "Its only history is with me." I looked inside, it was a beautiful symphony of wood, leather and chrome.

"It's beautiful," I said admiringly and then I turned to look at him and added, "I could not imagine you driving anything else, *it's so you!*" He smiled at me as I climbed into the passenger seat. I could feel the soft cool leather against my skin and noted that it really was in immaculate condition. I imagined it looked exactly like this when it came from the factory.

"How do you maintain a car like this?" I asked in wonder.

"I had a few problems with it when it was new, but I have connections in London and these days it rarely troubles me. It has been well looked after." Seeing my look he added, "You do what is necessary to exist in a mortal world."

Darius sat beside me and started the engine that was unexpectedly quiet, it almost purred as we pulled out of the barn.

"And you remain anonymous in this?" I asked incredulously. Darius smiled.

"You would be surprised. In the dead of night an old black car can be inconspicuous, even one as beautiful as this. People see only what they allow themselves to. You never knew I was in London watching you for all those months," he said, emphasizing the point.

"People walk past each other, without the slightest indication of those other people's lives. People that are fearful or sad put on a mask and they project a different persona to the world that is different from the one that really exists. Why would seeing an old car in the middle of the night seem sinister to a casual onlooker? Most people do not even see it. Mortals can be very unobservant," he added.

We drove over the desolate moors and I watched the creeping mists rise up and obscure the landscape all around us. Occasionally the thick cloud cover would break, enabling the moonlight to momentarily light up the shadows and reveal a windswept tree, a clump of gorse, or a few ramshackle farm buildings down in a valley. As the light faded once more they disappeared and were lost again in the blackness, leaving only the remnants of their dark shadows.

The roads were empty of any other vehicles and there was no artificial light of any kind. If it had been a clear night I knew I would have been able to see thousands of stars lighting up the sky. Tonight the only illumination shone from the Wraith's headlights, reassuringly guiding the way ahead. The moors by day could feel remote, but by night they felt truly wild and desolate; far from any distractions of modern life or the living. We passed through this enchanted landscape and I felt that we were on top of the world, a world in which we could have been the only two inhabitants. We two, immortal and mortal shrouded in the protection of our ghostly apparition of a car, for even *it* seemed to disappear into the shadows and the damp clinging mists of the night.

I wondered how many times over the years Darius had made this trip. As if reading my thoughts his voice interrupted my musings.

"This is an easy journey by car now," he declared. "By horse it used to take days and the roads were often treacherous; particularly in winter. An occasional inhospitable coaching inn along the roadside, made the dangers all the more apparent. Travelling back in those days could be very dangerous, especially at night," he concluded. I smiled to myself, conjuring up an image of a highwayman again.

"Why London, Darius?" I asked, curiosity getting the better of me. "Surely there are closer cities for you to go to?"

"These days there are," he answered. "Years ago London was all there was. The local cities that you see now were little more than small towns if they existed at all. Besides, everything I know is in London or here on Exmoor. This has been my life." He paused before continuing, "The journey only seems long to you because of your perception of time, but in my life this is but a brief moment." His words were not said to hurt me, but I found their content pained me considerably.

"Am I but a brief moment?" I asked, feeling slightly dejected. He turned to look at me; even in the dim light his eyes showed sincerity.

"You could never be, I can live a lifetime with you," he said reassuringly. Although I was comforted by his words, I was however, disturbed by the thought that my life would fade in but a few moments compared to Darius's life. That thought played on my mind as I stared out into the blackness. Could I bear the thought he would endure endlessly without me? Would there be someone else like me in another hundred years or so? Darius sensed my feelings, and he placed his hand on mine.

"Madeline, I would never want to find someone else, for me there is only you. What is important is now and the time we have," he said gently.

"I know," I said quietly as I tried to dislodge the negative thoughts. I rested my head on his shoulder. Darius was right, it was the time we had that mattered. I changed the subject for a more agreeable one.

"How long does this drive take in this car?" I asked, realizing it must take a great deal of time, for this was a very old car and I couldn't imagine it speeding down the motorway at eighty miles an hour.

"About four hours." I lifted my head and stared at him. Darius's eyes met my own.

"Then how on earth do you make this journey in the middle of summer? When there can only be four or five hours of darkness." I had just realized Darius wouldn't have much time to get to London in the height of the summer months; what if he got delayed?

"I have another house," he said casually and obviously amused. "I was wondering when you would figure out that this journey would be impossible during the summer months." I sat in silent amazement.

"The other house, where is it?" I said at last.

"It is in the county of Wiltshire just outside a small remote village named Crossways." Darius saw my look of amazement and began to explain. "Years ago the only roads in these remote areas were trackways. An ancient, long distance trackway crossed Wiltshire and this route was widely travelled by people who wished to cross the country. I regularly stopped at a particular coaching inn along this trackway, owned by a man called Benjamin Grey. He was relatively a young man, but he was dying of tuberculosis. The inn did not bring him much profit as there were more popular establishments nearby. He had no family left for both his wife and young daughter had died of influenza." Darius paused for a moment remembering. "We became acquainted and he agreed to sell the property to me."

"Acquainted?" I questioned.

"He was dying anyway. I just gave him the option of a quick and painless end, rather than the suffering he was enduring," he answered, matter of factly. "In return for his quick death he signed the property over to me. I actually liked Benjamin," he added. "There have not been many people I can say that about."

"Did he know then?" I asked, realizing what Darius was telling me. "He knew about you?"

"No, not at first, but I would stay there on my way back and forth to London and we engaged in several conversations. Obviously at the end he knew." Darius continued, "Once he died I closed the inn to the public, although on occasion I did have cause to accommodate a weary hapless traveller." I shivered. Darius looked at me and changed the direction of the conversation.

"A few years later new more direct roads were built and no-one apart from a few locals bothered with the old trackways. So the surrounding property has remained unchanged and undisturbed. It is no longer an inn, but a house named Chantille."

"Did you name it?" I questioned, now more interested than ever.

"Yes, the original name was Crossways Inn, as it was built close to the point where the old trackway crossed an ancient Roman road—hence the name. Chantille was Benjamin's dead daughter's name. I thought it was a beautiful name and appropriate to name the house after her, seeing as she had died in the house." I was fascinated by his story and I longed to see this house named Chantille. I turned to him.

"Can we go there?" I asked in earnest. He smiled at me.

"Not tonight, but I will take you there." My mind was intrigued; just when I thought I knew everything about Darius he still managed to surprise me further.

CHAPTER TWENTY THREE

The Museum

The constant purr of the engine and the darkness all around eventually lulled me to sleep. I awoke some time later and saw at once that we were no longer in the countryside, but entering London. The bright city lights hurt my eyes for a few seconds before they adjusted to the new surroundings, but I had fallen asleep with my head resting on Darius's shoulder and now I was acutely aware of the stiffness in my neck from the awkward position.

"Why didn't you wake me?" I asked indignantly.

"You looked so peaceful," he replied looking at me.

"How far do we have to go?" I said, sitting up straight and rubbing my sore neck.

"We are very close now."

A few minutes later we pulled into a narrow alleyway between several tall imposing buildings. Darius turned the car sharply and we were confronted by huge double wooden gates that seemed to open automatically. Darius guided the car between them and the gates shut behind us. We had driven into a small walled courtyard and directly in front of us were double garage doors set into the back of a large building. These doors opened as if by themselves before I realized that Darius had some sort of remote control device by his side, which made me smile. He drove the car into its garage and turned the ignition key. The engine's purr faded and Darius turned to me.

"What is so amusing Madeline?" I allowed my smile to widen.

It just seems strange that you have such modern things, like remote controls." I said, indicating the device. "It is from the age of technology and you are not." Darius considered my words for a moment. "I have to exist in this age, despite being born of another time so I have to learn and progress. The world today moves faster than it ever has and unless I have the ability to move with it, I will get left so far behind that my existence would be difficult. Besides," he added cordially, "even I can see the usefulness of some electronic devices."

I stepped out of the car and I saw that we were standing in a large concrete bunker with no windows, only a metallic looking door set into the back wall.

"This is my museum," Darius announced as he produced a key and unlocked the door that enabled us to enter. At first I could see nothing, but as my eyes grew accustomed to the subdued light, I saw stacks of old boxes lining a narrow corridor. We walked through, past the boxes to a heavy steel security gate that revealed another locked door. Darius opened both doors and turned to face me.

"We are very safe here," he said as if in response to an un-asked question. As he passed into the room before me, he flicked on a switch and at once the room was illuminated by subtle lighting; we were in the museum.

I stared in wonder at the sheer enormity and quantity of it all. Rows of glass cases were filled with collections of pottery and ornaments, cases of books and stacks of old maps sat on long tables. Many ancient and yellowing documents filled every available surface along with several jewellery boxes and photographs. I felt like I had stumbled into a treasure trove and I was initially too stunned to speak; I just stared in amazement. I turned to Darius in disbelief.

"You collected all these things?" Darius shrugged.

"Some of it was my mother's," he said pointing to the paintings and the pottery. "But when money is no object and you have all the time in the world, I suppose you can acquire a lot," he added bemused.

It was strange hearing him talk that way for I had never thought of Darius as being rich before. After all, he didn't do anything that would indicate that to me, but as I thought about all the land he owned, Ravens Deep, this building with all its contents, the house in Parson Place and Chantille, I was certain that he must be extremely wealthy. Of course it was of no consequence to him, having all the money he could ever have wished for; it could not buy him what he longed for most, the one thing he craved—peace. I moved closer to him.

"Do you even remember what's here anymore?"

"Mostly, but not everything," he confessed.

We walked amongst the treasures and he told me various interesting facts regarding the acquisition of each item, or to whom it had once belonged. I was a little disturbed to learn that many of the small items had been removed from victims over the years. According to Darius, bodies were less easy to identify without personal trinkets. We negotiated our way through the room's entire length and I saw that we were approaching the back wall with another door, which Darius unlocked and we entered into the space beyond. It was an small empty room with a heavy metal gate, secured in place by a heavy chain and padlock. Darius indicated beyond the gate.

"Through there is the rare bookshop I told you about, but there is no way through from here. The lock is securely sealed in case the padlock ever got broken. No mortal has ever entered the museum until now," he added, looking at me.

"The people who work in there, they are not curious?" I asked inquisitively.

"I pay them well not to be curious," he replied. "They believe it is an old warehouse filled with junk. I already told you they believe me to be some rich eccentric who just pays them handsomely for running a book shop."

"Then why do it? Why risk any exposure?" I asked in amazement.

"It is useful to have some contacts who will do your bidding," he paused for a moment, "like leaving magazines in hotels," he continued, watching me with amusement. I shook my head in disbelief.

"If I ever had a problem getting here or was unable to conduct business in the hours of darkness, they would be of use to me. You have to think of all the possibilities Madeline." He thought for a moment and added: "You need to have some subjects loyal to you." I laughed at his words.

"You make it sound like you are royalty—some mysterious prince," I said mocking him.

"If that were so, then you would be my princess," he said agreeably. "Come with me and I will show you some of my favourite things."

He led me back amongst the various tables piled high with papers to a glass cabinet and reached in to extract an object for me to examine. It was a decanter made of gold, and it was extremely heavy. It took my breath away, as its beauty was almost indescribable; it was undoubtedly one of the most beautiful objects I had ever seen.

"It is encrusted with emeralds, rubies and pearls," Darius remarked casually. "It has a matching bowl," he said, retrieving the bowl from the cabinet. "They are from ancient Persia." The bowl was just as elaborately adorned.

"They are beautiful," I said in awe. "What were they used for? Not wine surely."

"No," Darius replied. "It was the custom for the Shah and his privileged dinner guests to wash their hands prior to and after eating. A servant would pour the water over the diners' hands, from the decanter whilst at the table, and a second servant would catch the falling water in the bowl beneath. See how it has a concealed sieve in the bowl, to stop the water from splashing onto their fine clothes," he added. "Traditionally the water was scented with rose petals, in fact the custom still remains today even in more modest households."

Darius never failed to amaze me with his knowledge of so many things. I handed the decanter back to him and he replaced it in the cabinet and then turned to me.

"I have something for you," he said and led me through the jungle of treasure to a very old apothecary cabinet. He opened one of the drawers and produced a black box, which he opened. Inside was a necklace of silver filigree set with three stones which I supposed to be diamonds. It was an exquisite piece of jewellery, beautiful and unique, unlike anything I had ever seen before. Darius unclasped the silver chain.

"This was made for the Persian princess Barsine for her wedding day. The diamonds are African yellow diamonds, but now they are known as Iranian Yellows. You will see in the daylight their true colour and beauty," he said as he pulled my hair to one side to place the necklace about my neck.

"I cannot take that, it's obviously priceless," I gasped. Darius ignored my protest.

"It is priceless and is mine to give to you," he answered. Too choked to say much else I remained silent until he had fastened the clasp.

"How does it look?" I said looking into his eyes which were firmly fixed upon mine.

"Beautiful," he replied before turning to another box. Upon opening the small box he produced a thick band of delicate filigree gold. I stared at it bewildered.

"Who did this belong to—another princess?" I asked cordially.

"No, my mother," he said quietly. "This was her wedding ring, honeysuckle and roses entwined in gold." Darius took my hand and fitted the ring onto my left hand ring finger. I looked down at its shining brilliance.

"It fits perfectly," I said in amazement, feeling overwhelmed by the gesture.

"I know, you were meant to wear this ring," he said before he kissed me lightly. "It just took me so long to find you." I pulled back from him.

"Do you believe in fate, Darius?"

"Why?" he looked at me puzzled.

"I was wondering that if you had never seen my name, would you have found me.

"I don't know … maybe." He hesitated for a moment. "I was meant to find you," he said with conviction. "It was meant to be."

"I often wondered why I was called Madeline," I explained. "It was not a common name. Was your mother reaching out from beyond the grave when they named me? Was it our destiny to meet? Did fate bring us together?"

"Whatever it was I am glad that it did," Darius remarked. "But we will never know for sure." I stood watching him and wondered if he knew the answers to the questions asked since the beginning of time. After all, he would know what was possible and what was not, wouldn't he?

"What do you think happens when you truly die?" I asked now, fascinated to hear his response. Darius seemed to think about the question in detail.

"I honestly don't know," he said at last. "There may be another world, but not like mortals believe. The fact is the majority of mortals, people and creatures alike, do turn to dust to replenish the earth. We come from nothing, therefore we must also return there. It is the way of the natural world," he concluded.

"But some do survive in another form," I said looking at him.

"Yes," he agreed. "But it is not a good thing to survive, look at me forever falling into despair, it is not the natural way of things."

"But what about ghosts and other supernatural beings?" I pressed. Darius considered for a moment.

"They are not real; they too have gone, but their energy, their aura is suspended in time. Forever falling, but never fallen."

He made it all sound so sad. The implication that a ghost remained forever suspended in time and never at peace, even if it wasn't real, seemed to me a pitiful state to be left in. Darius turned towards the door we had entered earlier.

"It is getting late and we need to leave," he remarked.

"You do not stay here?" I asked surprised.

"I can, although you will be more comfortable at the house." Seeing my confused look he said: "The house in Parson Place."

"Is it close?" I felt that I had totally lost my sense of direction and now I wasn't sure what part of London we were in.

"It is two roads from here," he continued, "but there is an alleyway that provides a short cut. That is the reason I chose that particular house, so I would be close to the museum." Darius went through a ritual of locking everything and we passed through the garage. I retrieved my bag from the car and he locked the doors behind us. We walked in the darkness with the shadows gently enveloping us and the quietness of the early hours was comforting for our presence together in the city.

Darius had not exaggerated when he said the house was close, it was a very short walk. We did not enter Parson Place through the front door, but through a gate set into a brick wall at the rear of the property. We entered into a small courtyard and then moved across to the side of the building, where there was another metal gate that covered the side door. Darius unlocked both doors and we entered into a small compact kitchen, devoid of any of the usual type of clutter that you would normally expect to find. From this room we went into a hallway, and that led through to a front living room. Contained within this room were the standard museum quality furnishings that I had become accustomed to being around Darius.

The dust indicated that no-one had sat in here for many years. Darius, seemingly very in tune with my thoughts tonight turned to me. "I do not spend much time in here, but mostly in the library."

The library was filled with books and I didn't even have to pick one up to know they were rare and extremely valuable. Darius continued the tour of the house and we walked up the stairs. The whole house felt very regal, with its high ceilings, ornate plaster-work and intricate door casings, but nothing less than I had come to expect as I knew how Darius appreciated the beauty in everyday things.

There were three bedrooms and a bathroom, all contained beautiful vintage furnishings and every room had heavy velvet or damask curtains obscuring the windows. I took in the interior of the house and a feeling of deja'vu came to me. It felt like the first time I had walked into Ravens Deep.

"Where do you sleep?" I suddenly asked as I knew Darius never slept in a bed by day.

"I will show you," he said and a slight feeling of dread went through my mind.

"It's not another chamber is it?" Darius smiled.

"I know the chamber at Ravens Deep disturbs you so. It is really not that sinister," he remarked, looking amused at my obvious discomfort.

"I know," I said. "It just seemed a little horrifying." In truth, I had tried not to think about that chamber too much, as it did in fact disturb me and I had not entered it since the first time.

"Don't worry, you will not find this quite so claustrophobic." Darius led me down to the basement, via a set of back stairs. Metal grates covered two small window openings from the inside. The walls were made of a rough red brickwork and the basement was empty apart from a couple of old boxes. He lit a candle and took my hand before leading me around the side of what I initially thought was the back wall. To my surprise a door was concealed in the darkest shadows of the corner and Darius opened the door to reveal a dark room, a chamber of sorts, and the inevitable coffin. Darius pointed to the trap door in the floor and explained that it led under the house into old tunnels that were long since forgotten.

"Where does it lead to?" I asked in amazement.

"They lead under the roads and connect some of the old houses," he answered. "Many have been sealed up, but this one leads to three tunnels, one of which connects to an old crypt in a nearby church. The crypt itself remains sealed, so there is no access from inside the church." He added, "In an emergency I would easily be able to unseal it and escape. The tunnels are empty. No one ever goes under there and you can seal this trapdoor from above, so no one can mistakenly enter from below."

"What were the tunnels used for?" I asked in wonder.

"Years ago they were probably used as escape routes, especially the one leading out of the church, or smuggling routes up from the river Thames. There are various old derelict houses around this area that still have their tunnels unsealed," he continued, as the flickering candlelight cast dark eerie shadows all around us.

"Today they are useful passageways and tunnels to get rid of unwanted corpses, I have had to make use of them on several occasions over the years." I felt myself go cold and stared at him in horror. Seeing my look of anguish, he looked at me directly.

"You wanted all of my life, well this is it!" he said with sudden coldness.

"I know Darius, I just don't need to know all the details," I replied just as coldly, trying to compose myself and repress the images that my mind was conjuring up. I felt like I was listening to some bizarre horror story; if it wasn't quite so chilling, it was amazing.

I forced myself to remain cordial given the circumstances. Darius knew only too well the effect his words would have on me and right now the demon in him was trying to surface and provoke a negative reaction in me.

I looked down at the coffin. "Have you never slept in a bed?"

"I lay in your bed," he remarked icily.

"But you always leave me," I reminded him. "Whenever I awake you are gone," I said softly. The demon seemed appeased since Darius's coldness just as suddenly disappeared and he returned to his normal self.

"When I sleep you know I am vulnerable. It is better that I remain hidden and a coffin gives essential protection. At first it felt right to sleep in a coffin because of what I am, a fitting place for the damned," he remarked with almost a sinister smile. "Even though it was frightening being contained so, but over the decades I have grown accustomed to it and now I feel too vulnerable if I don't," he reasoned.

We left the basement behind and walked back up the stairs to the main part of the house.

"I have to leave you alone for a while," he said, "then I must rest." He kissed me very quickly and I noticed his skin was chilled. "I will not disturb you when I come back. You are very safe here, Madeline. You may go anywhere in the house, but do not leave it." There was an underlying threat in his voice.

"I won't, I promise."

He left via the side door and I heard him lock both doors as he went out into the night. I walked to the kitchen and wondered why he had turned so cold towards me down in the basement. Maybe that cruel cold streak surfaced when he was confronted with reality and the inner demon had more control. I knew I had to deal with it; it was a part of his life and now I was a part of that life too. It wasn't as if he killed people for fun; he needed to do it in order to survive and I knew him well enough to understand that he was tormented by what he was.

If he can bear the torment, I would have to as well.

I tried to reassure myself that everything was going to be all right and I wiped away the tears that were now running down my face.

In the kitchen I opened the cupboards and to my surprise I found there was a set of crockery and cutlery. I had brought a kettle, so I could at least make some tea. It had been a long night and I knew I should sleep, although

I was curious about this house filled with more mysterious things, so I resigned myself to thoroughly explore in the daylight and before Darius awoke the next evening.

I walked upstairs to the biggest bedroom and pulled back the covers from the bed. Dust filled the air and suddenly feeling better than earlier, I smiled to myself.

Immortals may be educated and refined, but they knew nothing about housekeeping!

We spent four nights in London and the hours I spent alone were filled with wonder at the contents of the house. There were beautiful items in the house, exquisite paintings, ornaments and rare books to keep me amused and all these discoveries filled me with great delight. When I questioned Darius about all these objects d'art allowed to languish in the museum and here, he merely replied,

"Take anything you want, if it pleases you."

I soon discovered that Darius was quite jaded with all his possessions—he had so much. The collection had grown in vast quantities over the years and I felt he just collected now for the sake of it and he was not really aware of everything he had acquired.

I decided to take two paintings back with me to Ravens Deep. They were so beautiful and I didn't have to examine them closely to know they were originals. Darius had exquisite taste and the snob in him would never have allowed him to acquire a fake of anything.

I think Darius finally realized that I was not so much of a threat to him in the city as he had first anticipated, but I did obey his warnings and did not leave the house without him. I did not wish to provoke that inner demon.

Darius was correct in his assumption, that mortals only really see what they want to and we moved amongst them in the night time hours, without bringing any unwanted attention to ourselves. Darius did not even look out of place in a city like London. Since the gothic revival, it was fashionable to look deathly pale and sinister and even with the vivid glass like quality of his eyes, anyone would have been fooled into thinking that they were just beautiful contact lenses.

In truth, I felt Darius was quite at home and comfortable in the city, he knew no real attention would be drawn to him. I suspected that it was me that he was more concerned about. That I might remember, or miss this life and wish to return to it and to a normal existence but it was not what I wanted and I assured him of my longing to remain by his side forever.

After four nights in the city, I could sense his agitation and I knew he longed to be back at Ravens Deep. I also had begun to miss the peace, tranquillity and beauty of the moors. When Darius said it was time to leave, I had no regrets.

CHAPTER TWENTY FOUR

A Sacrificial Site

We left the bright lights of London behind and my thoughts once again turned to Darius's house that I had not yet seen. I changed my position and looked at him in anticipation.

"Will you take me to the house in Wiltshire?" I asked, "just for one night?" From our present location I knew we could be there in a little over two hours. He gave me a questioning look before returning his attention to the road ahead.

"Why tonight?"

"I really would like to see it and it would be very easy for us to go there tonight and then continue on to Exmoor tomorrow night," I reasoned. He didn't answer me straight away, he was obviously thinking my plan through. "I will take you there tonight," he said at last, "but it will not be as comfortable as the other houses and there is nothing in the house to keep you amused."

"I am sure I will manage," I said smiling at him, "besides, realistically we will only be there for a few hours."

Later, as we approached the Wiltshire countryside, the landscape seemed to transform completely. Wiltshire was famous for its chalk uplands, vast plains and of course its most famous monument; Stonehenge.

"Do we pass close to Stonehenge?" I asked, as an idea was beginning to take root in my mind. "Yes very close," he replied. I looked at him excitedly.

"Can we stop at the stones? The weather is perfect; there is almost a full moon with no clouds in the sky." He didn't answer, but returned my smile with his own, which I took to mean that he was agreeable to my request.

Some time later we approached the ancient ruin and I thought how mystical and magical it appeared as it rose out of the darkened earth and was bathed in the bright moonlight. The road on which we travelled seemed to roll up and down over the ancient burial mounds and most of the landscape was devoid of any trees. The only notable exception was a large clump opposite the ancient monument. We headed for this copse and at our near approach I could see it hid various buildings; a mixture of touristy gift shops, a visitor centre and other out-buildings. Now it was deserted, as we had arrived in the early hours of the morning. Darius passed by all these buildings and chose to stop at the far end of a designated parking area. He parked very close to the trees and as we walked away, I noticed that the Wraith's silhouette seemed to vanish into the obscurity of the darkened foliage.

We crossed the deserted road and walked up the slight incline. Salisbury Plain stretched out before us. From the road the stones had looked large, but now standing so close to them I was in awe of their magnificence, which was enhanced only by the moonlight casting mysterious shadows all around them.

In recent years the fences that barricaded this ancient monument had come down, in response to the protests of the people and quite rightly so, as I believed everyone should be able to walk around these stones—not just a select few. Now I could not help wondering just how many druid priests had worshipped at this site and how many pagan festivals had taken place here. I took hold of Darius's hand and we walked round the megalithic ruin in silence. I ran my hand over one of the upright trilithon stones and wondered how many countless other people had also touched this very stone over the centuries.

We walked into the inner horseshoe made up of the preseli bluestones and as soon as I entered this area, I could feel their power and their magic. There was energy here and I wondered if all stone circles possessed that same energy as I considered the message they wished to convey, for I was certain this mysterious site had some real purpose; some reason for its existence.

"What do you suppose this was really used for?" I asked, looking at Darius.

He looked up at the stones.

"There have been various theories over the years," he said considering. "The ancients may have used it for sacrificial purposes, but there has also been a belief that it is a temple made for the worship of ancient earth deities or even an astronomical observatory," he remarked.

"There are so many mysterious things you cannot expect to understand them all." He released my hand and bent slightly to place his hand on one of the fallen sarsen stones.

"Do you feel anything?" I asked, fascinated to find out if he felt their energy too.

"I feel death," he answered cordially, looking up at me from under his eyelashes. I laughed at his remark.

"You would say that, knowing that people were probably sacrificed here and we are standing surrounded by hundreds of burial mounds."

"What do you feel?" he said, now amused at my comment. I turned from him and walked into the centre of the horseshoe. I stood still for a minute, then turned to look at him.

"It feels like a place steeped in mystery and magic and I feel that there is an energy here. It is something I have never felt before." Darius was now sitting on one of the fallen stones watching me.

"Tell me you feel it too," I said, walking slowly towards him. "I am not just imagining it, am I?"

"No, there is something here," he said suddenly alert. As he spoke he reached forward and pulled me down beside him.

"What is it?" I whispered, feeling suddenly anxious. "We are not alone."

I turned and looked at the stones directly behind me, half expecting to see an apparition of some kind—but there was nothing. I turned back to Darius, but he had vanished. I jumped; I had not felt him move from my side. My heart was racing and it felt eerily quiet. I sat still not daring to move. I hoped there wasn't anyone else here. If there was ... I dreaded Darius's reaction to that possibility.

A sudden movement made me turn my head quickly to see a hooded figure wearing a long dark robe move out from the shadows of the stones, his face obscured by the material of the hood. I felt my blood go cold and the sensation of fear made its full impact felt throughout my entire body.

What should I do? Where is Darius? Maybe he will just walk by and keep walking, I could avoid eye contact. Just ignore him and he will go away.

All these thoughts and more ran frantically through my head before I saw Darius move into my line of sight. His silhouette obscured the hooded figure from me even though they were only a few feet away. I shuddered, sensing a frightening situation about to unfold. The robed figure seemed to be trying to talk, but a garbled sound was the only noise that came from him. I moved from my position on the stone and stood up. I could see clearly that Darius's hand was gripping the figure's throat. Darius must have seen my movement because his head turned suddenly in my direction.

Stay there! Were the words that came to me, but I knew he hadn't spoken. I quickly sat down again in fright.

What should I do? What could I do?

Darius was about to kill someone here right in front of me and every instinct inside my head told me that I had to stop him. "Darius," I implored softly, "please don't." My heart raced frantically and I held my breath in anticipation of what might happen.

Darius gave me one last look before he dragged the robed figure behind an ancient stone, out of my sight.

Suddenly my breath came back to me in a stifled gasp; I was shaking and could feel myself sobbing quietly. I was frightened and shocked. This had started out as a perfect evening, but now I knew we shouldn't have come here. It was my fault and another death on my already guilty conscience. Then I began to think that perhaps

Darius would not harm him—but whom was I kidding? I closed my eyes and silently chanted.

Not here, not in this sacred place.

"Why not?" Darius's voice startled me. I opened my eyes. "For a modern day druid what better place for his sacrifice, than in a sacred place like this?" he said darkly. I looked up at him, my vision slightly blurred from my tears. He reached down and pulled me up close to him, his hand was very warm; in fact his skin was hot.

I stood motionless. I was frightened of the situation, the implications and the horror, but I could think of nothing to say. I already knew that he did this all the time, the only difference was, I had witnessed it tonight.

I was forced to ask myself the question; did it make me love him any less? Darius knew of my inner conflict and spoke gently to me.

"If you want me to exist then this is how it has to be," he reasoned.

"I want you to exist," I echoed, "more than anything else." He brought my hand to his lips and kissed it.

"Go and get into the car, Madeline." I unsteadily made my way down the incline, trying not to glance in the direction of the body that lay crumpled at the foot of the stones. I felt sick and tried to will myself not to think about what I had seen.

Just as I reached the car hidden in the shadows of the trees, a bright light emanated from the base of one of the ancient stones.

A sacrificial fire!

CHAPTER TWENTY FIVE

Chantille

We left the expanse of Salisbury Plain behind and drove again into the night. We progressed west for a few more miles and we were silent. I was unable to shake the memories of earlier and I knew Darius sensed my feelings; he was most likely calculating the best way to deal with them.

I closed my eyes and tried not to think and when I finally did open them, I realized the landscape had changed dramatically. We were driving through dense woodlands and our sudden decrease in speed drew my attention to the probability that we were close to our destination.

Darius brought the car to a stop and I looked up to a pair of wrought iron gates, which were already opening to allow our passage through. We passed through the gates and then progressed between a narrow avenue of oak and beech trees; too numerous to count.

The headlights of the car suddenly brought the house into view. It seemed to stand silent and forgotten, buried deep in this Wiltshire wood. The car stopped and the reassuring purr of the engine died, leaving the air noiseless and still. Darius turned to me.

"Welcome to Chantille."

My eyes met his and in that moment, I was not thinking about the house or where we were, my only thoughts were of him.

"Darius how can I deal with this? I know I am weak and my feelings vulnerable to the horrors of your immortality. I wish it was not, but it is ... I can't just brush them aside easily."

"I know," he said softly. "I feel your pain, Madeline."

I looked away from him and stared down to my tightly clasped hands. I tried to continue evenly, but knew I was failing to steady the inconsistent tone of my voice.

"My every instinct tells me of the horror, the terror and repulsion I should feel and yet when I look at you, I don't see that. I see only my love for you, powerful and all consuming." I paused briefly, "I feel sometimes as though I am being torn in two," I said in anguish looking back into his eyes. Darius took my hands in his own.

"You have to forgive and then forget what I have done, it can be no other way," he replied gently.

"I know that, I do," I answered weakly. "Because I also know regardless of what you have done, or will do, I love you more than any pain and anguish I feel."

"I know," he said softly. "This life, this existence is worth it only because of you." With those words he pulled me into his arms and we sat wrapped within our love for each other.

"Let it go Madeline," he said at last. "We have to move forward from this night, forget what you have seen tonight." He continued to soothe me with his words for a while and as I listened to his voice and the way he spoke, my own anguish seemed to melt away and when

I stepped from the car the feeling of despair left me entirely.

With renewed interest I looked up at the house that stood before us.

"It looks very old," I remarked. I could see even in the dim light that its limestone walls were spotted with lichen. It was an interesting property, with its mullioned windows and undulating tiled roof and various prominent chimneys protruding above the roof line. Even without taking a single step inside, I imagined it would be reminiscent of a moment in time that has long since passed.

"It dates from the mid seventeenth century," Darius said interrupting my thoughts. He took the key he had been holding and fitted it into the lock. We entered through a studded oak door, our footsteps sounding eerily loud upon the flagstone floors. We continued forward through the hall and entered into what would have been the main saloon. The furnishings still were arranged into several seating areas and I discovered later that this was by far the largest room in the house.

Darius removed candles out of a Jacobean candle box that rested on a table directly inside the door. He lit several candles and an old oil lamp, to enable me to see better and explained that the house had remained as he had acquired it and had never been updated. To a modern girl like me that meant: no plumbing, electricity or heating. Although I did see that there was an old stone fireplace with a black empty grate in the wall, and I could imagine that it would have cheered the room significantly when it had been lit, but now the air felt static and chilled.

It was just as I had thought; this house belonged to a different moment in time. Left alone and abandoned for so many years and not a living soul had entered this house until tonight. Darius told me that nothing had been touched or removed in all those years, so as I saw it now was how he had acquired it shortly after Benjamin Grey's death. That notion did give me a peculiar feeling and I wondered if all his belongings and those of his wife and child still remained. It was almost as if I expected to hear the echoe's of their voices filling the rooms and I shivered inwardly. Darius glanced at me and explained that he never spent any time in the house, only in the cellar. It was a matter of necessity that he came here during the summer months and I nodded in understanding as we continued walking around. The oil lamp now accompanied us, allowing a soft glow to light our way.

I saw the comfortable armchairs strewn with tapestry cushions, an old piano that stood forlorn in a corner and the beamed ceilings and oak panelling that were in evidence throughout the property. I briefly looked into various rooms, cluttered with old worn furniture before we reached the staircase. It was steep, rickety and narrow and we made our way upwards to the main bedroom.

"You will be comfortable in this room," Darius said smiling at me.

"You are not leaving me are you?" I asked nervously. I really didn't want him to leave me alone here. I was acutely aware that I did not want to witness Benjamin Grey or his family members manifest themselves in front of me. After everything that had happened tonight, I didn't think my nerves could stand any more shocks, however benign the intention.

"No, I will stay with you until you fall asleep, but there is nothing to be afraid of," Darius said reassuringly. I gave him a weak smile.

"It just feels a bit creepy in here. The sort of place you would expect to be haunted," I offered in explanation. Darius smiled at me.

"I thought you didn't mind ghosts," he said cordially. I hesitated before answering.

"Just make sure I am really asleep before you leave me," I said, trying to sound braver than I felt. "Where will you be?"

"There is an old cellar; I won't take you down there. You would find it ... even more creepy," he answered with amusement in his voice. "When you wake you can explore the house, you will not disturb me and you are quite safe here." I averted my gaze from him and looked down at the bed.

"When did someone last sleep here?" I asked, eyeing the blankets and covers with distaste. Darius thought for a moment.

"1877," he said at last.

That disclosure made me feel very strange, in fact the whole place did. I really could believe that I had travelled back in time; nothing moved, nothing touched for over a century. Impervious to my reaction Darius lay down on the bed and pulled me after him, his body was close against mine and my breathing shallowed as he fixed me with his steady green gaze that captivated my attention. His lingering kiss tempted me further and his touch sent an erotic shiver through my body as his pursuit of enrapture continued, and my earlier feelings of being haunted diminished as I succumbed to his sensual seduction.

"I love you Madeline," it was barely a whisper. He tightened his hold on me and I forgot how unclean or ancient any of the surroundings were. There was only him and I, and caught up in my desire for him, nothing else mattered.

I awoke around midday—alone.

I had been totally unaware of Darius's pre dawn departure to the cellar. I got up quickly and started to make the bed, but soon realized that the covers on the bed were as I had supposed extremely dirty and dusty. Instead of remaking it, I ended up stripping the bed entirely and discovered that the mattress was ancient and made of some kind of straw. Next time I would bring new linens with me, but for now I gathered up the old and stuffed them in an old wooden chest that sat under the window. I opened the antique wardrobe, and found within it several vintage dresses and gentlemen's clothes. Just as I had suspected, all the personal possessions of the Grey's were still here; I quickly closed the wardrobe feeling almost as if I was trespassing on their memories.

I walked down the stairs and headed outside, I had realized last night that this old house contained no bathroom, only a stone outhouse of a very rough construction. Water had to be drawn from the old well at the rear of the property, which much to my dismay was icy cold.

The garden was mainly overgrown, but there was an extensive rose garden. The roses were all of old fashioned type and I bent to admire their fragrant perfume. Over the years they had grown large and ungainly, tangling themselves around their nearest neighbour; it was in the garden that I spent most of the afternoon.

The house although fascinating, was covered in decades of dust and grime and without any running water I could not even begin to try and clean anything. Maybe a future project, I thought to myself, but for now I could do nothing and unlike Darius's other properties, there were no books to read.

As the sun began to disappear I began to think about Darius. I was certain that the cellar led directly off the kitchen; earlier I had opened a door and discovered a narrow staircase leading down into the depths of the earth. I hadn't wanted to disturb him if he was down there, also fearing the unknown I had quietly closed the door again.

I walked back into the main saloon and focused on the piano sitting in the corner. I sat upon the wide wooden stool and lifted the heavy lid that concealed the keys. One by one I depressed them, it sounded in tune, but what did I know—I couldn't play anyway. However, I spent the next hour playing with the keys as I tried to string together the various notes to make a recognizable tune. The time passed quickly before I had a sudden sensation of not being alone. I looked up to find Darius sitting on one of the chairs watching me. I allowed my hands to fall from the keys in a reaction of surprise.

"How long have you been there?"

"A few minutes," he replied and I silently acknowledged how much it unnerved me that he was able to enter a room or be within my presence and initially I was totally unaware of the event.

"I wish you wouldn't do that," I said slightly annoyed. He laughed as he rose from the chair and came to sit beside me, but his extreme closeness chased away any displeasure I might have felt before.

"Can you play?"

"Of course," he said confidently and the instant his fingers touched the keyboard, some classical piece that I was vaguely familiar with resonated from the piano. "Bach," he said casually, "or I can play Mozart," and to prove his point the music changed dramatically.

Darius I soon learned, was an accomplished piano player and I sat entranced at his skill as his fingers seemed to glide effortlessly over the keys. He finally stopped playing and turned to look at me.

"Are you ready to go home?" he asked.

"Yes," I replied sincerely.

We locked up the house and I realized that I hadn't seen the car all day. I asked him what he had done with it.

"In the stable," he said. The stable was large and he opened the double doors to show that at one time, it would have accommodated a sizable carriage. Now, the Wraith stood there in all its splendour. The various stalls were complete with original fittings and housing items of saddlery, but also in these stalls were mechanical pieces, they looked like car parts, and at the far end which would have originally housed a second carriage, there was another car almost identical to Darius's—another Wraith. Darius smiled, enjoying my obvious surprise as he explained its presence here.

"Over the years I have used it as a spare parts car; I don't even think it is capable of driving anymore, but its useful to keep a replica in case I have need."

I was astonished at his words, it seemed that Darius thought of everything, but then again I supposed he had to. "So you're a mechanic as well?" I asked in my own amusement.

"I do what I have to, but I admit I would prefer not to." He paused. "It is a matter of necessity for someone *like me* to have to do this." I looked at him bemused.

"Yes I can see that. You are by far too refined and educated to ever have been a mechanic and it must play havoc with your nails." I remarked trying to keep the tone even in my voice. Darius lowered his head and looked at me with slightly narrowed eyes.

"If you have finished amusing yourself at my expense we should leave," he said dryly and he opened the car door for me.

We left Chantille behind and headed for Exmoor, a few more hours and we would be home. Once again I could feel the moors calling, but this time the calling was to both of us and it was telling us that we belonged there together.

CHAPTER TWENTY SIX

An Evil Interlude—Part 1

Our return to Ravens Deep really did feel like coming home and we settled down once again into the routine of our life. It seemed that the peace and tranquil ambiance of Exmoor was calming to Darius, whilst in London he had appeared more tense; more on edge, but perhaps it was my presence there that had made him so.

Several weeks had passed, he no longer left me alone and I accompanied him whenever he went to the city, and I was content that once again, I had some connection with the outside world. Darius rarely left my side in his waking hours; even then it was only to venture out into the middle of the night and then to return to me as if he had merely taken a midnight stroll. I tried not to let my thoughts get the better of me; if I didn't think about what he was doing, I could almost believe that side of his life didn't exist—almost.

Now, I sat in the library on this warm afternoon and my attention was on some bank paperwork that I had recently picked up from my flat in London. I still owned the flat and knew that I should probably sell it, after all, I doubted that I would ever return to live there again. It seemed pointless just letting it sit empty, to mention nothing of the chore of collecting any mail and ensuring that the monthly standing orders were paid. It was apparent that Darius did not like me visiting there; it was a constant reminder of a former life, but he understood that while I still owned the property I did have an obligation to ensure the affairs were kept in order. Darius had never suggested that I sell it and I supposed that it was still a good investment, as property values had been climbing steadily.

Despite all of Darius's wealth, he was shrewd when it came to business matters and he probably knew that it was a valuable piece of real estate, but to me it was becoming an inconvenience and I firmly made up my mind that I would talk to Darius about selling it later. My mind was completely engrossed in these thoughts, so it was a complete surprise when I was suddenly jolted back to the present moment, by a shrill ringing from the mound of paper before me. I visibly jumped; it seemed such a strange noise and so out of place at Ravens Deep.

I was a little shocked just to hear a phone ring after so many months; I had always kept the phone charged in case of emergencies and it was reassuring to know that I wasn't entirely cut off from civilization. But this afternoon I had used it to call my bank in London and I had not immediately switched it off in my usual style. I also did not want to disturb Darius, as even though he was far away in another part of the house, the sound of such an unfamiliar noise might wake him. I was never quite sure how good his hearing was, but like all his other senses I imagined it was much sharper than my own. I hurriedly lifted up various papers to find the phone's hiding place and answered quickly, expecting it to be a wrong number, but listening to the voice at the other end, I knew I could not have been more mistaken.

"Madeline? Is that you?" The voice was familiar to me.

"Yes," I answered cautiously as I wracked my brain to think who this person was and how they could possibly have this number.

"Madeline it's Charlie."

I hesitated before I answered as the feeling of relief, which quickly turned to shock, pulsated through me; my thoughts suddenly became a blur.

What was Charlie doing calling me? More to the point; why was Charlie calling me now? I hadn't seen or spoken to him in months.

"Hello Charlie," I could not keep the surprise out of my voice, as his voice sounded disturbingly near to me.

"Where are you? You sound very close," I asked, holding my breath in anticipation of his answer.

"If you are still on Exmoor then I am close; I am in Beaconmayes." I could hear the frivolity in his voice. I, however, found no humour in his words; those words hit me like a bolt of lightning—I had to think fast.

"Why are you here Charlie?" I questioned, hoping beyond hope that he didn't want to see me, but at the same time sensing a foreboding premonition that he would.

"Madeline are you alright? ... you sound a bit strange."

"Yes, I'm fine. Why are you calling me?" Maybe I sounded a bit dismissive, but it was for his own good, I reasoned. Charlie hesitated before replying.

"I have been trying to reach you for days," he began, "and in the end I thought I would just drive down and see if I could find you." At that point I think my heart stopped for several seconds; this was not good. My heart now began racing and I was feeling sick from the implications of this situation. I was lost for words and remained silent.

"Madeline can you still hear me?"

"Yes," I replied quietly as Charlie continued in a cordial tone.

"I have great news. Your book, the novel that you left at my flat, I submitted it for publication on your behalf and it's been accepted. Isn't it great?" I was stunned at his words, butsoon found my voice again and forced myself to respond.

"Really?"

I had forgotten all about my novel. When Charlie and I had broken up, my heart was not in that book anymore and the memories of where I had written it was too painful for me. I had left the manuscript with Charlie half expecting him to throw it away, especially after the anguish I had put him through, but he obviously had not. My mind was swimming as the revelation was going through my head.

My novel was actually going to be published.

Charlie's voice interrupted my thoughts.

"Is that all you have to say?" I could hear the disbelief in his voice.

"I'm sorry ... I am just in shock that's all," I said truthfully, although the novel wasn't the only cause for my shock right now.

"Yes I know it must be a surprise," he continued, "I guess hearing from me too ... seeing as I am here now ..." he hesitated again. "Can I come and see you?"

"No," I replied a little too quickly and regretted my tone instantly. "What I mean is … it's difficult." Making up my mind quickly I said, "I will come and meet you. There is a park on the outskirts of the village with a duck pond and a couple of benches. I'll meet you there in an hour," I said looking at the clock. It was only two o'clock; I had time to meet him.

"OK," he said cheerfully. "See you in an hour."

I switched my phone off and sat thinking.

Wow—my book going into print; to be published. That is amazing.

I was aware of a feeling of gratitude for Charlie not having thrown it in the bin after all. Although Charlie being here in such close proximity to me wasn't good, but I reasoned that if I had refused to see him, it could have made him all the more curious. However, deep down the thought of seeing someone I knew well actually gave me a sense of excitement; although that excitement was mixed with a doubt. I would have to be careful how I handled this situation.

I can't let him know anything, the details of where I live or especially who with.

Then there was Darius; what was I going to tell him? … I would worry about Darius later I concluded to myself.

My mind was spinning and I knew I had to think this through very, very carefully. The next forty minutes flew by and still the confusion in my mind was unresolved. Even as I drove towards Beaconmayes a constant thought kept nagging at me:

I shouldn't be doing this. I shouldn't be meeting Charlie, Darius would not be happy if he knew.

I drove through Beaconmayes and it appeared as always; the perfect sleepy country village that I now knew so well. People here now vaguely recognized me, but that in itself was no threat. On the rare occasions that anyone ever inquired as to where I lived, I would always name a bigger town several miles away.

I parked my car a little way from the park and walked slowly as I tried to collect my thoughts.

Was meeting Charlie a bad idea?

I thought about Samuel Dunklin and a feeling of dread came to me.

No, I will not let that happen, I can protect Charlie.

As I entered the park I saw him a little distance away from me, standing by the pond.

Charlie instantly turned in my direction—he had seen me. Not waiting for me to reach him, he started walking purposefully towards me. We approached each other and his face lit up in a smile, answered with my own.

"Hello Charlie, it's good to see you," I said warmly although I was aware of my feelings of apprehension. "Madeline, you look great," he said as he leaned forward and kissed me lightly on the cheek. It was a simple gesture, but it unnerved me.

"You really do look good," he emphasized giving me an appreciative look. "The country air must certainly agree with you. How long has it been now?"

"A good few months," I answered casually.

"You look well too. How is the business?" I tried to keep the conversation light and casual, but my stomach was tying itself in knots; I was nervous.

In fact he really did look good, his skin had a healthy glow and his eyes sparkled with a happiness to see me, but I recognized that look and it made me take a step back. I knew I had to be as straightforward as I could.

"Charlie it really is good to see you, but I am with somebody else now," I said and hoped that he would take it well.

"I know," he said softly. "I mean I thought as much," he said, looking slightly crestfallen. "I guess I could tell by the way you acted on the phone." Seemingly undaunted by this piece of news he smiled at me.

"Tell me, why do you keep your phone switched off so much?" he asked cordially.

The tension eased between us and I felt myself relaxing.

"Too many distractions," I said lightly with a small shrug. "Where are you staying?"

"In the Beaconmayes hotel, it's very small and a bit basic, but it serves its purpose," he answered looking at me. I didn't like the thought that I was his purpose and the reason he was here. I sat down on the bench feeling uncomfortable again as he continued.

"Who is this new man in your life?" he said, "Anyone I know?" he added jokingly. I could tell he was trying to remain nonchalant, but it wasn't working; there was an underlying strain in his voice.

"It's no one you know," I answered casually. "Tell me about the book," I said trying to divert his attention somewhere else. He paused as if he were going to say something, but then seemed to think better of it.

"It's great isn't it? It's Blaketon's, you remember the big London publishing house? I actually thought about our company publishing it for you, but you know we don't really handle that kind of publication. I couldn't have offered you anything like the deal that they have been discussing. In a few years from now you might be a famous author." He seemed genuinely excited.

"I always thought you could do it, you know," he remarked wistfully. Then tried to inject some humour into his words by cordially adding, "Who knows, perhaps the publicity and book signings may come quicker than you think."

My head was suddenly swimming. I knew that could-n't happen, I had to remain anonymous and Darius would be furious if I brought myself that kind of attention. I turned to Charlie.

"Charlie, I do not want any publicity, none at all. And I don't want it published under my name, I want a pseudonym," I stated firmly. Charlie was staring at me, clearly puzzled.

"Why would you want that?" he asked in astonishment. I sighed.

"It really is something I cannot talk about. I cannot have anything to do with it. Any commissions you can keep, after all, it wouldn't even have been considered for publication if it wasn't for you; besides I really don't need the money." Charlie just sat staring at me incredulously. He finally spoke.

"Madeline what has happened to you? I thought you would be ecstatic, but instead you are acting like it is a huge inconvenience to you." He seemed clearly hurt.

"I am sorry Charlie, please don't think that I am not appreciative, I really am, but my circumstances have changed. My life has changed and it is not as important to me as it once was." As I spoke I absently brought my hand to my face to push my hair back. Charlie grabbed my hand.

"You are married?" he said, glaring first at the ring and then at me.

"What?" I answered in surprise. I looked at him he seemed distraught. I had been correct in my assumption that he had put on a false bravado when I had mentioned someone else.

"Charlie, you didn't think that we would get back together again ... Did you?" I asked, astonished, but as I looked into his eyes I could see that had been on his mind. I was shocked. "Why would you think that? We haven't seen each other for months. All the anguish and pain I must have put you through in London. Besides, I thought you had met someone else," I said, staring at him.

"I did meet someone else," he said quietly. "I thought I would get over you; forget you completely and make a new life with her ... but she wasn't you," he said looking at me directly. "I realized that I had to find you again, but I should have known that you would have forgotten me so easily."

His final words had bitterness in them and he paused for a few moments.

"Does he make you happy? *Your husband*, are you really happy?"

This was awful, I knew that I was hurting Charlie all over again, but I had no choice.

"Yes Charlie, I am." Seeing his look of total deflation, I continued, "But I want you to be happy too." I paused. "You and I ... we were never meant to be," I said gently.

"I always believed we were," he said looking at me with distaste. He hesitated for a brief moment. "How long have you been married?"

"A few months," I answered cautiously. We sat in silence and I could sense his shock; the atmosphere felt very tense between us and I wished I could make it easier for him.

"Charlie you should leave Exmoor today," I said slowly. "What we had is gone and I know there is someone for you out there, someone that could make you happier than I ever could." He looked at me.

"It's him isn't it?" he said directly.

"Who?" I asked bewildered.

"*Your husband*," he said emphasizing the point, "he is the one that doesn't want you to write. He's taken away your passion for life!"

I was angry. How dare he. With Darius I had more passion than he could ever know existed, but I forced myself to remain calm. Charlie was angry and upset himself and I had hurt him yet again. I coolly turned to him.

"Charlie whatever you may think, this is the life I have chosen." I tried not to sound too blunt as I added; "Besides it's none of your business. If you want to publish my book go ahead. I will sign whatever paperwork you need, but it must be sent to my London address … if you decide you don't want to, then I will understand your decision. I did care for you once, but it was not meant to be. You have to accept that." I sighed, "Charlie … I don't want us to part with you thinking that I never cared."

"I know you cared," he said quietly. "Just not enough, and I am only sorry that you never felt the same way about me, Madeline, as I do about you. We could have had a good life together, you and I." I looked at him, shaken by the impact of his words.

"I have to leave, Charlie," I said getting up and feeling distressed myself.

"At least give me your address and home phone number, so I can keep in touch. I may need to reach you regarding the book," he added tactfully.

"No, I don't think that's a good idea given the circumstances, do you? You have my cell phone number, I will turn it on in the mornings. If you need to contact me regarding the book, call me early in the day." A few moments passed and I spoke without hesitation. "You should leave, Charlie, go back to London … there is nothing for you here," I concluded a little coldly.

"I am leaving tomorrow morning anyway," he stated simply. I relaxed. At least he wasn't planning to try and see me again.

"I have to leave now," I said.

"OK … I really need to get back to the hotel as well," he answered with a forced smile, but we both knew that he had no pressing reason to go back yet. We walked back to my car in silence and I turned to him.

"Well I guess this is it," I said, smiling at him and feeling an unexpected pang of regret. "Good-bye Charlie." I turned to open the car door.

"Wait, Madeline." I turned back to face him and in that instant he pulled me to him and kissed me, taking me completely by surprise.

"What are you doing?" I asked, both annoyed and amazed by his action. He grinned at me.

"For old time's sake," he said apologetically. I shook my head in disapproval, but smiled back at him. "Bye Charlie," I repeated as I got into the car.

"Good-bye Madeline," he said softly.

Charlie stood watching my car pull away and he stayed in my mirror as I put more distance between us; then I saw him turn and walk away.

As I drove out on the road towards Ravens Deep I checked my mirror several times, just to make sure Charlie hadn't followed me, but the road behind was empty. I felt strangely sad, for even though we had broken up months ago, this meeting today seemed so final; like an end of an era. I wondered what I should say to Darius, but maybe it was better to keep quiet, I didn't want to provoke any reaction in him.

When Darius entered the living room some hours later, he found me sitting on the floor with my back against the sofa; absorbed in an old book. He sat upon the sofa behind me and pulled my hair aside and leant down to kiss my neck. His kiss at once sent a spine tingling shiver through my body and I immediately discarded the book. I turned and responded to him instantly. My thoughts were caught up in the heat of the moment, but somewhere in my mind I absently mused that it was so unlike the earlier kiss with Charlie.

Darius abruptly pulled me to my feet and firmly held me back from him, staring at me, his eyes wide with rage.

"What have you done?" His voice was like thunder and his accusation sent a wave of fear through my entire body.

"N ... Nothing," I stammered horrified.

Oh my god, he knows, he read my thoughts.

I almost felt myself go white and a cold chilling sensation passed through me that made me shiver.

"Darius ..." I faltered as he looked so angry that I thought he might actually strike me. I felt my throat go dry as I summoned the courage to try again. "Darius, please don't look at me like that, I haven't done anything ... it was nothing," I said trying desperately to clarify my words.

"You have been with him and it is nothing?" he snarled at me and I could feel his hold intensify.

"Please, Darius, calm down. I haven't," I insisted.

"You cannot lie to me. Your thoughts betray you every time," he snapped coldly.

"I am not lying to you," I insisted, "it is not what you think." I quickly related brief details of what had occurred earlier in the day. "He knows nothing of this place or you, he only knows that I am married and I will not see him again," I concluded breathlessly. Darius was considering my words, figuring out if I had met Charlie because I had really wanted to see him again.

"At least you have got one thing right today," he said sarcastically. "You will not see him again." I didn't like the way he said those last words and now I started to feel panicked.

Releasing me Darius demanded: "Where is he now?" I stared at him in fright, I knew I couldn't tell him; I was too scared of what he would do, but I couldn't lie either. He was right in his observation that my thoughts would betray me in an instant. Darius was staring at me intently now as though trying to pry the information from my mind.

"Why?" I challenged, terrified for Charlie's safety.

"Just tell me, Madeline," he said impatiently. He looked very threatening and I knew he was extremely angry, but if I told him. ... I didn't want to think about that possibility. I took a deep breath summoning up the courage to speak the next words.

"I won't tell you Darius. I won't let you hurt him. He means nothing and he will leave and be gone by tomorrow. Just let him go."

"Madeline I am not in the mood to be bargained with. Do not me make me hurt *you*!" He said viciously. His words were chilling to my ears and he moved even closer to me, his presence towering over me and intimidating me completely. Darius's eyes narrowed.

"Why are you trying to protect him if he means nothing to you?" My eyes held his and I could see the rage consuming him. "Do you wish to be with him again?" I could feel that rage increasing in intensity by the second.

"No," I answered instantly.

"Then make me believe that, tell me where he is," he demanded aggressively. I was unable to tear my gaze from his. The energy from within him forced me to obey his demand as the voices that resonated from him terrified me.

I tried hard to resist, but my resolve was diminishing and the name Beaconmayes hotel flew from my lips. I gasped as I felt my mind and eyes had been released from their captivity. I averted my gaze, but then summoned up the courage to look at him once more, and saw that the intensity had gone and so had the voices. Now, I was extremely frightened not only for Charlie, but also for myself. Darius's demeanour told me he was very capable of hurting me at this moment and I stood unmoving, anticipating some action from him, but he remained still as he glared angrily at me.

"You should be careful Madeline, your thoughts do betray you," he repeated, "and you can keep nothing from *me*." He gave me a bitter smile before moving away soundlessly. I breathed easier for a moment until I realized he was at the door and about to leave.

"Where are you going?" I asked in a tense whisper. Darius turned and looked at me.

"Out; I have an appointment to keep," he remarked sadistically.

"Darius please don't." I ran to him. "Darius, please, you don't need to do this," I said frantically as I tried desperately to find something to say that would make him remain with me. I brought my hand up to his arm. "Please Darius... please stay here." He looked down at my hand in contempt.

"It is not advisable for you to be this close to me right now," he remarked coolly and I instantly withdrew my hand, then he shot me a disdainful glance as he left the house slamming the old oak door behind him.

I didn't quite believe what had just happened. For a long moment, I stood staring at the empty doorway before me; then I felt panic.

What have I done?

I suddenly heard a car start up; my car. I looked at the table, my keys were gone and I knew in an instant exactly where he was going.

What shall I do? I have to warn Charlie. I have to do something. I wouldn't let this happen.

In a horrifying hopelessness, I searched for my bag and retrieved my phone. I quickly dialled the operator to get the number I needed. After what seemed like endless hours the phone finally connected to the Beacon-mayes hotel.

Why isn't anyone answering?

I desperately hoped Charlie would be there, and at last the receptionist answered and finally put me through to Charlie's room. It seemed as though I waited another eternity as I listened to the constant ringing at the other end. I audibly sighed with relief when the receiver was at last picked up and I heard Charlie's voice at the other end.

"Hello."

"Charlie, it's Madeline," I began, my heart racing and my voice trembling.

"Madeline? ... are you OK? You sound ..."

"Shut up Charlie," I ordered, "just listen to me. You have to leave the hotel now... just get out." The silence at the other end was deafening. "Charlie are you there?" I said frantically.

"Yes, Madeline, I am, what is it? You sound terrified." He sounded shocked.

"Charlie please leave now. You are in terrible danger, please believe me!" I was crying now. "Please Charlie, do as I ask, please leave now."

"Danger from whom?" he questioned.

"I cannot say. Please Charlie, you're wasting time, just get out. I have to go." I turned the phone off, praying silently that he would think my tone dramatic enough and sense the urgency in my voice to just get out of there.

I was distraught, if Darius found him what would he do? Just frighten him or worse? It was the worse I couldn't bear. I hoped with every ounce of my being

Darius would miss him and think he had just left. Then I would be able to calm him down and make him see reason before he thought about going after him in London.

I could do nothing more; I sat and waited for Darius to return.

An Evil Interlude Part 2

Charlie stared at the receiver in his hand. Madeline had sounded terrified and there had been an urgency in her voice that he could not dismiss. Making up his mind quickly, he threw his few belongings into a bag, and after taking one final look around at the room he walked downstairs to the hotel foyer. The receptionist seemed startled by his sudden announcement that he had urgent business in the city and needed to leave straight away and he stood patiently while the girl behind the desk searched for a pen, in order to make out his invoice.

Charlie was aware of a sudden chill. A premonition, he wondered, or was it just Madeline's words making him jumpy and on edge? He hoped that she was all right, but he still did not know where she was and he could not go to her, but her words had undoubtedly disturbed him. Although he reasoned to himself that perhaps she was just being over dramatic, even so, there had been something in the tone of her voice that had unnerved him. He was sure that she had been crying and that alone had made him feel that he should obey her wishes, but he was mystified to know the reasons behind them.

Charlie tapped his fingers impatiently on the countertop and wished the girl would hurry up with his bill.

He wondered if she were intentionally being so slow to annoy him and tried not to allow her unhurriedness bother him. Instead he wondered what situation Madeline had got herself caught up in, but she had said she was happy and she had looked good. It hadn't appeared that anything awful was happening to her.

He knew he should forget her, especially now that she was married, but there was that constant hope that she might have wanted to come back to him. They could have salvaged what remained of their relationship and made a new start. He would have taken her back too; even now he knew that he still would. Deep down he knew he was being foolish and that he should resign himself to the fact that it was over between them once and for all. And maybe she was still suffering from effects of the breakdown, in reality who would want to harm him here? No one knew him.

Charlie took the receipt from the receptionist and walked outside to the car park, located to the side of the hotel. It was very dimly lit and he could barely make out his car parked next to the hedge at the very back. He absently thought that Exmoor seemed exceptionally dark tonight which was helped by the fact that the moon was hidden behind the heavy cloud cover. In the distance Charlie could hear a slight wailing that moaned soulfully from across the moors as the winds gusted up from the coast and he shivered slightly.

Suddenly he thought he heard a noise, a footstep perhaps, he turned, but the car park was empty. He shivered again as the wind blew right through the thin material of his shirt, making him quicken his pace. He unlocked the car door and threw his bag across to the empty passenger seat, before he attempted to climb into the driver's seat.

All at once something gripped him firmly and he was thrown back with vicious force against the cold metal. Initially Charlie had gasped from the pain and shock of the impact, now he caught his breath and felt anger build as he clenched his hand into a fist. He tried to swing his arm upwards with force, but it was instantly trapped in a vice like grip. In a mixture of shock and fear he looked up. Charlie stared with disbelieving eyes, into the face of his aggressive attacker.

A thought raced through his mind:

Was this what Madeline had meant by that phone call?

His aggressor leant closer and as Charlie's eyes adjusted to the shadows, he felt a terror like no other. He was certain that it was a man, but it was not; it was altogether more sinister and more demon-like. The skin was pale and through the thin fabric of his clothes Charlie could feel the coldness of that flesh creeping over his skin. But it was the eyes, so intense and fierce, burning into him that frightened him beyond all measure. He tried to tear his gaze away, but he could not; their effect was so powerful and hypnotizing that he was aware of all the strength he possessed slowly ebbing away. He could only stand motionless like some puppet waiting to be manipulated.

Charlie struggled to make sense of what was happening, as the demon loomed closer. He was certain he could sense extreme animosity and utter hatred from this being before him. Its shadow was slowly enveloping him; then he heard a voice as cold as ice.

"She is mine."

As the chilling words penetrated his head, Charlie's thoughts flew to Madeline, just as he was aware of an intense pain on his neck. He could feel the venom flowing through his veins before he felt himself falling, his own life force ebbing slowly away as he faded into darkness...

An Evil Interlude Part 3

I nervously waited for Darius to return as I listened to the constant reassuring tick of the clock on the mantle. It seemed as though endless hours had passed before I heard another sound in the distance. A noise that got steadily louder as it approached; and I recognised the familiar resonance of my car's engine. I remained seated, trying to keep calm.

I can handle this, Darius will be angry that he has missed Charlie. He will probably blame me, but he will calm down after a while.

I summarized to myself how it would be and then I shivered, waiting with anticipation for the door to open; I did not have to wait long.

Darius entered moments later, throwing my keys on the sideboard with unnecessary forcefulness and slamming the door behind him. His eyes were wild and my heart was full of dread as he crossed the room to where I sat.

"You dare to betray me?" he said with savage vehemence. "Did you think that I wouldn't know?" He spat the words at me and the initial fear I had felt grew in its intensity and was consuming my whole being.

"No, I haven't," I began to tremble. Darius's full brutal force emanated from him and his next words struck even more fear into my heart.

"Where is the phone?" he demanded in an icy voice that seemed to cut through the air.

If I had thought about refusing him I was acutely aware that this was not the time. My hands were shaking as I reached down and pulled it from my bag. Darius snatched it away and dropped it onto the hearthstone, then he stamped heavily upon it; shattering it into a hundred fragments. I was horrified by his actions and what he would do next and I frantically began to talk.

"Darius, I couldn't let you hurt him, you must understand. He was no threat to us."

Darius stared straight at me, his gaze un-nerving me entirely.

"He is not a threat to us now," he corrected coldly with a cruel smile playing around his mouth and I shuddered as the meaning of his words sank in.

"No! You didn't?" I jumped up facing him. "Tell me you didn't." I was almost pleading as my heart pounded faster still. Darius didn't answer. He just stood observing my reaction and he actually seemed to be enjoying my pain, but as the realization hit me he knew that he didn't need to say any words, the satisfied look and almost contemptuous smile on his face told me the truth.

I stared at him horrified, initially too shocked to move, then I felt myself losing control.

"How could you?" I cried as the tears starting to stream down my face. Some inner impulse made me raise my hand to strike him, but he caught my wrist in his hand, laughing.

"You cannot hurt me," he said before his lips pressed together in a bitter smile.

"You killed him?" I asked again, not wanting to comprehend the fact. "How could you do that Darius?" I asked almost choking on the words.

"But I didn't, you did!" His voice was chilled and calculating, allowing his words to have the maximum impact upon me.

"What?" I asked incredulously.

"I may have performed the physical deed, but it was you who killed them both. Him and Samuel Dunklin, it was you who sealed their fate." His voice was cruel and sadistic. "And they died because of your involvement!" he said, making his meaning very clear. The venom in his words sounded incredible to me and I stared at him full of loathing.

"Don't look at me like that," he said, his eyes narrowing.

"Why?" I snapped. "Because I might upset you, because you might get angry and you might do something you regret," I said provoking him. "I hate you," I added, and in that instant I did. I pushed past him and ran into the garden. I heard his voice behind me.

"Leave me alone," I cried, as my legs felt that they were unable to support my weight any longer and I sank down to the stone steps. The endless tears I cried were for Charlie and for Samuel and as my tears began to falter I sensed I was not alone. I looked up to find Darius leaning against the door post watching me.

"When you have finished crying over *him*, perhaps you will learn not to defy me again," he remarked coldly.

"Go away," I responded just as coldly, but he remained.

Very soon the cold winds had started to chill my skin and I shivered. Darius voice broke the silence of the night.

"Madeline, I do not have the tolerance for this ridiculous emotion," he remarked impatiently and I stared up at him in amazement.

Ridiculous emotion, how dare he!

"You can go to hell," I stated viciously. He approached me silently and swiftly and snatching my arm he pulled me up from the stone step.

"I am already there," he said bitterly and I looked at him with disdain.

"You murdered someone I once cared for and you expect me not to be upset?" I asked in amazement.

"It is clear I cannot trust you; you will not leave here again on your own," he stated avoiding my question.

"Or what?" I challenged.

"Madeline, do not make me continue this conversation, I have made my decision."

"I do not make you do anything, that is clear. You have no concern for my feelings only your own," I snapped at him.

"You wanted this life," he reminded me bluntly.

"No, I wanted a life with you. I opened my mind to accept what you are and as distasteful as it all is, I accepted it all … I even accepted what you have to do, but at no point did I expect you to kill everyone I have ever known or spoken to."

"Then you are naive," he stated calmly. "The boyfriend wouldn't have given up. I could hear his thoughts and they were only of you. I will not share you with anyone," he said as he pulled me to him.

I tried to push him away, but he was too strong and held me tight. His kiss was fierce as if he was daring me to doubt his total possession over me, then after a few minutes he relinquished his tight hold.

"Don't ever doubt my determination to destroy anyone that comes near you." he stated icily.

My head hurt, my eyes hurt and I felt sick knowing Charlie had been thinking only of me when he had died. With Darius's overwhelming possessiveness I felt suffocated and I couldn't stop shaking. I tried to turn away from him, but he would not allow it and instead he pulled me firmly to him again, refusing to let go, until I had no choice but to submit to him.

Although despite my rage and emotional state of mind, I also needed to be held. I needed someone to tell me that this was a bad dream, a nightmare that I was going to wake up from and everything would be all right; even if the one to do it was the monster whose arms now surrounded me.

Eventually my anguish subsided and my rapid breathing eased and when Darius spoke to me his voice was calm, but commanding.

"Madeline, look at me." Reluctantly I looked into his eyes and once again I was mesmerized by him, his voice and his words eased my pain, he made me believe in him again and I found him irresistible once more. I stood there listening to him and watching his cool steady gaze and after a while, what had happened this evening seemed less horrific.

I knew he was hypnotizing me, enchanting me again. Only he knew how to speak to my very soul. This power he possessed over me made my anguish less and his reasoning chased away all the sanity within me. He truly was my enchanter and I knew; there was no longer a mortal person alive that I cared about, for me there was only the immortal.

CHAPTER TWENTY SEVEN

Ashes to Ashes

Exhausted after the night's events, the morning slipped un-noticed into the afternoon. The shock and numbness I felt throughout my entire body very slowly began to dissipate and eventually I must have fallen asleep, for I was aware of my mind succumbing to the blissful release of falling into a deep dreamless state of being.

When I opened my eyes some time later, I felt peaceful and calm until the memories of only a few hours before came flooding through my head. Then I wished it was all some horrific nightmare, and now back in the reality of wakefulness I could forget it all. But I couldn't for long— it was real, and now I had to face the torment again.

Darius did not appear after sunset and I became extremely unsettled. I felt unable to do anything, but wait with an awful sense of foreboding. It was almost ten o'clock when he finally did walk through the door; his clothes were dishevelled and a faint smell of smoke entered the room with him.

I tried not to speculate what he had been doing and I dared not ask—I dreaded his answer. We regarded each other coolly for several moments; Darius was probably gauging my reaction to his presence before he spoke.

"Are you feeling better?" he asked at last. I watched him coldly, really wanting to say: *Actually no, I feel awful and terrorized because you just killed Charlie!*

But I masked my thoughts as best as I could, instead I just nodded in response. He crossed the room to my side and sat down beside me. He took my hand in his and the smell of smoke increased at his nearness to me.

"What have you been doing? Have you been near a fire?" In spite of myself I was concerned, I knew how dangerous that was for him. He smiled, sensing my concern for him. "I'm fine; I just had to take care of a few details." My thoughts flew to Charlie.

"What details?" I asked in almost a whisper, not wanting to hear the words, but needing to know. Darius sat studying me for a few moments.

"You do not need to know, Madeline," he said simply.

"Yes I do," I whispered fearfully as I looked into his eyes. "I need to know. It's Charlie isn't it?" I was feeling sick to my stomach. I did not wait for his response before I continued. "I have to be able to lay his ghost to rest, I need to know where his body is," I concluded, feeling daunted by my own words. Darius sat observing me for a few minutes further then he calmly explained.

"Last night I moved the car and the body into the woods out of sight. I returned tonight and disposed of them properly."

"Where?" I asked in barely an audible whisper, "where is it?"

"I burnt the car and now its shell lies in a deep ravine." He paused for a moment before continuing. "The body was burnt separately in the woods." Indifferent to my look of utter horror he added, "It was best Madeline, I buried the ashes and no trace will be found." I looked at him in anguish.

"Does it matter to you? Does it ever play on your conscience? Do you even feel the horror of it?" I asked bitterly. I felt his grip tighten on my hand, not in a threatening way, but more as a way of reassurance. "You make me aware of the horror of it," he said almost wistfully. I felt my bitterness slowly fading. "In the end it's a matter of survival and that instinct is great in us all; even you," he observed. I remained silent, thinking about his words.

So it is done, Charlie's body burnt to ashes in some unmarked grave in the woods. His car, now a burnt out shell in some remote ravine.

I turned to Darius.

"Someone will come looking you know, people will look for him."

"I know," he said gently. "But what will they find? They will find nothing," he said in answer to his own question. "He checked out of the hotel of his own accord—thanks to you," he added almost amused. I on the other hand had the words: a*ccomplice to murder* racing through my mind. Darius interrupted my thoughts. "At least you saved me the trouble of having to dispose of anyone else last night," he said with almost a sinister smile on his face.

"This is not amusing Darius," I said coldly.

"No it isn't, but you must see the irony," he remarked. I ignored his comment as I knew only too well the truth in his words; I had lured Charlie right into Darius's path. I shuddered at the very thought as Darius continued.

"People go missing all the time, en route to and from places. People will look, but in time they will forget—they always do. It will be recorded as unsolved on the police report, along with the hundreds of others that are still unaccounted for."

A shiver ran down my spine as I stared at him. He looked at me in amazement as he observed my reaction to his words. "You must know this?" he insisted, staring at me. I shook my head.

"Maybe I have just led a sheltered life." I remarked dryly. "What happens to them all?" He paused, thinking for a few moments.

"Many people, seemingly happy people just up and leave one day. They go and start a new life, change their identity and leave behind anything they once knew. Unable to cope with their current life they choose to find another. Others are just taken."

"Taken? What do you mean … by you?" I asked, giving him a puzzled look.

"Me, others like me, or psychotic mortals." He looked pointedly at me. "It is not only the immortals that are capable of horror."

"I know," I said quietly. We sat in silence for a few moments and Darius turned to me with an expression of concern.

"You cannot go into the village," he stated. I looked at him with wariness. "Darius, I know you are still angry that I went to meet Charlie yesterday, but I have to buy food, I cannot exist here with nothing," I replied calmly.

"I know … but you may have been seen yesterday."

"I wasn't," I insisted. "There was no-one else in the park." Darius looked at me. "There is always someone watching when you least expect it," he observed. "We will go to London for a few weeks. It will be safer for you there." Seeing my look of dismay he added, "we will return in a few weeks when enough time has passed and he is forgotten about."

Only a few weeks, is that how long it took to forget someone? For the searches, the inquiries to stop and for his name to be added to the ever-growing list of unsolved disappearances?

"Darius," I said looking at him directly. "Do you think I would be as ruthless as you, were I immortal?" Darius looked at me in alarm.

"Why do you ask that?"

"I am curious I suppose. I just wondered if women had the disposition for immortality. If your mother or sister had become un-dead, would they have endured immortality as you have or would they have perished unable to deal with the emotional side of it all?" Darius seemed ruffled by my words and was gauging my thoughts, he appeared to come to the conclusion that I merely wanted an answer to the question. Although it did make me wonder why he seemed so troubled by my line of questioning, but he hesitantly began speaking.

"I believe women are actually more ruthless than men," he replied. "Men can lead great battles and campaigns and carry out evil deeds, but normally it takes weeks of planning and calculations; sorting out the details. A woman on the other hand sizes up a situation and acts instantly, you only have to look at a mother defending the life of her child. She will act ruthlessly and defensively and pay the ultimate price with her life, if there is not an alternative way out. Whereas a man will look for a way out first, he will look for a way to calculate."

He paused. "Women definitely have the disposition for immortality, probably more ruthless killers at the end of the day with less conscience about doing it."

"You really think so?" I asked incredulously. "You think that I would not have a conscience?" He looked decisively at me.

"You would see the necessity and your logical thought process would tell you what had to be done. You would not allow your conscience to get in your way and you would justify your actions with your logic." I looked at him and I knew he was right, that was precisely how it would be. Maybe I wasn't so unlike him after all and despite my despair and protest of what had recently occurred, deep down he knew that too.

CHAPTER TWENTY EIGHT

Underground Tunnels

The next evening we relocated to London and in the days that followed I reluctantly settled down to life at Parson Place. Initially I was irritated not to be at my beloved Ravens Deep, but I understood Darius's way of thinking. It could be a risk for me to remain on Exmoor right now and I wondered how many weeks we would have to stay away.

Even though no-one knew my whereabouts, I still half expected that fateful knock at the door and the police to be standing there with their questions and accusations directed at me, but as the days turned into weeks, I began to feel confident that was not going to happen.

The horror of Charlie's death slowly began to fade from my thoughts and once again, I became self absorbed in the security of the relationship that I shared with Darius. Initially I had been content to read books and discover the house's own treasures; I had delighted in the amazement I felt at opening door after door and finding the beautiful clothes that belonged to Darius hanging in the ancient wardrobes. Many of them were modern, but there were outfits that belonged in some costume museum; they were decades old. It was during this time that I became aware of the fact that Darius never threw anything away.

However, those discoveries had not held my interest for long and although when Darius was with me my discontentment was less, I found that when I was alone, I was bored. I had cabin fever and I longed to go out and about as I once had. Just to be able to venture into the garden would have been sufficient, but there was no garden at Parson Place and I felt imprisoned.

I did not dare to cross Darius and go out on my own. I knew Darius's warnings were not just his possessiveness; there was a real danger for me; I could not risk someone recognizing me and asking me questions. I needed to keep as far away from the public eye as possible, or at least until Charlie's disappearance had become old news.

It was a cold mid November evening and very dark outside. I looked at the clock which told me that it was already past eight. I had felt restless all day and now, sitting alone, I could stand it no longer.

Darius where are you?

He was always with me by now and perhaps foolishly I made up my mind—I would go to him; he had to be awake by now. Cautiously I opened the basement door and walked down the stairs. I made my way to the room at the back of the basement and very quietly I opened the door. The coffin was open and empty; Darius was not here, but he wasn't in the house either, I was certain that I would have known. Now, my concern was growing—where exactly was he? My eyes came to rest on the floor.

The trapdoor.

I am not sure what suddenly gave me the courage to attempt to open the trapdoor. Curiosity I supposed, mingled with a sense of concern for him. I pulled up on the iron ring and was mildly surprised at how heavy it was. Undeterred though, I persevered and found that with force I could lift it and found myself looking down into a black hole. I let the trapdoor rest in an open position and moved quickly back through to the basement and up to the kitchen to get my torch.

A few moments later I was cautiously peering into the hole again. I allowed the beam from the torch to illuminate the passageway and saw that there was an iron ladder attached to the side of the wall, roughly a foot beneath the floor that I was standing on. I got down on my hands and knees and shone the torch down the dark passageway. It was just an empty tunnel and the beam of light reflected off the glistening wet floor below.

I cautiously got a foothold on the ladder and climbed downwards. I hesitated at first, but then with determination I began to make my way along the tunnel which was notably cold and damp combined with a distinct smell of decay that seemed to cling to the ancient mouldering walls. After I had walked a few hundred yards the tunnel suddenly divided into three. I shone the torch down each of them in turn; they all appeared the same. I choose the middle tunnel and continued walking as various thoughts plagued my mind.

I shouldn't be down here. I should go back, but where is Darius?

I did feel scared and questioned my own actions, but I was also intrigued to find where this underground maze would lead to. I was still conscious of the fact that this might not have been a good idea, but my own sense of adventure kept me moving forward.

It probably dead-ends anyway.

After a few hundred yards my torch light suddenly illuminated another ladder fixed to the wall. I shone the light upwards until it rested on another trapdoor. I climbed the ladder and pushed upwards, the trapdoor moved slightly. I pushed harder and sent it crashing down on to the stone floor above sending a cloud of dust into the room.

What are you doing? Go back before it's too late.

But I didn't go back; my curiosity had taken over any sensible thought. I pulled myself up and into the room. As the dust settled I saw it was an old basement of a derelict house, just as Darius had told me existed. I could see the destruction in the ceiling, either ripped apart intentionally or fallen in from years of damp and decay. The room was empty of any furniture and only old newspapers yellowed with age littered the floor.

I moved across the room and opened a door which led into another basement room, similar to our own in Parson Place. An old stained mattress rested in one corner and cardboard boxes mixed with piles of cloth were heaped in a pile in the centre of the room.

The smell of methylated spirits came to my senses at the same time as I heard a muffled noise. I took a step back in wariness and instantly turned my attention to the pile of cloth that all at once moved into the air.

The tramp eyed me suspiciously as he staggered to his feet. Instantly I reacted to the sight before me and made for the door. I pushed through and almost hurled myself down through the hole in the floor—but I was not quick enough.

My hair was seized by rough hands and I felt the excruciating pain as the tramp dangled me precariously by it, since I had lost my foothold on the ladder that led down into the passageway. The pain subsided as a strong hand grasped one of my flaying arms and unceremoniously hauled me back into the basement room.

"Let go of me," I yelled indignantly. The tramp merely laughed nastily before he spoke.

"I don't often get visitors as pretty as you ... especially not ones who come into my bedroom of their own accord." This statement seemed to amuse him and he displayed an idiotic grin which allowed me to glimpse his badly decayed yellowed teeth.

"Just what am I going to do with you?" he said almost to himself as his eyes glittered dangerously. I could tell by the way he looked me up and down, what he thought he was going to do with me, it wouldn't be good. From the smell of his breath I knew that he had been drinking, but he wasn't by any means drunk and I began to realize the full implications of this situation. I was also aware of his filthy fingernails digging into my flesh and I hoped that I would not catch any disease from him as I tried in desperation to extract myself from his grip.

"Just let me go and I won't tell anyone that you are here," I began. He narrowed his eyes and brought his face closer to mine.

"You're not going anywhere," he stated menacingly and I immediately realized the futility of trying to negotiate my way out of this situation. Instead I brought my free hand up and dug my fingernails into the softest part of his cheek, before ripping them in a downwards

motion to gain as much effect as possible. Simultaneously I started to scream at the top of my voice; in the
hope of un-nerving him at the very least. Crying out in
pain and anger, he gripped my other wrist and the weight
of his body pushed me to the floor.

"No one can hear you scream down here," he hissed
maliciously in my ear. I was unaware of the intelligence
of the words that flew from my mouth, only that I
shouted and screamed under his suffocating force. All
the while I tried desperately to twist my body from under
the dead weight of him. This, however, didn't seem to
deter him—it only succeeded to arouse him further.

I could feel myself weakening and I knew his resolve was
not diminishing, so in a frantic effort of desperation I
grabbed a handful of his dirty hair and pulled on it hard.
This action seemed to have no effect, but I managed to
get my hand to his face and raked my nails across his
flesh in the hope of gouging his eyes out. All at once he
let out an agonized scream and suddenly I felt his head
move backwards in what appeared to be a completely
impossible angle.

His heavy weight seemed to lift from me, as if by
itself, before it went crashing into the wall on the far side
of the basement. Astonished, I looked up.

Darius stood before me.

The coldness I saw in his eyes resurrected my terror
once more, but his expression was unfathomable. It felt
as though he was looking straight through me as his eyes
did not seem to register any type of emotion. Darius
turned from me and approached the tramp's body, which
was now convulsing strangely in some reflex of recent
death, or maybe he wasn't dead, but only in a paralyzed

state of being. I realized what Darius was about to do and turned my head; I couldn't watch this.

Slowly I rose from my position and climbed down the ladder, shaking uncontrollably. I leant against the stone wall for support, without it I knew I would collapse in a heap on the floor.

A few moments later as I fought to gain control over the situation, the corpse of the tramp landed at my feet. I screamed in horror and fright as I pressed myself against the wall. Darius landed softly beside it, his gaze unwavering from my own horrified stare.

A trickle of blood ran out the corner of his mouth and I recoiled in horror. Still he did not speak, but he retained that same unemotional look in his eyes. This was worse than any words he could say to me. Why didn't he say something?

"Darius... I'm sorry."

Darius turned suddenly and I did not even see his arm move as he brought his hand up. I was only aware of the intense pain across my face and I fell to the floor unable to comprehend the shock of what he had just done.

"You could have died tonight!" His voice was like ice. "And you still might!"

The venom in his words stung more than the sting of his hand and with those chilling words he left me sitting on the floor in the dark tunnel. I could hear the soft noise of the corpse being dragged after him. I sat very still hardly daring to breathe and trying to stop the tears from falling, as I listened to the sounds moving further and further from me. My cheek stung and I was aware of the blood on my hand as I touched my now swollen skin— his nails had cut me.

Was that what he had meant, when he had said that I might die tonight? If I was bleeding so profusely in front of his eyes would his control diminish completely? I held the fabric of my top to my face as I tried to staunch the blood flow. I knew that I had to stop the bleeding before Darius came back.

The tunnel was very dark and although a faint glow of light came through from the trapdoor above, I could barely see a few feet in front of me. I knew my torch was back up there somewhere, but I was too afraid to go and search for it. Instead I just sat huddled on the damp floor until my ears picked up the faintest of noises. Was Darius coming back? I listened harder—it was getting closer. It was not a normal footstep, more like the running of tiny feet. Not Darius after all, but the other possibility was just as fearful to me; London was full of rats.

Oh God, please not rats.

I got up quickly and climbed up onto the lowest rung of the ladder and that was how I remained, trying to keep my feet from touching the floor as I waited for the fearful things that I knew would come out from the darkness.

It felt as though an eternity passed, before I heard a soft sound and I strained my ears again to hear better; I could see nothing in the dark tunnels. To my complete surprise Darius appeared directly in front of me. I climbed down from the ladder and nervously stood facing him.

My throat had gone dry.

"Why did you come down here Madeline?" I felt relieved at how calm his voice sounded and I felt myself breathe easier.

"I … I was worried," I stammered, I didn't know where you were and it was late." He regarded me coolly, weighing up my answer.

"No, you wanted to know didn't you? You wanted to experience the torment first hand."

"No," I said at once. "Why would I want that?"

"I don't know," he sighed. "But now that you have my love, I hope you are satisfied in your quest."

"It wasn't a quest," I protested. He dismissed my protest with a shrug and took a step closer to me. He brought his hand up to my face and traced the outline of the cut he had left with his fingernail, making me wince as it was still tender.

"You are a danger to me here, a danger to my existence by your careless actions," he said softly and then more resigned, "but I cannot let you go."

"I don't mean to be a danger to you," I said quietly, "and I don't want you to let me go." Darius pulled me into his arms and then bent to kiss me, but the mental picture of what he had just done and the sight of the dried blood on the corner of his mouth made me withdraw.

"I can't, Darius—not right now."

He smiled faintly at my expression, but he ignored my protest and held me firmly. I felt unable to breathe and despite my objections, he kissed me forcibly. I was acutely aware of the slightly metallic taste of blood. Not his or mine but someone else's and with it came the horror that I was being forced to endure. He was making me experience the worst and darkest part of his existence and telling me in no uncertain terms, that I was a very much a part of that darkness.

He finally allowed me to push him away and I glared at him angrily.

"How could you?"

"Easily, and if you ever do this again I will make you watch when I kill them too," he replied sadistically.

CHAPTER TWENTY NINE

The Question of Immortality

I never dared to venture down into the basement again, let alone open that trap door. I knew Darius did not make idle threats and I was certain that he would not hesitate to carry out that particular warning. So for a few more weeks, I had to content myself with the house in Parson Place and wait for Darius to decide when the time was right for us to return to Ravens Deep.

In all, we spent five months in London and we were both impatient to return to the peace and tranquillity of the beautiful Exmoor countryside. I missed being close to the sea, the rugged beauty of the coastline and the magic of waking up to the scenery of the moors. Above all, I felt I had left a part of myself at Ravens Deep and I wished to go back and reclaim it.

After our return, I discovered that there had only been brief inquiries into Charlie's disappearance, and this had only occurred because a staff member had remembered him staying at the hotel. His picture had appeared on the news briefly, but it was apparent that he had told no one of his expedition to find me; therefore my anonymity had remained intact.

There was not even any line of questioning being directed at me, as I had half expected, when I eventually visited my flat in London. I had anticipated a message or some inquiry from a long forgotten connection—thankfully there was not. After all, I was only an ex-girlfriend whom he had not seen or spoken to in months, as far as anyone else was concerned. Why would there be any speculation that I had anything to do with his disappearance? It wasn't even a murder case, as only a missing person report had been filed.

Now, I believed Darius's statement when he had told me that no one would find the remains of the body. I could imagine that Charlie's file had already been relegated to some dusty shelf in the police department.

Darius had been correct in his assumption that people soon forgot; sadly it was old news. This month a sudden disappearance of another person, in a neighbouring county, filled the headlines.

After that interlude, time passed for a while without incident. We divided our life between Ravens Deep, the museum and Parson Place, with occasional visits to Chantille. The months turned into another year and the bond between us grew stronger.

I had struggled, many times, with the ethicality of our love and our relationship and I learned to overcome any feelings of remorse I might have ever felt. I had accepted a long time ago the implication of Darius's existence, but it was after Charlie's death that I knew: there was no going back.

If I had ever considered walking away or leaving, it would have been then, but I had stayed because I couldn't walk away from Darius. I needed him; I needed to be with him and I felt that I could not live without him. We connected with one another on a level that I didn't believe existed between ordinary mortals, but I also knew that it was not my decision to make; Darius would never have allowed me to leave.

These days the horror of his immortality seemed more apparent to me in the city. Every time he left me alone in the house on Parson Place, my mind would conjure up vivid images of the dark, dank passageways under the very streets where mortals walked; they were completely oblivious to the corpses being dragged beneath them. I was aware that in order for me not to lose my mind, this feeling of horror had to be laid to rest, for I had no choice—my destiny was to remain by Darius's side.

Eventually I did find the willpower to push the negative feelings aside and relegate them to the very depths of my mind. I focused instead on only the positive thoughts, the happiness we found in one another and I tried to enjoy being in the city with him.

Together we partook in things he had never dreamed of doing; we would hire a private box at a theatre, normally only reserved for royalty or VIPs. I soon learned how easy it was to obtain certain privileges open only to an elite group. It seemed money could open any closed door and it was easy to silence any sort of questions, providing you were willing to pay the price.

Having extreme wealth definitely had its advantages. Money was not something I thought about anymore, as we had more money at our disposal than we knew what to do with. I lost count over the years of how many theatre tickets I purchased. I paid handsomely and always in cash which ensured our entry via the side and back doors, away from the usual crowds. A privilege normally only enjoyed by the famous.

In this manner we moved amongst the ordinary mortals, with them, but always apart. This enabled us to experience numerous productions of the opera, classical renditions of ballet and fine theatre; we both revelled in all the fine arts London had to offer. Darius's world expanded significantly, as he came to realize with me at his side he could participate in a life within the city that he had never experienced before

I managed to persuade Darius to let me leave the house on Parson Place during the day. It was strange not to have him by my side, but it was easier for me to take care of details regarding my former life in the daylight hours. I visited my flat once a month to pick up any mail and ensure everything was in order. I closed every account I had ever opened, except my bank account, and ensured there was always enough money to pay the standing orders I had in place. Now, I kept only the electricity and water turned on at the flat and they were the only obligations I had to worry about.

I had mentioned to Darius about selling the flat, but he had predicted the property market would rise again and that it was still a good investment, so I had let the subject drop. I wondered exactly why we needed all these investments, but I guessed that Darius only knew how to keep making money and it was in his nature to maximize everything to his best advantage. Then again, it did give him another safe haven in the city in case of an emergency.

My past experiences and the path I had chosen to follow made me cautious around people and I tried not to engage in any unnecessary conversations or encounters, but I did amuse myself by purchasing exquisite clothing and beautiful accessories. Soon I discovered that the seduction of being able to buy anything you wanted was quite time consuming and I finally understood why Darius constantly acquired new treasures.

On occasions when we did appear in public, it must have seemed that we truly belonged, mixing amongst London's wealthy elite society. Obviously unknown, but our appearances frequented the right circles, which in itself allowed our air of mystery to remain intact. There were of course the inevitable encounters with other mortals, but we kept them brief and inconspicuous.

We were caught up in the happiness of being in each other's company and we needed no one else. Although Darius could be very charming when it suited him; his potent charisma, mixed with his obvious education and refinement, earned him an instant respect from anyone who crossed our path.

I was convinced that he did indeed possess the ability to hypnotize mortals. He used his sultry beguiling tone as he spoke, and under his bewitching influence, a mortal might not be certain that they had actually encountered him directly, perhaps thinking they imagined participating in a conversation. I witnessed almost a daze like stupor of these individuals for just a few seconds as we left them. Then on observing them further, they would return to their senses unsure of their exact engagement with us.

Perhaps it was a good thing, as there was no doubt we made a striking couple. Darius was tall and dark with cat-like eyes that mesmerized and captivated. He always dressed in dark stylish clothes and he carried himself both effortlessly and gracefully. I, by comparison was petite and slim, my blonde hair now cascaded to my waist and framed my pale delicate face. My eyes, although less vivid, matched Darius's and my beautiful clothes were worthy of any top fashion house.

Darius had learned over the decades how to exist amongst the mortals. I knew that was the key to his very survival and the fact he had remained for so long. Regardless of whatever conflict raged within him; he moved easily amongst them.

I wondered if it had always been so, or had he learned such self control because of me? I on the other hand felt nervous at these brief encounters, always mindful that I may witness something that I did not care to see. In those moments I lived my life on a knife edge, waiting with bated breath, forever watchful that a scene from a horror movie might play out before my very eyes; I alone knew, only too well, what he was capable of.

Darius would sense my discomfort and that in itself amused him, but he would reassure me that he would never subject me to any unnecessary horrors and I would relax again for the moment.

However, one evening whilst in London his reassurance tested me to its fullest extent. We had just left a theatre and I was caught up in the excitement and wonder of the fine production we had just watched. I revelled in the details of the story whilst Darius and I walked hand in hand through the various patrons of the theatre that remained milling around in the street.

With my eyes only for Darius, I was totally unaware of the faces of the people that we passed by, but abruptly I had to acknowledge the reality that other people did indeed exist, as I was suddenly aware that someone had said my name.

In astonishment I looked for the source of the voice, and I felt Darius's tightened grip on my hand.

"Joe?" I had to stifle a gasp of horror.

Charlie's father!

"Madeline, I thought that was you." I looked at him. I hadn't seen him in a long time, but his face was drawn and I was certain he had aged prematurely; no doubt brought about by months of worry and concern over his son.

I had to think fast.

"How are you Joe?" I said forcing a smile. I didn't know what else to say to him and I could feel my face burning, as I was very much aware that I didn't want to hear the next words out of his mouth; but it was inevitable that they would come.

"Actually Madeline ... not that good," he faltered. Then he said the words I was dreading. "I don't know if you heard, but Charlie disappeared ... he just upped and went one day. Nobody has heard from him since." Joe's eyes were staring into mine and I felt myself go cold.

"I am so sorry, Joe, I really am," I half choked, I felt terrible, but as I spoke the words I felt Darius's grip tighten even further, and his penetrating gaze burning into me.

I tried to ignore him.

"Have you seen him at all?" Joe asked expectantly, as his eyes almost seemed to plead with me to give him hope. I felt close to tears and didn't know how to answer. There was no hope; but how could I tell him that?

"No I'm sorry Joe, I haven't seen Charlie recently." I paused. At least it wasn't a complete lie. "You know things were difficult between us."

"I know but ... well I thought, you of all people might have had some contact with him. "I cringed inwardly at his words. "Charlie cared for you a great deal, you know," he added, much to my discomfort.

"I know, Joe," I said sympathetically, "but it was over a long time ago between us … besides … I am married now." The words almost stuck in my throat, but I had to say them to prevent him from talking about Charlie, I felt distraught and Joe's underlying distress was obvious and heartbreaking.

"Perhaps he will be in contact soon." I heard myself say the words, but I was shocked at my own response. What the hell was I trying to do to him? In desperation I glanced at Darius. Joe seemed to realize for the first time that I was with someone as his gaze left me and he stared at Darius. It was a longer than necessary look and I was mindful of my silent pleading with Darius not to react. Joe took a step back.

"I'm sorry Madeline, I didn't mean to be the bearer of bad news, I should be congratulating you."

"No it's fine, I really am sorry Joe," I said sincerely. Joe seemed to resign himself to the fact that I had not seen Charlie. He looked deflated and I felt terrible.

"Well, I have to be going," he said as he made a soft despairing sound. "It really was nice to see you again Madeline and I should give you … both my congratulations."

"Thank you," I said forcing a smile. Joe smiled back at me and glanced quickly at Darius again, before he turned and disappeared into the crowd. I looked up at Darius. He was watching Joe depart and an unexpected darkness seemed to surround him that made me suddenly nervous.

"He could be a problem," he remarked in a calculating way. I squeezed his hand tighter,determined not to let it go.

"No, don't even think it," I said with authority. Darius glanced down at me, but before he had time to respond I continued. "He is not a problem. Think of the consequences, Joe is a well known man, an owner of a successful publishing company and he is well liked and rich. It would be too much of a coincidence if his son disappears, then the father disappears. It would not go away, too many questions would be asked." My voice was confident as I added, "Besides, we must be on at least two or three different surveillance cameras. Think about it, our image caught on tape as the last people seen speaking to him before he disappears."

Darius studied me, smiling faintly at my words. He knew I was trying desperately to save Joe's life, but he also knew the words I spoke were correct; he knew as well as I did that London was full of cameras.

"Maybe you are right," he said at last, "it may be better to let him be."

"Will you promise me Darius, that you will leave him alone?" I pressed. Darius regarded me coolly for a few moments.

"Unless he crosses your path again, he will be safe from me," he stated. I felt somewhat appeased for the time being and relieved that Darius had seen the sense in my words. It was a shock seeing Joe tonight and to realize the trail of anguish Darius had left behind. Darius turned to me.

"It's only you and I that matter, remember that." I looked at him and smiled weakly as I tried to put any thoughts of Joe and Charlie far from my mind.

We walked through the city streets in silence until we came to a familiar building, the museum, where Darius wanted to retrieve a book and I happily accompanied him. The museum had also become a source of my own amusement, I enjoyed discovering the many treasures that had been locked away for so many years. I had spent hours sorting through old documents and books, cataloguing the artefacts he had acquired over the years. Occasionally I would remove an object from the museum and take it back to Ravens Deep; the house was now filled with many beautiful and priceless pieces.

The rare bookshop also earned Darius a regular income and he made a handsome profit from its sales. I only ever witnessed a couple of meetings that took place between Darius and one of his *subjects*, as he referred to them. It was but a brief exchange of words and paper-work. Every few months the sales from these priceless books would accumulate enough cash to pay for the running of the shop or to spend.

Some of it would be used to arrange for yet another treasure to be acquired. The *subjects* would handle any transactions, as the artefacts were always shipped to the bookstore. Darius would then retrieve them in the hours of darkness at his convenience.

It was a fine tuned operation, but I often wondered what went through their minds when they met Darius year after year and his appearance never changed. Although recalling Darius's own words in which he had told me once: "Money can buy you loyalty and silence, if you are willing to pay enough."

More time passed and I felt we were truly a part of one another. The longer I spent with Darius, the more I began to think of myself as immortal, and normal people began to feel strange to me. I had quickly learned that Darius was a creature of habit and he liked the routine of things. I supposed after one hundred and seventy years plus, anyone would get a little set in their ways.

I tried hard to accommodate his routine and did not seek to defy or anger him too often, but I was not always willing to accept his decisions. Those were the times that I enraged him and caused the ever present darkness to surface. Inevitably it was I who had to back down as always, the moments of witnessing his terrifying nature shattered any illusions I may have been under that it could be any different, but time heals most wounds and eventually they became but brief shadows in our life.

However, there was a cloud looming on the horizon, one which hung over my mind and plagued my soul; the question of immortality haunted me. I had often witnessed the demon that terrorized Darius, and I had to ask myself; was his suffering worse, because he was alone in it? Even though he tried to describe to me what it felt like, I could not even come close to imagining how all powerful it was for him at times. How could I possibly know the terrible toll it took on his very being; and that made me question my own mortality. How much time did I have on this earth to comfort him, to remain by his side? One day sooner or later the inevitable would happen; I would die. Whether it was by natural causes or something else, it would cause us to be parted.

These days I did not fear for my life, in truth, I don't really think I ever did. Despite what Darius was, I was confident that he loved me more than anything else and I felt completely safe with him.

However, a disturbing contemplation remained with me night after night, and when Darius was present it took all my willpower to conceal my thoughts from him, but I knew that soon I had to confront both him and my inner torment; for it was growing stronger.

CHAPTER THIRTY

A Fatal Kiss

Four years had passed since my return to Ravens Deep, so perhaps it was natural to contemplate my existence, as I reflected on this life that I had chosen. I was caught between the happiness I had found with Darius and the inescapable horror and isolation that came with this reality. I sat alone now, and not for the first time, I wondered what would have become of me, if I had never met Darius.

Would I have married Charlie? I didn't think so.

I was certain that I would have just moved through life incomplete; never knowing the feeling of being totally, utterly captivated by another being and I could reason that I was privileged to have been allowed to enter a forbidden realm, where I had borne witness to a legacy which was very much a part of both my history and my future.

Darius had once said that it was a cruel fate that brought me to him, but I knew that it would have been more of a tragedy not to have fulfilled this destiny.

However, there was an unforgettable torment to this unfathomable life; immortality and the consequences that accompanied it. I rationalized that every relationship had its negative moments—the bad phases. Darius and I, we had a down side, episodes that tested our relationship to its fullest extent; our down side was just a little extreme.

In retrospect if I could have done it all again, would I have done anything differently? And I knew the answer to that question was a resounding—no.

I had just celebrated another birthday and with the passing of that date came a reminder of my inevitable fate; the foreseeable fate of every mortal. That one day no matter how good or bad we are, it is our destiny to ultimately die. Our bodies will turn to dust and our own personal points of view, along with our unique desires, likes and dislikes will simply vanish into thin air. Only remembered for a short while by the loved ones that we leave behind. Maybe because of this latest event, I was haunted by the fact that I was getting older year by year whereas Darius was not. In recent days I had mentioned to him that I was actually now older than him in mortal years, but he had merely smiled and told me that age had no importance. He had not really paid attention to the words I had spoken or the agonizing meaning behind them. But alone again, they came back to disturb my peace of mind, along with the cold harsh reality of what would happen to me in a few years from now.

Right now, I was still in my twenties and I had no justified reason for concern, but what about when I was in my forties, or much older if I lived that long? Darius would still be twenty five and he would still look young. His hair would still have the dark lustre and shine of youth. There would never be wrinkles or lines on that perfect skin, no moles or age spots that come with the terrible tragedy of aging.

How could he possibly love me when I was seventy? That thought haunted and tormented me. I didn't want to change, I wanted to be young and beautiful and forever by his side.

Another poignant reality had also crossed my mind; when I was much older would I love him? A twenty five year old immortal. Would I be able to kiss him with the same passion that I could now? Would I want to?

I was prepared that I might provoke his anger and I was aware that his reaction might not be good, but for months now I had learned to master the technique of concealing my thoughts when he was with me and I wondered just how much longer I could keep this up. It was wearing me down, and sooner or later I would let my guard down and he would find out. I finally reasoned it was better that he hear the words I chose to speak, rather than perceive what was on my mind.

The sun had set and I switched on the table-lamp, which immediately cast a warm glow around the room. I took a seat on the sofa and Darius walked through the door a few minutes later; sitting down beside me. I tried to keep the conversation light and casual, but he seemed to have already sensed my unease.

"What is it Madeline?" he questioned me with concern in his eyes. I took a deep breath preparing myself for his reaction. I tried to keep my mind clear so it would be hard for him to read my thoughts; at the same time I summoned up the courage to begin.

Darius was watching me intently.

It was now or never. I had to say the words right now, another minute and I would lose my nerve. "I want to be with you always, Darius," I began.

"You will be, I will not leave you," he said, looking slightly confused at both my tone and the words. "What is it? What has happened?" His gaze was unwavering and I began to feel nervous; I could tell Darius sensed it too.

"This is not a decision I have come to lightly," I remarked, evading his question. "I have thought about this in depth." I paused as I wondered how I was going to say the next words.

"Thought about what?" he said warily as he narrowed his eyes. I hesitated as I tried to find the right words to continue, but as I looked at him I saw the wariness vanish and it was replaced by a comprehending look of horror.

He knew—he had sensed my thoughts.

"Madeline, don't even say the words to me, I will not listen!" he said with sudden aggression. He stood up abruptly and moved away from me. I was not about to be so easily dismissed. I got up and followed him. He turned, looking down at me.

"But Darius ..." I began.

"No," he said brusquely. "How can you even think it?" The disbelief was apparent in his voice and I could feel my heart racing as I moved closer to him. My well-rehearsed speech sounded strained, even to my own ears.

"Darius, will you still love me when I am old? When my hair is grey and skin wrinkled?" He looked at me in anguish.

"I am immortal, do you think that matters to me?" he asked incredulously.

"I don't believe you," I answered sharply and I knew I was provoking him. "Even though you say that now, one day it will matter to you." My voice was trembling and even as I continued my voice betrayed my own distress. "Besides, even if it does not matter to you, it does to me," I said, gaining the courage to proceed. "This way I can be by your side forever, we can go on just as we are now, nothing will change." He stared at me with eyes that were now ferocious.

"You think nothing will change!" he retorted abruptly. "What about the demon you will become? The hunger you will not be able to satisfy? The craving that will not subside?" He kept his eyes fixed intently on me and he shook his head in despair.

"You will kill indiscriminately, people you once knew, once talked to in casual passing. Don't tell me nothing will change!" His voice was loud and frightening, but I was determined to continue.

"I don't care, Darius, nothing and nobody matters, only being with you forever. If I have to become immortal to do that; then I will gladly give up my mortal life." He stared at me as if in shock and seemed momentarily lost for words.

"I cannot believe the words I hear you speak, Madeline," he said at last. "You know how I struggle constantly with the horror of what I am, don't ask it of me. It does not matter to me that you will get old, only that you have a peace in your life that I do not."

I could tell by his demeanour that he was very irate and was fighting to keep that anger under control, but I was unable to back down. I knew I could not leave this hanging between us and I had to make him see this situation from my point of view.

"It matters to me though," I retorted. "Knowing I will grow old and you will stay young forever and it *will* matter to you one day too!" I hesitated briefly. "It is inevitable, you said so yourself." I challenged.

As we glared at each other the terrifying darkness that once disturbed me was darker than I had ever known. His presence more menacing, and if I ever believed he would kill me—it was in that instant. He moved closer to me, his eyes belying the anger and danger within as he hissed out the next words.

"Everything I have done to protect you, to keep you safe, it has all been for nothing! Do you really know what you are saying?" I was witnessing fury that I had never known before, the intensity of his force seemed to shake the whole room, but caught up in the heat of the moment, it seemed to provoke and fuel the irritation within me.

"If you really loved me you would allow me to be with you for ever," I said bitterly, moving towards him.

"I never thought your vanity would be your demise, Madeline!" Darius spat the words at me. I took a deep breath in an effort to calm myself as I tried to think of a plausible response.

"I am not vain, only realistic, I know I will not be beautiful forever, but through you I can be." I could feel the tension in the air and the silence was deafening as I glowered at him. He in turn, held my eyes in an unblinking stare for a few moments before he hastily turned from me, which broke the trance. He stepped away from me, but I anticipated what he was about to do and reached out quickly and caught his arm.

"No Darius, you are not going to walk out on me as you always do. I want you to realize I am deadly serious, I want this."

Darius rapidly turned making an indescribable noise of anger. His hand was a blur as he grabbed my throat and squeezed hard; his nails were digging into my flesh.

"You want to die, is that it?" he snarled. "Do you want me to kill you now?"

I was unable to breath, terrified by his action and extremely aware how easy it would be for him to cause my demise right here and now. I could only gasp and tear at his hands while I fought for breath which was getting more difficult by the second. My head suddenly seemed to get lighter before he released his grip. I stumbled against him before I steadied myself and choked to regain the consciousness I had felt slipping away from me seconds earlier.

"Darius please ... understand what I am asking," I pleaded. "I only want to be with you." I was trembling and my voice sounded strange. "Why is that so terrible?" I questioned as I struggled to regain my self control and calm my breathing. He was frightening me and I hadn't expected him to act so violently. My fear grew as he continued staring at me and I felt the intimidation of his whole being as his eyes burned into mine.

Darius held me in his murderous gaze for a few moments longer and then he dropped his voice low.

"If I make you like me I really would be a demon," he said grimly. "What if I didn't love you anymore? Has it ever occurred to you that maybe I am only capable of loving a mortal. If you were to become immortal you might not interest me anymore!" He lowered his head and narrowed his eyes as he emphasized the point, "I would be forced to kill you!" The words were spoken viciously and to hurt me, and I looked at him with contempt.

"If I could make you mortal by condemning my own soul, I would do it for you," I remarked coldly. "I believe you would love me no matter whether I were mortal or immortal, if I did change you would not." He shook his head, his expression unreadable.

"You know nothing of the things that you talk of," he stated bluntly. "How could you, for I have protected you from the horrors of it," he remarked, almost to himself. He was towering over me, sinister and horrific, and a chill ran through me as he grasped my wrist. "Come with me, I will show you the horror of what you want," he said, pulling me after him towards the front door. I protested loudly and strongly which only seemed to make him more resolute.

He threw open the front door and dragged me after him into the night. I was terrified of what he might do and pleaded with him to release me. Undaunted by my pleas and the fact I was ripping at his hand with my nails, he dragged me through the garden. Frantically I tried to reason with him

"Darius let go … this is madness for goodness sake … let go of me." I repeated, struggling to free myself from his grasp. I felt very afraid of where he was going to take me.

"Where are we going? … Darius stop." Despite my constant protests he refused to release me and I had no option but to be dragged along behind him. I begged him incessantly, but his grip remained firm.

As we reached the ivy curtain and the hidden doorway I had more than an uneasy feeling, I started to feel sick. I had not entered that chamber since the first time and did not want to go in there now. I tried again in my pleading, hoping to appeal to the gentler side of his nature.

"Darius stop it please, I do not want to go up there, I know what's in there," I said faintly. Darius turned to me with a twisted smile on his face.

"Do you, my beloved? Do you realize what it's like?" he asked sadistically as he pulled me closer. I was struggling in his arms by now, but he only tightened his hold on me. He half carried, half dragged me up the stairs with him until we reached the dark chamber, then he released me into the room in front of him.

His body blocked the staircase, so I had no option but to move backwards, deeper into the chamber. I shivered as my eyes grew accustomed to the gloom and I believed I could feel the rage building and his dark menacing stare burning into my eyes. Suddenly with one quick movement he bent forward and threw open the lid of the coffin with force. I did not initially comprehend what he was about to do; I remained rooted to the spot.

"Why don't you climb into the coffin, since you are so eager to spend your life as an immortal," he invited icily, taunting me further.

I felt him lean closer to me, I could feel his breath on my skin and sense the evil intention in his mind; he suddenly seemed so dangerous to me. I shuddered, panic building within my whole body and I began to tremble from the fear of what he was going to do.

"Stop it Darius," I said sharply, trying not to sound intimidated. I moved slightly to his side, in order to push past and run back down the stairs. He however, had anticipated my movement and was too fast and too strong for me to compete with. All at once he lifted me in his arms and I found myself hurled violently into the coffin.

The lid was forcibly shut on top of me and I heard the sickening snap of what could have only been the latch closing. My mind was full of terror as I pleaded with him to open the lid. I could hardly breath or move, the claustrophobic sensation of being shut in such a confined space panicked me. I shrieked in angry protest, but as the shock of what he had done developed, my body began to convulse and I started screaming at the top of my voice, but my screams felt stifled.

I tried to calm myself and then I pleaded with him again and again to let me out. All the while my skin felt like it was on fire as the air continued to diminish around me. Through this confusion of sensations, my mind felt as though it were exploding in my head with the words: *How could he do this to me?*

After endless appalling moments I stopped pleading; my throat was seizing up. My long hair had wrapped itself around my neck and now felt as if it were strangling me. I tugged hard on a handful of strands, but I was laying on the majority of them and I could not tear it away from my neck; it was sticking to my damp skin and soaked by the tears that had spilled down my face.

I tried to steady my breathing, which had become laborious, and to remain calm, but after a few more seconds I began to feel myself lose control again.

"Darius?" I implored him frantically.

I held my breath and listened carefully in the terrifying darkness, but I couldn't hear anything.

I didn't know if he was even there.

I strained my ears further to listen for any sound apart from my own frantic heartbeat, the chamber it seemed was deathly still and silent, the only sound was coming from me. In the fragility of my mind, I felt beyond terror now. I could feel the hysteria diminishing along with the little air that was left.

I knew I had to get out; otherwise I would die very soon.

A tormenting voice in my head told me that Darius had left the chamber and I was all alone here. I tried to push that thought away, but my already rapid breathing was increasing by the second and the awful questions begged for an answer. Would he leave me here to die? I thought he might, he had been angry enough.

Now I really was fighting for breath, I was gagging—there was no air.

The terrible thoughts came back, they raced through my mind and reminded me that I was going to die here; he was going to let me die!

But then I thought I heard a noise in the darkness and I called his name, but my words did not articulate. I screamed, but no sound came to my ears. With my failing strength I attempted a last effort to push the wood in front of my face, but it remained rigid and unyielding. In final desperation I raked my nails across the hard surface of the wood and felt my nails breaking, along with the sticky wetness that I knew to be my own blood.

It was at that moment the petrifying reality hit me; I was being buried alive in my very own tomb.

I was crying, suffocating in silence, but with my last strangled breath I summoned the will to voice my terror once more, but my throat was closed; I was gasping for the air that wouldn't come, my life was diminishing and my being fading into darkness.

Suddenly the coffin's lid flew open and a cold rush of air came at me. I could barely make out Darius's silhouette as he stood over me. I was too caught up in gasping the first breaths of the precious air that I needed so badly that I was almost oblivious to him picking me up, but as my gasps for breath intermingled with frantic sobs, I knew that I was in his arms.

I clung to him with all my strength and he carried me down the stairs and out into the cool night. The fresh night air filled my lungs instantly, making me feel extremely light headed and weak. Darius eventually moved back into the house and back to the living room. Minutes passed and my tears finally ceased and I reluctantly released my grip on him, but I was still shaking and caressing the shock I had endured inside the coffin.

I wanted to hate him, I wanted to push him away from me and take down that candle from the mantle and burn him to ashes, but I knew I couldn't, because deep down I didn't hate him and despite the horrific ordeal he had just put me through, I still loved him unconditionally.

He sat holding me in his arms until my shaking came under control. My vision was still blurred from my tears and it took a few moments for me to see his face more distinctly and then I saw his anguish.

"I would do anything to protect you from immortality," he said quietly. My voice was still trembling and my throat still felt partially closed as I softly whispered to him.

"What will happen to you when I am gone? You said once that your life would cease too. How can it?" His gaze was unwavering from my eyes as I continued. "When there is no one to save you from the darkness, no one by your side and you are alone again in your immortality for endless years, how will you endure it? I know you could not bear that anymore, I know how tortured you are and will be again." I hesitated briefly, catching my breath.

"With me by your side forever we can stay together, we will forever remain at Ravens Deep for all eternity. We can shut out the mortal world and exist in our own world." As I looked at Darius my vision gained clarity. He sighed looking weary and broken.

"Madeline, do you really think I can do that to you, when the very last part of my mortal emotion loves you so desperately?"

"But doesn't the immortal part love me too?" I whispered.

"Yes," he said sadly, uttering a sound of despair. "Madeline, I cannot do this to you." "Yes you can, "I pressed gently, "I could not bear to lose you even in death and no matter what you do to me, I cannot be apart from you ever." I paused, allowing my voice to gain some momentum.

"If you love me you would not deny me anything. You once told me that you would not deny me anything if it made me happy," I reminded him. "To be by your side for eternity, with you to guide me through the torment of it all would make the horror less for me. It wouldn't be the same for me as it was for you. You will teach me how to exist."

I pulled him close to me, his penetrating gaze seeing clearly into my mind.

"Wake up my immortality, I can see the hunger in your eyes and *my blood* will be the sweetest because you love me so," I said seductively, willing him to do my bidding. He stared at me with a haunted look in the depths of green.

"What if I kill you instead?" he demanded. "Have you considered that?" But despite his words I could tell I had worn him down. His skin felt cool to my touch and I knew he had to feed soon.

"My remains can wait forever in that cold stone sarcophagus in the churchyard, but I will be gone, or I can be by your side forever," I answered. I could see the darkness in his eyes once more, but now it was mingled with a deep desire.

As I entwined my fingers in his hair he brought his mouth to mine. The tears were now falling freely down my face and Darius drew back and looked into my eyes. I could see his torment, his pain and anguish, but I closed my mind to his conflict and whispered to him.

"If you truly love me then do it. Do it now and I will be forever with you." I closed my eyes and grasped his hair even tighter. I felt his breath on my cheek and his lips on my throat, until finally I cried out in pain at the sting of his kiss on my neck.